Laurean Brooks

©2021 Laurean Brooks

Published by Scrivenings Press LLC
15 Lucky Lane
Morrilton, Arkansas 72110
https://ScriveningsPress.com

Printed in the United States of America

All rights reserved. No part of this publication may be reproduced, stored in a retrieval system, or transmitted in any form or by any means—for example, electronic, photocopy and recording— without the prior written permission of the publisher. The only exception is brief quotation in printed reviews.

Paperback ISBN 978-1-64917-123-8

eBook ISBN 978-1-64917-124-5

Cover by Diane Turpin, www.dianeturpindesigns.com

(Note: This book was previously published in 2017 by Mantle Rock Publishing LLC and was re-published as is when Scrivenings Press acquired the publishing rights in 2021.)

All characters are fictional, and any resemblance to real people, either factional or historical, is purely coincidental.

All scriptures are taken from the KING JAMES VERSION (KJV): KING JAMES VERSION, public domain.

Endorsements for Laurean Brooks

HALF-PRICE BRIDE is an enjoyable, satisfying read, and well worth TWICE the price! Seriously, this story has it all: Endearing main characters and engaging secondary characters, a gorgeous setting, and a storyline that'll grab your attention on Page One and won't let go until you reach The End. My advice? Make space on your "This One's a Keeper" shelf, because you're gonna read it more than once!

— *LOREE LOUGH, USA TODAY BESTSELLING AUTHOR OF 125 5-STAR, AWARD-WINNING BOOKS, INCLUDING READER FAVORITE 50 HOURS*

Acknowledgments

I would like to acknowledge the Mantle Rock Publishing staff for the great job they do. Two of those who run the well-oiled machine include Kathy Cretsinger, who ensures everything is up to par, and Diane Turpin, who created my beautiful book cover. I would also like to thank beta reader, Phyllis Rundell, for her eagle eye. Great job, Phyllis.

I would like to dedicate this book in memory of Mrs. Frances Stairs and Ms. Marcie Shewmaker, two sweet ladies who encouraged me at the onset of my writing. Both have since passed. You will never know how much your support and enthusiasm meant to me. You would not let me give up.

Chapter One

Bartlett, Tennessee
Late August 1884

Emily Hammons stepped up to the post office window and smiled at the silver-haired postmistress. "Miss Preston, do you have any mail for us?"

The petite woman turned and pulled an envelope from the Hammons's slot. "Yes, Emily, here's a letter addressed to you." She adjusted her wire-rimmed spectacles and frowned at the envelope as she slid it forward. "I hope it's not bad news."

Emily's throat constricted when she read the return address. Dr. Wendell O. Clemons, DDS. She had waited four weeks for this letter. Now that it was in her hands, she was petrified.

The postmistress studied her with curiosity. "I'm sure it's not," Emily replied, sliding the letter inside her skirt pocket away from the woman's prying eyes.

She hurried down the dirt road that led to her home, entering the woods and taking the worn path that culminated at the back door of their rambling farmhouse. The house she'd shared with her mother and her brother until Mama passed away last summer.

Six months later Roy took a wife and moved her in. On that cold December day Louise burst through the front door, peace flew out the window.

Emily sank down on the back steps and gazed up through the giant oak tree. Its foliage spread over this part of the house, shielding the screened-in back porch and kitchen from the summer heat. Its shade provided a welcome relief. The rope swing hung as sturdy as ever. Emily had begged her brother for a swing. Roy climbed high up in the tree and tied the rope to a strong branch. She relived the times she'd gripped the rope, run out, and arced around it, sometimes skinning her knees on the rough tree trunk. But she didn't mind. Nothing she'd experienced compared to the freedom of soaring through space.

Emily pulled the envelope from her pocket. She'd found an ad in *The Commercial Appeal* near the end of June and replied with the information the next day. The ad read:

"Texas dentist seeks healthy, attractive young woman of nice proportions to marry, and to assist in dental practice. Will be well provided for. High school diploma required. Please send tintype of self and record of grades. If interested, I will reply."

Six weeks passed before the dentist replied. Why had he insisted on seeing her grades? Was she afraid he'd be bound to a simpleton? She studied the writer's artistic flourishes. One might think a woman had penned it. The previous letter was the same, only much thinner.

The message inside would seal her fate if she followed through with her plan. Marriage was meant to be a binding contract, holy in the sight of God. How could one know a person's character merely through letters?

Like other young ladies, Emily dreamed of being courted,

falling in love, and ideally getting married to the man she loved. Instead, she had agreed to a union with a stranger through only two brief correspondences. Most folks claimed a perfect union did not exist, but Emily believed God had the right mate for everyone.

She wouldn't have answered the ad if she had seen any other way out of her dilemma. Her sister-in-law had made it clear that Emily was to move out as soon as she graduated. Since Emily's graduation, her nagging had increased.

"It's high time we did somethin'." Louise's clamoring voice blasted through the screen, jolting her. What had riled her sister-in-law this time?

Emily was seventeen when Mama died and left the farm and house to Roy. Their mother's one stipulation—that Roy would take care of his sister—had no legal papers to back it. Without papers declaring Emily as an equal owner of the house and farm, she had no say.

She had cooked, cleaned, and worked on the farm. No one else gathered eggs or kept fresh straw in the hens' nests. Neither did they offer to help shovel manure out of the chicken house and spread it over the garden.

Panic seized Emily. She could not marry this stranger! Pulling a match from her pocket, she struck it against the rough tree bark. Holding the match below the envelope, she watched the flame burn down near her fingers. No. Burning the letter would not solve her problems. She blew it out.

Roy said something she couldn't hear. He and Louise argued a lot about money, and about Emily.

"I've had it with her!" Louise's angry voice pierced through the screen again.

This argument was about Emily. The drought had damaged their cotton crop. They depended on the sales to get them through to next year's harvest. Her brother's budget was already stretched, and Emily's presence added to his burden.

"What are you suggestin'?" Roy growled.

Louise's whine reached Emily's ears. "Roy, you know as well as I do, that it ain't rained since mid-June. We've done sold off our best livestock to pay the feed bill. The mercantile will be wantin' their money next. We ain't makin' ends meet as it is. What do you think'll happen when the baby comes?"

Emily had learned of the overdue bill when she'd set a basket of eggs on the counter at the mercantile, yesterday. Mr. Barker inspected each egg without looking up. "When do you reckon Roy will be in to pay his bill?" he asked.

Emily was surprised her brother's account was overdue. Roy only charged items out of necessity and paid within the week.

"As soon as he gets the money," she'd informed the store owner.

Mr. Barker was not given to complaining but worry creased his face. "This drought ain't helped, but it don't look like it'll let up any time soon. I have bills, like everybody else."

"I understand," Emily had replied. "Keep the money for the eggs and put it against our bill."

Once more Louise's words pierced the screen. "If you don't tell your sister, I will."

The words sounded like a threat. Emily wasn't surprised, but why didn't Roy defend her?

Roy's voice boomed, "I know what you're thinkin', and I won't stand for it!"

Emily's fingers closed around the envelope. Answering the dentist's ad was her only solution. She had searched the *Help Wanted* ads in *The Commercial Appeal* since early spring. Few jobs were open to women. Every listing, besides domestic help and waiting tables, called for prior experience.

Why hadn't God worked things out between her and her sister-in-law? Was He trying to teach Emily patience, or was He telling her to leave home? If the letter revealed what she suspected, she would be on her way.

If their pa hadn't deserted them for the silver mines eight years ago, things would be different. Mama would still be alive. Emily was sure of it.

"I know you promised your mama you'd take care of Emily," Louise persisted, "but she's a grown woman, now. And she's got the smarts that come with a high school diploma."

Emily flinched when the house shook. Her brother was given to stamping his foot in a fit of temper. "I won't throw my sister out!" he yelled.

Pot lids banged in response. Louise was displaying her own brand of temper. "I never said that, exactly. But there's got to be a way to get your sister out on her own. If she just had a job to pay for her upkeep… Em'ly's been graduated three months, and what's she got to show for it?"

Louise cut in before Roy could answer. "Nothin', that's what. When your mama made you promise to look out for her, she didn't mean forever. Em'ly's a grownup. She could find a payin' job somewhere. Like Memphis. I'm not sayin' she don't help out around here, but when this baby comes, we'll be hard-pressed to feed an extra mouth. And, I won't let this baby go hungry."

Tears stung Emily's eyes. She was the "extra mouth." Was that how her brother felt, too? Anger replaced the tears. Louise couldn't get by one week without her help. It would serve her right to suffer a little.

No, Mama had taught her to forgive offenses. But their mother had not seen the real Louise. Forgiving wasn't easy when the person spewed hurtful words every day. Ma died before Roy married and Louise's true colors surfaced.

"Louise, there ain't no jobs around here," Roy argued. "I talked to Mr. Barker. He said I was the fifth one to walk into the mercantile and ask if he could use some help. Said he couldn't afford to hire nobody, even if he wanted to. Times are hard on everybody."

A wet dishrag slapped against the counter before Louise spat,

"There's Memphis. It's not that far, and it being a big city, your sister could find some kind of work there—plus a boarding house to move into."

Emily tore open the envelope, her hands shaking. As she pulled out the folded sheet of paper, two large bills and a smaller one floated to the ground. She picked them up and gasped.

Did a train ticket cost this much? She'd heard train fare was high, but this was absurd. Emily sucked in a ragged breath before unfolding the paper. Closing her eyes, she prayed, "Lord, if this is Your answer, I will obey."

She unfolded the paper and read the straight-to-the-point note.

Miss Emily Hammons,

Your grades are impressive. After replies from other applicants, it appears you are best suited to fill the positions of wife and assistant. I trust you have strong limbs and therefore, no problem standing for extended periods.

Enclosed, find money to cover train fare from Arkansas, to Abilene.

Urgent: Arrive before August 15th. We will wed immediately.

Bring wedding dress. Please telegraph to inform of arrival time.

Wendell O. Clemons, DDS

A tear slid down Emily's cheek. The missive was cold and formal. It held no hint of affection. If the dentist's biggest concern was his wife's ability to stand for extended periods, why didn't he just hire a sturdy man?

Could affection ever flourish between them? It sometimes did in these cases. Or so she'd heard. What if she and the dentist found each other repulsive? Could the marriage last?

Exactly how much did he expect from her? Did he want a wife who would bear him children? Emily shuddered. She wanted children, but not under those conditions. If this letter was God's answer to prayer, why had a dark cloud enshrouded her?

She read the last line again. *"We will wed immediately. Bring wedding dress."* A shiver skittered up her spine. The man allowed them no time to get acquainted.

Her mother's wedding dress, tucked away in the trunk, had surely yellowed. Emily would have to see if it was salvageable. She wished she could send the dentist a curt reply that read, "No thank you, Dr. Clemons. I must decline your ridiculous offer."

Emily swallowed her pride and faced the facts. She had no job, and young men were in short supply the South. Even before The War Between The States, some had left their families behind to venture as far west as California, to seek their fortunes in gold and silver.

Emily closed her eyes. "Lord, this will not be easy, but I will step out on faith and trust You. Thy will be done."

A pot lid clanged again before Louise groused, "We have to do somethin', now! No use puttin' it off. If your sister just had a beau or a prospect of marriage, things would be different. But Emily has scorned every man who's tried to court her. She's too high highfalutin' for'em."

Was Louise referring to Homer Collins, the hog farmer on the far side of town? She'd dropped strong hints about the fifty-year-old man with two kids older than Emily, and two almost her age.

Or had her sister-in-law meant Carl Goodwin, who lived in a shack down the road. Carl, in his forties, returned from the war with an alcohol addiction. His wife had stood all she could before taking the baby and leaving him with five young'uns. The oldest child was sixteen, the youngest not yet in school. Emily did not want to start a marriage with a passel of kids.

It was time to make her presence known. Emily tucked the

money inside her skirt pocket and rose. She climbed the steps and opened the screen door and stepped inside, letting it pop closed to announce her arrival.

Louise stood at the stove. She turned and glared before whirling back around to stir a boiling pot. Roy's face flushed. He scratched his temple. "You get somethin'…from the post office, Sis?"

Emily held up the envelope. "It's addressed to me. A marriage proposal." The spoon in her hand dripping, Louise spun around. "Marriage proposal? Who'd be proposin' to you? Why you ain't even courtin' nobody."

Anger burned in Emily's chest. "If I was, it would be my own business." She immediately regretted her harsh words.

Before her sister-in-law could retort, Roy blurted, "Who's the letter from, Sis?"

"A dentist. I answered a mail-order bride ad in the *Commercial Appeal*." She handed him the letter and envelope.

Louise threw up her hands. "Well, in all my born days! I ain't believin' it. Let me see that letter."

Roy sat in the rocker with the letter in hand. Louise pranced into the living room and peered over his shoulder.

Roy finished reading and rubbed the back of his neck, the way he did when he was faced with a tough decision. "It's short and sweet, for sure. I don't know, Emily. Somethin' don't set right about this letter. Why would a dentist want a wife and an assistant rolled into one? And why would a man advertise for a wife, unless he was ugly as old Butch?"

As if Roy had offended their lazy hound dog on the porch, Butch raised his head and howled. Emily suppressed a giggle before she replied, "I don't know. it's only the second reply I've received. It's been six weeks since I first answered his ad."

Rubbing her swollen belly, Louise piped in, "You're saying, all you know about this man, you could stuff in a thimble?" In the sweltering heat and with the baby due in two months, her sister-in-law was bound to be miserable.

Emily sighed. "The man is Dr. Wendell O. Clemons, he's twenty-nine, and he's a dentist. He sounds respectable. I sent the information he requested, and this is his reply."

"Let me see that letter again." Louise yanked it from Roy's hand, smoothed the page, and admired the stationery. "Fancy writing paper is a good sign this man has plenty of money. And his penmanship is fancy. Dr. Clemons sounds respectful enough. He even asked your arrival time, meaning he's considerate enough to meet you at the depot."

She turned to Emily and winked. "You should've asked for his bank statement since he requested your grades."

Emily bit her tongue to silence it. Roy's wife was the reason she had decided to leave. Why didn't she leave well-enough alone?

Louise read the brief message again and looked at Roy. "Says something about enclosing train fare. Is there any money in that envelope?"

Of course, Louise would ask. Money stayed foremost on her mind. In this case, Emily needed to be cautious.

Roy looked inside the envelope. "Nope."

Emily pulled one bill from her skirt pocket and held it up. No need to show them the rest. She had no clue what it cost to take a train from western Arkansas to Abilene, Texas.

Her sister-in-law stared longingly at the money. "Now, wasn't that generous of him? At least he's true to his word. Where does this dentist live?"

Roy flipped the envelope. "Abilene…Texas? Why, Emily, that's halfway across the country! I don't know if I should let you go. Anyway, how do you plan on getting there, if I do?"

"What do you mean, if you should let her go'?" Louise grumbled. "Your sister's a grown-up. Emily can make up her own mind. You can take her to Memphis to catch the ferry. Once she crosses the river, she can catch a train to take her the rest of the way. It's purely simple."

Louise worried her lips. "Emily, when are you planning to leave?"

Roy glared at his wife before turning back to Emily. "I don't know, Sis. What if this dentist ain't all he claims to be? What if–?"

"Nonsense," Louise's shriek clamped Roy's mouth shut. "Emily's got more wits about her than you give her credit for. She can make it there safe and sound, by using a little caution. She knows not to speak to strangers."

The remorse in her brother's eyes made tears pool in Emily's. "Is this what you want, Sis?"

No! Emily wanted to scream it from the rooftop. But what choice did she have? At least she would be out of her sister-in-law's hair. She met Roy's concerned gaze. "Yes. Don't worry. I will telegraph or write after I arrive, so you'll know I made it there safely."

Louise waved the letter. "He wants you there by the fifteenth. Today's already the thirteenth. You'd best start packing. I don't mind helping."

"I can do it by myself, thank you," Emily quipped.

Roy's brow furrowed. "There ain't no way I can even get you to the ferry before the fifteenth. I've got to finish getting in the hay tomorrow, and the next day I have a meeting with Mr. Strickland. You'll have to be a day late."

Emily's heart skipped a beat. Roy was meeting with the banker? Was he applying for a loan? This confirmed she'd made the right choice. Time would tell if it was the right choice for her.

Over supper, Louise couldn't stop talking about Emily's departure. Once, she got so excited, she tipped over her milk glass. Emily worried about her tardy arrival but couldn't see why one day would make a difference. She would telegraph Dr. Clemons along the way, to inform him of her delay.

While Louise sat on the porch swing with Roy, Emily washed the dishes. When she'd dried and put them away, she slipped into her bedroom and pulled her mother's wedding dress from the trunk. The musky scent of the rose sachets tucked around it invaded her nostrils.

She spread the dress across the bed to inspect it. Although it was slightly yellowed, the garment remained beautiful. Papa had paid a high price for it twenty-five years ago. He'd boasted his bride was the prettiest to ever grace *The Commercial Appeal* society pages.

Emily pulled out a valise and packed a change of clothes and a few personal items inside it. She tucked the money for train fare and coins from egg sales, inside her purse.

After replacing her mother's wedding dress in the trunk, Emily laid three slightly worn dresses of her mother's on top. She had remade the dresses for herself, to bring them up to fashion. An exemplary seamstress, Emily was blessed to have a treadle sewing machine. If she'd had the fabric, she'd have stitched shirts for Roy, added to her own wardrobe, plus made dresses for Louise.

Mama always said, "Kill'em with kindness," but she hadn't lived long enough to witness Louise's overbearing ways.

EMILY AND ROY reached the landing in Memphis by noon on August 15. The ferry arrived an hour later, and two sturdy boys loaded her trunk onto it.

Roy pulled Emily into a warm embrace. "Sis, be cautious and stay alert. You may have a wait when you reach the other side of the river. Take a seat inside the depot. Hold onto your bag and purse. You never know what kind of riffraff might be hangin' around."

"I'll be fine." Roy's words warmed her heart. He still treated her as if she were ten years old.

"Well, I'd better start home, if I want to get there by dark. Let us know when you reach Abilene, so we won't worry." He stepped back and gripped her shoulders. "And, if things ain't on the up-and-up with that dentist, you hop on the next train and head home. You hear?"

Emily nodded, knowing she wouldn't return. Yes, Roy would worry, but Louise wouldn't give her a passing thought. Mama had said plenty of times, "No house is big enough for two women." She and her sister-in-law were living proof of it.

After giving her brother a peck on the cheek, she stepped onto the ferry and gripped the rails. A cool breeze blew off the river soothing Emily's warm face as she watched Roy's wagon pull away. While the Mississippi waters sloshed onto the tipping ferry, reflecting the overhead sun, Emily clutched her stomach wondering how early settlers navigated this river and kept their food down.

The ferry didn't reach the other side soon enough to suit her. The ferrymen set Emily's trunk on the bank. How would she transport it to the train station?

As she frantically scanned her surroundings, a wagon rolled toward her and the stout driver yelled, "Fifty cents to haul your luggage to the train! Can take three passengers."

Emily waved and ran toward him. "Sir, I need a ride!" While he halted his team, she dug in her purse for two quarters.

The man hopped to the ground and grinned. He tipped his hat as she dropped the coins in his palm. "Thank you, Miss. I'm Hal Smith, proud to be of service."

Mr. Smith and a ferry worker loaded her trunk onto his wagon. When they reached the depot, a young man attached a ticket to her trunk and tore off the bottom section.

He handed it to Emily and raked her with an appreciative look. "Keep this stub to claim your trunk, Miss, once you reach your destination."

Emily thanked him and waved at Mr. Smith who was heading back to the ferry. She waited in line to purchase her ticket. To her dismay, the train fare took most of her money. Dr. Clemons had provided barely enough to cover it, and maybe one meal if she was lucky.

With a long wait for the westbound train, Emily settled on a bench.

She had read three chapters of her Wild West novel when the engineer shouted, "All aboard that are goin' aboard!" The rumbling train ground to a stop. Emily rose and boarded it with several other passengers.

Emily chose a seat and set her carry-on items in it. The stuffy interior of the train made it difficult to breathe. She pushed the window up halfway, then sat down. When the train picked up speed, soot swept in sticking to her clothes. She brushed off the specks until she realized she was wasting her efforts. She had to decide between an open window and an outfit speckled with soot, or a closed window and a pristine outfit soaked with perspiration. Emily chose the open window with a breeze.

At the second water stop, Emily ate the ham and biscuit she'd packed. She would eat a light breakfast in the morning and hope she had a little change left over.

Dusk fell as the train pulled into Little Rock. Emily got off to stretch her legs and use the facilities. She managed to sleep a couple of hours as the train rocked and lurched until the whistle jarred her awake.

A bald man across the aisle rolled his head and whined, "Looks like that engineer wouldn't blow that inferior whistle at every dinky little crossing."

The matronly lady next to him patted his hand. "Now Henry, don't make a fuss. It's bad for your heart."

~

SUNLIGHT STREAMED through the window when Emily woke to the train whistle and the conductor yelling, "Eastland, next stop! Ten-minute lay-over."

Emily brushed the sleep from her eyes and rose. This might be her last chance to send a telegram to inform Dr. Clemons of her tardy arrival. The lines were so long at previous stops, she feared she might miss the train. Thankfully, only four people stood in front of her now. After she paid for the telegram, she noticed she was down to two dollars

She boarded the train and as she sat down, a blonde young woman stopped in the aisle next to her. "May I sit with you?"

Emily smiled up at her friendly face and patted the seat next to her. "Of course."

"Thank you." The girl sat down and extended a gloved hand. "I'm Jessica Dawson, and I'm headed to Abilene."

Emily grasped her hand and introduced herself. "Abilene is my destination too."

Jessica set her valise at her feet. "My sister has lost her mind. Margie is marrying a virtual stranger, today. She answered a ridiculous mail-order bride ad from a man she's never met. We don't even know his last name. I knew she had answered the ad weeks ago, but when she got the reply on Monday, she pretended it was a big joke."

"Your sister was serious?" Emily asked. Did Abilene have a shortage of available women?

"Yes, she was. I should have suspected something yesterday when Margie dressed in her Sunday best and took the buggy to town. I offered to accompany her, but she said she wanted to go alone. When Margie didn't return by noon, Papa sent me looking her. I found our buggy in front of the depot. The ticket master remembered a woman fitting Margie's description, and said she'd bought a ticket to Abilene."

Jessica adjusted her hat. "I aim to meet this man before my sister makes a big mistake. If he doesn't meet my standards, I'll talk my sister into going home. Even if I have to hog-tie her."

Emily sighed. She wished someone had cared enough about her to persuade her to change her mind.

"I found a note on Margie's dresser after I returned from town. It read, 'By the time you read this, I will be on my way to Abilene, Texas.' She also wrote the intended groom had set the wedding for five p.m. August 16th. That's today. Then she added, 'Wish me well, Sis.'

"How can I when she knows nothing about this man? I don't even know his last name. She called him Oliver. He sent two letters, but she hid them. If Margie hadn't mentioned Abilene in the note, I wouldn't even know where to start looking."

"It's a good thing she did," Emily commented.

Jessica continued. "I think my sister wanted somebody to come after her, or why would she give directions to the church? It's across the street and a few blocks down from the depot. She said in the note that she was practically an old maid. Margie's twenty. She has plenty of time to catch a husband."

"How will you find her?" At least Emily didn't have to worry about locating the church. Dr. Clemons would meet her at the depot.

"I will find the reverend after I locate the Methodist Church. I'll ask him if he has a wedding scheduled for this afternoon."

Jessica brushed a black speck off her dress sleeve. "It's a good thing we wore dark outfits. They may be uncomfortable in this heat, but the soot doesn't show up as bad."

Emily wished she'd put as much thought into her decision to marry the dentist. Doubts plagued her as the train rolled closer to Abilene. Why was the dentist in a hurry to marry? Did he merely need an assistant to dispose of rotten teeth he pulled from patients' mouths, and someone to clean up vomit after they wretched? Or did he have a nefarious reason for rushing the wedding?

Jessica interrupted her musings. "Do you have kin in Abilene?"

Emily's cheeks burned. How could she give Jessica an honest answer without revealing too much? She wasn't proud that she'd resorted to answering a mail-order bride ad. "I received an invitation to come to Abilene," she finally replied. A twinge of guilt pricked her conscience.

Jessica patted Emily's hand. "It'll be all right. My aunt invited me to move to Houston, but Papa wouldn't stand for it. Said the big city was no place for a young lady. I stayed mad at him for a week even though I knew he was only trying to protect me.

"Papa smothers us. It's why Margie ran away. Don't think it hasn't crossed my mind too," Jessica huffed. "We're not children. I was eighteen in May, and Margie turned twenty in June. If I do leave home, it won't be to marry a virtual stranger."

Emily flicked soot from her bodice, happy that Jessica was airing her problems with her sister. This prevented her from asking Emily questions. Questions she would rather not answer.

Could she go through with her marriage agreement with Dr. Clemons? Would he pass the standards she had set for a life mate?

Emily drew a long breath as the conductor shouted, "Abilene, next stop! Departing passengers, collect your bags."

Chapter Two

Emily's gaze flitted over the crowd bustling about the depot. Through the sooty windows, wagons rolled along the busy street, churning out dust as drivers rushed to their destinations. Everyone seemed to be in a hurry.

Emily glanced across the street at the Tin Cup Saloon. Horses tethered to the hitching posts swished their tails. Mama had warned her never to go near any place that served strong drink.

Jessica gave her bodice a final brushing before pulling Emily into an embrace. "It was nice talking to you. "I wish you well with your aunt. I hope you find her without any trouble."

Guilt flooded Emily. "And I hope you find your sister before the wedding."

"So do I." Jessica picked up the valise she'd set on a vacant bench. "I'd better hurry if I want to interrogate Oliver before the wedding. If you have a long wait, you're welcome to attend the wedding. The church is just down the street. If the groom passes muster, the ceremony will begin in two hours.

Jessica sashayed toward the exit wedging herself between

two bulky men with cigars protruding from their mouths. She flashed them a smile and said, "Excuse me, sirs."

Emily's gaze wandered over the crowd. How would she know Wendell Clemons? He hadn't described himself yet insisted on a tintype of her. Was he tall and thin, or short and stocky? He hadn't even suggested they wear a certain item by which to identify themselves. Had he received the telegram she sent earlier that morning?

A thin man in a gray suit stepped inside the depot. Was this the dentist? No. He carried a traveling bag and stepped up to the ticket window.

Emily decided to check on her trunk. When she was assured it was in good hands, she found a vacant bench and sat down to open her book. According to the large clock on the wall, Dr. Clemons was late. So much for her idea that punctuality topped his list. She rubbed the back of her neck, stiff from sleeping in a sitting position.

Thirty minutes later, he still hadn't arrived. She fought panic by inhaling a calming breath. The dentist probably had to perform a procedure that took longer than usual. His patient might have become nauseous. You could not predict these things. Emily sighed, relieved she wasn't there to clean up the vomit.

She had read three chapters when a voice above her asked, "Miss, may I assist you?" The station master stood over her, his eyes filled with compassion.

"No, sir. Someone is supposed to meet me. He should arrive soon."

"If you say so, Miss. Let me know if you need anything." His words suggested she wasn't the first young lady who'd had a lengthy wait at the depot.

"Thank you, sir."

Emily read three more chapters before checking the clock again. Ten minutes of five. Dr. Clemons was almost two hours late. She squirmed on the hard bench her backside numb. She could sit no longer.

A church bell pealed in the distance. Was this bell announcing the wedding of Jessica's sister? If she looked anything like Jessica, she would be a beautiful bride.

She could stand the wait no longer. Wendell Clemons had either forgotten her or changed his mind. How could he have forgotten her when she had telegraphed him this morning?

Roy was awaiting a telegram, but she couldn't send it until she had something to report. And with only a few coins remaining, she wanted to hang onto them.

Emily rose and walked up to the ticket window and caught the station master's eye. "Sir, may I leave my bag here? I'm going to take a walk and stretch my legs."

"Certainly. And what is your name, so I can attach it to your bag?"

"Emily Hammons. Oh, and if Dr. Clemons should show up, tell him I will return shortly."

The man's brow furrowed. "Clemons, the dentist?"

"Yes, sir." She started toward the door.

"But—Dr. Clemons is at the church. That's the bell clanging now. He's—well…"

"Thank you, sir. I will find him," Emily interjected as she stepped through the door. Dr. Clemons was attending a wedding instead of meeting her at the train station? He could have had the decency to send someone to pick her up. She might just tell him that. Following the pealing bell, Emily walked until she reached a white clapboard church. The wooden sign above the door read Abilene Methodist Church. The bell stopped pealing and a moment later an organ began to play the wedding march.

An overflow crowd stood on the porch. Judging by the number of people in attendance, Jessica's sister must be marrying a prominent citizen. Anger fueled every step Emily took. She had a good mind to tell the dentist their wedding was off. She fanned her face glad she was wearing a hat. The organ music ceased as she walked up the church steps to the porch. The double doors had been propped open, probably to allow fresh air to circulate.

The crowd pressed in as she sliced through to reach the doorway. With a bit of effort, she managed to get a slight view of the altar beneath a hefty man's arm that he'd rested on a shorter man's shoulder. The rancid odor from his armpit made Emily catch her breath.

She managed to smile at the hefty man. "Excuse me, sir, I'm a friend of the bride's sister. May I stand in front of you to view the ceremony?"

He flashed her a toothless grin and stepped aside. Emily thanked him, but now a tall, redheaded cowboy blocked her view. He looked down at her and winked. Her heart did a crazy flip at the green gleam in his eyes.

"Stand in front of me, pretty lady," he offered. "You're short enough I can see over you."

With effort, she pulled her gaze from his mischievous one. Emily had often been teased about her lack of height. "Thank you." In front of the cowboy, no one blocked her viewed. She returned her gaze to the congregation, skimming the crowd as the reverend opened his Bible. Where was Dr. Clemons? Was he the dark-haired tall man seated near the front?

The crowd pressed in from behind Emily. Sweat popped out on her brow. She pulled a lace handkerchief from her skirt pocket and blotted her face, careful not to inhale the odor of the toothless man behind her. While tucking the handkerchief away, she elbowed the tall cowboy.

He let out an exaggerated, "Oomph!" and clutched his stomach.

"I'm sorry," she whispered and returned her attention to the ceremony, about to begin. The couple faced each other. She had a good view of the groom's portly build, his long face and protruding teeth. Why had Jessica's sister decided to marry him? A veil covered the bride's face. Emily's gaze swept across the front pew and found Jessica seated in a shiny, blue dress.

The church fell silent as the reverend began reading scriptures about the sanctity of marriage. He finished and smiled at the couple. "Do you, Wendell Oliver Clemons, take Marjorie Ann Dawson to be your lawfully wedded wife, to have and to hold…"

Emily's jaw dropped and she strained her ears to hear more. Did he say, Clemons?

The paunchy groom rasped, "I do." His protruding teeth bared as he grinned at the bride.

The reverend continued. "Do you, Marjorie Ann Dawson, take Wendell Oliver Clemons to be your lawfully wedded husband…?"

Emily's heart skipped a beat. Wendell Oliver Clemons! Oliver was his middle name. But, why was he marrying Jessica's sister when he'd proposed to her and even sent her money for train fare?

Emily held her breath and watched the exchange. The bride's shoulders heaved as she fidgeted with her bouquet. No words came from her lips. A hush fell over the congregation.

"I…I can't…do this!" she squealed and tore off her veil, flinging it at the groom. It bounced off his portly girth and landed at the reverend's feet. The groom froze, his eyes wide and his mouth gaping.

A matronly woman seated near the aisle blustered, "Well, I do declare!" as Margie flew past her down the aisle, gripping her skirt in one hand and the bouquet in the other.

A gaunt man seated on the back row, slapped his knee and yelled, "Way to go, Clemons! Hope you have better luck with the next one."

Emily gasped. The next one? What did he mean?

An authoritative figure of a man waved his hands. "All right. Back up, folks. Clear the way!"

The crowd split forcing Emily and those standing behind her to move out to the porch, to allow the wild-eyed bride a means of escape. Gasping for breath, Jessica's sister stopped in front of Emily and shoved the bouquet into her stomach. Emily stumbled.

"Enjoy the flowers!" the bride shrieked before she hurried down the steps and marched up the street, her skirt still hiked.

The crowd pressed in causing Emily to lose her balance again. A muscular arm snaked around her waist. Before she could see the man who had grabbed her, the crowd pressed in again. Emily stepped back and tripped over a booted foot. The taut arm tightened around her waist and she fell backward.

With both arms flailing, she and the man plummeted off the porch entwined, hitting the ground with a thud. Emily was grateful for the human cushion that softened her landing. She pushed herself upright and found the red-haired cowboy studying her with amusement. Flinging his arm aside, from her, she rolled away from him.

While she struggled to catch her breath, the cowboy sat up and drew his knees to his chest. When he started to chuckle, she glared at him.

This is not funny." Emily brushed debris from her bodice. Worse, a pain shot up her ankle.

When the cowboy's green gaze raked her, beginning at her eyes and descending to linger near her ankles, she looked down and discovered her petticoats and a good six-inch of leg exposed. She flung the hem over her ankles, but not before the cowboy's eyes twinkled with mischief.

She could hear her mother scolding, "Shame on you, Emily. Ladies don't allow themselves to get into such predicaments."

The cowboy reached for his hat lying an arm's length away. Coppery hair curled over his sunburned ears, caressing his shirt collar. A ruddy complexion peeked through a light tan. His lightly sunburned cheekbones contrasted the tan on his neck. Emily guessed this was as close to a tan as he'd ever had.

He tugged the brown Stetson onto his head, his green eyes sparkling. "Miss, I beg your pardon. I lost my balance when the crowd split. That bride packed a wallop." Compassion filled his eyes when he saw her rubbing her foot. "Are you hurt?"

Emily winced. "I think I twisted my ankle. Will you help me up, please?"

He hopped to his feet and dusted off the seat of his pants. Pulling Emily to standing position, he slid an arm around her waist to support her. "Lean on me," he urged.

Balancing on her good foot, Emily clung to him and looked up at his smiling face. His green eyes reminded her of the first blades of grass in spring. She could get lost in them.

"Now, try putting a little weight on that foot. See if you can walk at all."

Emily cautiously set the foot on the ground and cringed when a pain shot up her ankle. She clutched him tighter, her breath coming in gasps.

"I'm sorry, Miss— Doc Simmons is inside the church. I'll see what's taking him so long."

"No need, I'll be all right." Emily had no money to pay a doctor. She let go of the cowboy and tried to limp to the porch. Another pain stabbed her foot, and she almost fell.

The cowboy grabbed for her again. "Don't try to walk on that foot. Let me get you seated on the porch. Then I'll go after the doctor."

Before she could protest, he scooped her up and set her on the edge of the porch, her legs dangling off it. "Stay here. I'll be right back."

"But—" Emily protested.

He held up his hands. "I insist. It's the least I can do. I came here to get the doctor, anyway. My ma needs him."

Emily nodded. At least her purse was still intact. For the good it did. With only a few coins left, she could not pay for a doctor's services. Still clutching the bridal bouquet, she raised it to her nose and sniffed. She should toss them but some of the flowers were not crushed and they smelled like heaven. Blue and orange lily-type flowers mixed with daisies and a flower she didn't recognize, made up the arrangement.

Emily twisted to watch the cowboy squeeze through the crowd on the porch. She was plucking the crushed flowers from the bouquet when two women who looked to be in their late fifties bustled out of the church and lingered on the porch.

The tall, willowy woman frowned down at her before looking away. The woman's graying, red hair pulled into a tight bun gave her a severe appearance, making her hawk-like nose appear sharper. The short, plump woman with salt and pepper hair walked within inches of Emily, her billowing skirts swishing as she came to an abrupt stop. With her attention focused on the tall woman, she didn't seem to notice Emily

The tall woman pressed a hand to her cheek. "Well, I declare, Louella! Have you ever seen anything like it? That young woman left Ollie at the altar. The poor boy's in shock." She clucked her tongue. "I'm afraid he will never catch a bride. His mama has spoiled him."

The woman called Louella snickered. "I expect when any woman takes a close gander at Ollie, even the prospect of his inheritance won't be enough to cinch the deal."

Emily's ears perked up. Inheritance? How did this relate to Dr. Clemons finding a wife?

The tall woman with the hawkish nose spoke up. "Ollie's time is running out. His birthday is at the end of October. He'll lose everything if he doesn't snare a bride by then."

Still gabbing, the ladies stepped off the porch. Louella gasped. "Why, that's only two months away. He'd best not be wasting time."

The pieces were falling into place. Dr. Clemons had insisted Emily arrive by a certain date, but she had arrived a day late. Was this why he was exchanging vows with Margie? Was he afraid he'd lose his inheritance? Who had made that stipulation, and why?

Chapter Three

⚜

Clint cut a sideways glance at the young lady Jessica had called Emily. She was upset with him. Huffing out a breath she stared straight ahead. He had carried his teasing too far.

Now she wouldn't look at him. Clint was puzzled by her strong reaction when he'd told her Clemons had proposed to three women. One might think she was personally involved.

He scratched his bristly chin in thought. Emily had befriended Jessica on the train, and Jessica's sister was the bride who fled the church. It could be reason enough, he supposed. Still, something didn't add up.

"I apologize for making light of the situation," Clint offered. "You've had a long trip, and I'm sure you're tired. As soon as the doctor climbs in his buggy, we'll head to the ranch. You can get a good night's sleep there. Doc was treating Clemons's mother when I left him at the church."

Most folks laughed at his jesting. Not Emily. He had hoped he could ease her tension. Instead, his attempt at frivolity had backfired, giving her a bad impression of him. Clint had come off as a braggart and flirt.

26

Emily was too young to be this serious. He understood why a young woman alone and far from home, would be afraid, but he wasn't sure what to make of her. She claimed to have embarked on a wild west adventure.

The idea of young lady striking out on her own didn't sit well with Clint. Was Emily running from something? For what other reason would she ride a train 600 miles? She did not appear to have an independent bone in her body. Emily's wide-eyed innocence and dainty build brought out his protective instincts.

Clint exhaled a long breath. Over analyzing got a man in trouble. He would blame Emily's injured ankle for her ill mood and leave it at that. He'd never known a man yet, who could figure out a woman.

He'd better set things straight between them before she bailed out of the wagon, injured ankle or not. Judging by the way she kept scanning the street and buildings, it was on her mind.

"Look, Miss Emily, I was only teasing. Why don't we introduce ourselves, so we won't be strangers anymore? I know your first name. I'm Clint McCall. You can call me, Clint." He tipped his hat. "I promise to be on my best behavior for the remainder of our journey."

Emily picked at the now-wilted bouquet she clung to. She had to be melting in that thick, dark suit she wore. It would be suitable for a cool climate, but cool days were few and far between in Abilene. And never in August.

She looked his way before facing forward. Was she afraid of him? He wouldn't harm a fly.

"How far is your ranch?" she asked.

"Nine miles, give or take. Two hours, if I let the horses move at their own pace."

So that was it. She didn't trust him. He could not fault her for it. She was a pretty, young woman, and he was a man—a stranger. Yet, she must have considered him trustworthy or she wouldn't have accepted his invitation. She had ignored his suggestion they introduce themselves, asking the distance to the ranch, instead.

~

TWO HOURS? Emily's breath caught. His ranch was farther than she'd anticipated. A lot could happen in that length of time. She'd hoped it was thirty minutes at the most. She knew little about Clint McCall, only his name and that his mother was sick. Anything could happen between Abilene and this cowboy's ranch. If there was a ranch. Had she lost all sense of discernment by accepting aid and a ride from a stranger? But she had no choice.

She'd taken a bigger risk by traveling to Abilene to marry another stranger. Accepting help from the cowboy dwindled in comparison. She almost laughed at the irony.

If her ankle wasn't throbbing, and the doctor would not be following them, Emily would insist this cowboy help her down from his buckboard, and she would...what?

The thought flew out of her head when she remembered the two dollars in her purse. She doubted that hotels extended credit to strangers. If they did, they would limit it to the prestigious upper class. She certainly didn't have enough to cover a night's stay in the fancy one she'd seen.

The cowboy twisted to look behind him. "There's Doc now."

Relief flooded Emily at the sight of the thin, bearded man, who rolled up in a buggy beside them and hopped out. He nodded at Clint and tipped his hat at Emily, before running up the steps and into his office

Clint released the brake on the wagon. "If we hurry, Doc will get back before dark. He prefers to be home before the sun goes down. He doesn't carry a weapon unless you count his stetho-scope as a deadly object. Who knows? He might use it to strangle an attacker."

A giggle bubbled in Emily's throat. She swallowed it. To keep the upper hand with this cowboy, she must appear cool and collected.

The doctor reappeared carrying a medical bag. He set it in his buggy and climbed up. "Let's go. I'll follow."

Clint clucked to the horses, shaking the reins. They took off and the doctor's buggy trotted to catch up. He lifted a hand and waved before dropping back a short distance. Emily returned his wave, happy to have the kind-faced gentleman as part of their entourage.

It was apparent to Emily, that Mr. McCall's mother lived at his ranch. Emily could keep her emergency money if she spent the night there. Tomorrow, when the cowboy took her back to town, she would look for a job. If there were no openings for bookkeepers, she could hire on as a clerk at one of the many stores. She was not sure where she would stay until she received her first week's pay.

As they rolled past businesses, merchants were closing up shop for the day, lugging their goods off the boardwalk. Across from the depot, the Tin Cup saloon burst to life. Tinny piano music and raucous laughter spilled through its bat-wing doors. Wolf whistles from unkempt men lounging on the boardwalk, pierced the air. Some spit tobacco. All leered at Emily as their wagon rolled past. Her stomach knotted as she turned to face straight ahead.

"Don't pay them any mind, Miss Emily," the cowboy said while slapping the reins to get the horses to move faster. "They usually start getting rowdy about this time of day."

They'd traveled a short distance when they reached a fork in the road. Clint turned the wagon toward a sign that read, Buffalo Gap, 19 miles south. Emily massaged her pulsating temples, longing for a soft bed. It felt like a week since she'd left home, even longer since she'd slept. Who could rest on a lurching, rumbling train?

Was it only yesterday she'd taken the ferry across the Mississippi? Roy was probably worried about her. She had planned to send her brother a telegram as soon as Dr. Clemons arrived at the depot. Since he didn't show up, she needed to save her last coins for emergencies.

What could she say to ease her brother's mind, anyway, when hers was spinning with questions about her fate? First, she must find a job and a boarding house. Otherwise, where would she have her trunk delivered?

Clint's brooding gaze studied her. "We should be there in less than two hours if the horses don't tire." He shook the reins again to urge them on. "My mother has a high fever and a hacking cough. I hope Doc Simmons has a miracle cure in his black bag."

Emily readjusted her hat. "It's hard to watch loved ones suffer."

"Yes, it is." Clint tipped his hat. "Miss Emily, we haven't been properly introduced. I told you my name, but I only know your given name. Where do you hail from?"

She hesitated. The less he knew about her, the less she would have to explain later. "Hammons is my last name. I'm from Bartlett."

"Never heard of the town. How far is it from Abilene?"

Emily sniffed. "Bartlett is a small town outside of Memphis."

"Tennessee?" Clint cast a sideways glance at the young woman. "You crossed the Mississippi in Memphis and came all this way on the train alone?"

She nodded but said nothing.

It didn't add up. Emily had no relatives in Abilene, but she had taken the train over 600 miles to get here. She must have had a good reason. She didn't strike him as the type who decided on the spur of the moment and acted on it. On the contrary, she appeared to be the kind of person who deliberated before each decision she made.

He shifted in his seat. The only way he could know the truth was to ask. "You came this far without the promise of a job? I would think a young lady of your intelligence, could have found work in Memphis."

Emily busied herself plucking imaginary lint from her skirt. Clint sensed that his questions rattled her. But he needed answers.

She raised her head and locked her blue gaze with his. "A few years ago, I started reading novels about the wild west. Since then, my dream has been to go west and see it for myself. Also, I read that Abilene is growing by leaps and bounds."

What she said about Abilene was true, but Clint sensed this young woman had a more pressing reason for leaving her home. "I'm afraid you're too late for shootouts and Indian massacres. At least around these parts. There are still skirmishes farther west.

"Saloons are as wild as it gets here. The White Elephant saloon just opened in May. Their sign has already been stolen once. But they hung out another one. The worst times to be in town are on Friday and Saturday nights. Trust me, you don't want to go inside a saloon. It's no place for a lady." She appeared innocent and gullible. Surely, she wasn't considering a job at one.

Emily sniffed. "I've read stories about saloons. And my mother warned me."

She acted as if he had insulted her. He'd only meant to give her fair warning, to protect her. "Any place where there's drinking or gambling is no place for a lady."

In the west, young women often ended up in saloons because they couldn't find any other means of support. It happened to his mother. But, thank God, that was in the past. The way she got out of it was another story.

Clint shook his head. This was no time to dwell on that. Not with this raven-haired beauty with eyes the color of Texas blue-bonnets, seated next to him.

He would hate to see her end up in a saloon. Surely, she had kinfolk somewhere. Miss Hammons seemed close-mouthed about her personal life. He might have to pry the information from her.

"Did you leave your family behind in Bartlett?"

Her dark lashes fluttered before she lowered them and clasped her hands together in her lap. A soft sigh escaped her lips. He'd ventured into forbidden territory. What was she not saying?

She finally raised her head but avoided eye contact.

"I lived with my brother in our family home. He married last winter and moved his wife in. This summer a drought put us in dire financial straits. With Louise in the family way, an extra mouth to feed might be too much."

"You, being the 'extra mouth,'" he said.

Miss Hammons ducked her head without commenting. Her words about her sister-in-law rang true. What was it Ma said about "too many cooks in the kitchen?" Without a job to help pay bills, this young beauty had become a burden to her brother. He imagined the sister-in-law was also jealous of Emily's looks. Too bad she didn't have a relative willing to take her in.

Or did she? "What about your parents? Are they still living?"

"I don't know my Pa's whereabouts. He took off in '79 to strike it rich in the Colorado silver mines. He promised to send for us after he got settled. We received one letter saying he had struck a vein and would soon send for us. My mother died last spring. The doctor said it was from a weak heart. I'm sure it was from a broken one. Until her dying day, she held onto hope that Pa would either send for us or come home. He did neither."

Clint detected bitterness in Emily's voice. He knew about men who contracted the fever to go west and strike it rich. Staying behind was a good decision for Emily and her family.

Clint was eight years old when his pa bought a covered wagon and they packed their belongings and left the L&M ranch in Texas for Kansas. His pa was anxious to claim a parcel of free land under the Homestead Act. At least he hadn't been struck with gold fever like some. Still, the decision proved fatal. He was killed in a dispute with a claim jumper soon after they moved into the lean-to he had erected for their temporary home.

With little money and no other means to make a living, Clint's mother made a decision that affected the course of their lives. She took a job in a local saloon but refused to do anything but serve tables.

They moved into a room above the saloon. Ma had seen to it that Clint attended the one-room schoolhouse at the edge of town, insisting he get a good education.

Not long into the job, his ma found a mail-order bride ad in the newspaper and replied to it. The man lived in Nevada and mined silver at the Washoe Diggings.

It turned out to be a terrible decision that almost cost them their lives.

Clint shook his head to clear the ugly memories. It did no good to relive the past. Slapping the reins, he urged the horses to pick up.

He would let Miss Hammons rest from his interrogation for the time being. Losing both parents was hard enough, but getting booted out of her home, well, that was too much. It took courage for a woman to venture the distance from Tennessee to Texas, whatever the reason. Courage or just plain foolishness? His gut feeling told him there was more to Emily's story. And he planned to find out by first gaining her trust.

～

EMILY TOOK IN HER SURROUNDINGS. The August sun was hotter in Texas than in Tennessee, although the air was not as humid. A twinge of homesickness struck when they passed a cotton field, reminding Emily of Bartlett. The cotton would be ready to pick, come October.

Emily fidgeted with her skirt. The cowboy had fallen silent. She was glad he had quit asking questions. They dredged up painful memories, just when she thought they were buried.

Pa's broken promise made Emily wary of men. Especially the ones who used their charms to get what they wanted. Clint McCall possessed that charm. If she had not twisted her ankle, she would have found another place to spend the night. Possibly rooming at the hotel with Jessica and her sister.

She shouldn't have mentioned her sister-in-law's pregnancy. Mama would have admonished her. A decent young lady did not speak to a man about a woman being "in the family way." The long trip had wearied Emily, loosening her tongue.

It wasn't her mother's fault that Emily's tongue had a mind of its own. She had tried to teach Emily discretion, to speak and act in a lady-like manner. But sometimes blurting out the truth seemed better than hiding it.

If blurting out the truth came naturally, why had she fibbed about her true reason for coming to Abilene? Taking a deep breath, Emily readjusted her hat. This was different. She could not divulge her real reason when this cowboy had boldly voiced his opinion about females who replied to mail-order bride ads.

Clint did not know her, and he did not acknowledge that extenuating circumstances might force a proper woman to take risks. Emily believed her decision had taken courage, not to mention, sacrifice.

Her mother had often warned, "Don't forget, there's a fine line between bravery and foolishness."

Emily thanked God that today, He had kept her from crossing

that line. If she'd known Wendell Clemons had proposed to three women, she would have ripped his letter to shreds and burned it.

Chapter Four

A smooth baritone voice interrupted Emily's thoughts. "The doctor will see to your foot after he sees to my ma." The redheaded cowboy had reappeared.

Worry lines creased his forehead. "Ma's had a hacking cough all day. I hope the doc has some medicine for it." He glanced around as if searching for someone. "Did you come to the wedding alone? I haven't seen you around town."

Emily brushed debris from her skirt. "Yes, I came alone. I arrived by train, this afternoon."

The cowboy frowned. "Who met you at the depot?"

"No one." Emily bit back her anger. Wendell Oliver Clemons had left her at the depot while he exchanged vows with another woman. He was not only a two-timer, but a lout. The cowboy did not need to know this. Emily was no longer proud of her decision. In fact, she felt quite foolish. What woman in her right mind promised herself to a man she had never met? It took Jessica's sister to help her see it.

"Are you in town to visit relatives?"

His green eyes pierced hers as if trying to read her thoughts. She closed her eyes. "No. I came here to—to look for a job." It wasn't a lie, because that's exactly what she intended to do, starting tomorrow.

He pointed to a large, wooden building on the corner up the street. "You haven't checked into the hotel?"

"No." Emily didn't have to look inside her purse to know she didn't have enough money for one night's stay.

"What about your luggage?"

"It's at the depot. I have a carpet bag and a trunk."

He removed his hat and raked through his copper curls. "Tell you what, we'll pick up your carpet bag now. You can stay at the ranch tonight. Doc will see to your ankle after he checks Ma. In the morning, we'll come back to town and pick up your trunk. I'd get it now, but I'm anxious to get back to Ma."

Before Emily could protest, he slipped one arm around her waist and the other beneath her knees, scooping her up. After a dozen long strides, he deposited her on his buckboard. "I'll tell the station master to hold your trunk overnight."

"But—"

"Don't argue. It's partly my fault your ankle is hurt." He climbed up on the wagon and sat down, clicking to the horses. The wagon rolled along the dusty street until the cowboy tugged on the reins and set the brake in front of the depot. "I'll just be a minute." He hopped down and stepped up on the boardwalk, tramping toward the train station entrance.

"Emily is that you?" a familiar voice asked.

Jessica Dawson stood beside the buckboard, squinting up at her, the last person Emily wanted to see. Not because Jessica's sister had stood at the altar with that awful dentist, but because Jessica was a stark reminder of how gullible Emily had been. Even worse, she thought Emily had come here to visit a relative. If the cowboy talked to Jessica, questions might arise.

"Yes, Jessica." Emily forced a smile, hoping the young woman would leave. She seemed to be in no hurry.

"Did you by any chance make it to the wedding?" The young woman blew out a breath.

"Yes. The sanctuary was packed. I stood just inside the door."

She would not admit that Margie's intended was also hers. And if Dr. Clemons D.D.S. owned the entire state of Texas, Emily would not marry him now. Honesty ranked high on her list for a husband. The dentist was a fraud and she'd been gullible enough to fall for his scheme.

Jessica propped her hands on her hips. "Then you saw Margie make a swift exit."

"Oh, yes." She held up the bouquet. "She gave me these. No, she shoved them into my stomach. Do you want them? The flowers are still fresh. I pulled out the crushed ones."

"You keep the flowers. I doubt Margie would appreciate seeing them again. They would be a bad reminder." She glanced around. "I wish I knew where Margie went."

Emily glanced toward the depot, relieved the cowboy had not appeared. If only Jessica would move on. "I saw her walking up the street in this direction. I hope she recovers quickly from what happened."

"So do I. I pulled Margie aside to talk her out of going through with the wedding. She wouldn't listen to me. I had a bad feeling about that shifty-eyed dentist. I could tell he wasn't for her. He wouldn't even look me in the eye. Judging by the packed church, you'd think Oliver Clemons was a highly respected citizen. I wonder why he was in such a hurry to get married."

Emily sucked in her lips. "I wondered the same thing." Should she tell Jessica about the conversation she'd overheard between the two ladies? No, she'd better not.

Jessica continued. "Margie took my advice at the last minute. I stood up and clapped when she ran out of the church. Oliver's mother gave me a scathing look, but I didn't care."

Emily gasped. "Oh, no! I'm glad I didn't see that. I would still be laughing."

Jessica crossed her arms in front of her chest. "It didn't bother me one bit. I was relieved that my sister had come to her senses. The woman started fanning herself and moaning. She turned as white as a sheet. Somebody went to get the doctor while somebody else brought smelling salts."

That explained why the doctor was taking so long. She hoped Mrs. Clemons had fully recuperated.

Jessica screwed up her face. "I didn't wait to see if Mrs. Clemons fainted. I had to cut through the crowd to try to catch up to Margie. But, by the time I got outside, she was nowhere in sight. I already checked the depot."

Emily adjusted her hat and slanted another glance toward the depot door. The cowboy was taking a long time and Jessica's chatter made her nervous. Emily's breath caught when she remembered the station master knew she'd been waiting for Dr. Clemons.

What if he told the cowboy? Emily wished she could hop down and go inside to see what was delaying him. She would if her foot wasn't throbbing. Instead, she took a calming breath.

Jessica threw up her hands. "Can you blame Margie for running out on Clemons? Did you get a good look at him? He could pass for a twin brother to Papa's mule."

Emily laughed. She shouldn't have. Poking fun at a person's looks was mean. But the dentist's long face and protruding teeth could easily earn him the nickname of "Mule Face."

Jessica gazed in one direction then another. "You didn't see where my sister the bride fled?"

"Emily pointed across the street. "I saw her walking in that direction, but no more."

Jessica's eyes narrowed. "Is your aunt inside the depot?"

"Actually…" Emily clamped her mouth shut when she saw

the cowboy swaggering along the boardwalk, her valise in his grip.

Tipping his hat at Jessica, he said, "I heard you asking questions about the fleeing bride. She went inside the Commercial Hotel. Over there." He pointed to the rough-lumber structure down the street. To Emily's relief, he hadn't heard Jessica ask about Emily's supposed aunt.

The cowboy turned his attention to Emily. "Is this your bag?" When she nodded, he set it in the wagon and climbed up beside her. Picking up the reins, he paused to acknowledge Jessica. "The fleeing bride is your sister?"

"Yes, I'm afraid so. My folks sent me here from Eastland, to bring her home. They didn't approve of her running off to marry a stranger."

The cowboy nodded grimly. "I understand. Well, I hope everything works out for all of you."

Jessica sighed. "Me, too. I'm just glad Margie came to her senses before she said, 'I do'." Her gaze slid from Emily to the cowboy seated beside her. "Is this man kin to you, Emily? Where are y'all going, if you don't mind my asking?"

Emily swallowed hard. "He is taking me to his ranch. And, no, it's not what you think."

Before Emily could explain, the cowboy interjected, "Miss Emily here, knocked me off my feet at the church. You could say, 'I fell for her'."

Jessica scrunched up her nose. "I see—I think."

Emily pasted on a smile. Oh, how she wanted to elbow the cowboy. "Everything will be fine. I fell off the porch when your sister shoved these flowers at me. I think I sprained my ankle. He's taking me to where the doctor can look at it."

Jessica's eyebrows rose. "Are you seriously hurt?"

"No. It's probably just a sprain. I'll be fine."

"Good. I'm relieved to hear it. Well, I hate to rush off, but I need to find Margie. She's probably hysterical by now." She nodded at the cowboy. "I'm Jessica Dawson. Nice to meet you, sir. I already met Emily on the train."

He tipped his hat again. "Clint McCall. Nice to meet you too, Jessica."

Looking at Emily, Jessica said, "Margie will be on the early morning train for sure." She hiked her skirts and hurried down the street toward the hotel, turning once to wave at them.

Emily returned the wave as the cowboy shook the reins to get the horses moving. "I'm going to wait near the doctor's office." Clint said. "Doc will stop in to pick up his bag."

As they rolled past the hotel, Clint's gaze followed Jessica up the steps. "My understanding is her sister came here in answer to Clemons's mail-order bride ad. The woman's lucky she came to her senses before it was too late."

His next words came through clenched teeth. "Any woman who answers an ad like that has to be either desperate or crazy. I don't think Jessica's sister was desperate. She looked to be an attractive woman who could easily find a husband."

Emily's breath caught. Desperate or crazy? Given two choices, she'd take desperate. At least she knew where she stood with— Was it Clint McCall?

He must never learn that she had also answered an ad from this dentist, accepting his proposal. Did the cowboy know something shady about Dr. Clemons? Emily licked her lips and faced him. "Isn't a dentist usually of high moral character? Or does Dr. Clemons have something sinister lurking in his past?"

Clint's full lips pulled into a thin line. "Let's just say Oliver's not the best marriage material. From what I hear, his mother still coddles him, while his father has tried to marry him off for several years. Now, the senior Clemons wants to retire and has stipulated his son must marry before he turns his dental practice over to him."

Emily frowned. This must be the inheritance the ladies on the church porch were discussing. "Why would his father require that?"

"The senior Clemons wants to ensure he has a grandson to pass his practice on to. Until lately, Oliver has shown no interest in courting. Since, he's worked himself into a frenzy, looking for a wife. He has to be married by the end of October because his thirtieth birthday is then. Oliver's father set that as the deadline."

Emily remained silent, questions rolling through her mind, while Clint pulled in front of Dr. Simmons's office and set the brake. What would she do? Where would she go? She was down to a few coins.

"You have to give the dentist credit for trying," the cowboy said. "He placed ads in papers in four states, and only got three offers. Clemons promised matrimony to all three women." Clint chuckled. "The only thing I can figure is he was planning to start a harem."

"A harem! I'll make him think—" Emily bit her tongue. She had overreacted. "You aren't serious. Why would any man promise marriage to three women?" If not for the delay in her travel plans, Emily might already be married to that despicable dentist

"I'd say Clemons had a backup plan. He figured two brides wouldn't show up, or else two would run like scalded hounds when they got a look at him." Clint slapped his knee and laughed. "He was right about this one, and I'm glad I was there to witness it."

Emily's hands clenched into fists. "That triple-timing Casanova!"

She held her breath, silently scolding herself. If she did not control her outbursts, this cowboy, would become suspicious. Her stomach twisted in knots. This very minute Emily might be riding off into the sunset with the three-timing Dr. Clemons. She stopped her wayward thoughts and silently thanked God that her trip had been delayed.

The cowboy's eyebrows drew together. "Take it easy, Miss Emily. Clemons's problems are no skin off your back. Just thank your lucky stars, you aren't one of his prospective brides."

She had already thanked God that she hadn't arrived before Margie. "Why didn't the dentist look for a wife in Abilene?"

The cowboy shrugged. "Maybe he did but got no takers." Thrusting out his chest, he boasted, "In case you haven't noticed, Clemons isn't nearly as handsome as Yours Truly."

Emily tried to suppress the smile widening her lips. The cowboy was fishing for a compliment, but she was not in the mood to pay him one. Yes, Clint McCall was handsome. His copper-colored hair and sparkling green eyes could capture any woman's attention. Just not hers. Not when she felt stupid and humiliated and he had made her feel worse.

If Emily had not been duped by the dentist, she might have found the situation comical. As it stood, she didn't think it was funny in the least. And if Mr. McCall thought he could make her laugh he was wasting his time.

Clint grunted. "Sorry to keep on about this, but can you imagine Clemons at the altar with all three brides?"

Emily giggled despite herself. "Yes, and all three brides fleeing the church."

Clint threw his head back and roared. "I wonder how many other bystanders would've been knocked off the porch."

Emily joined in the laughter. When she had pulled herself together, she asked. "Why did you tell Jessica, I 'knocked you off your feet'? I didn't appreciate the way you said it."

Clint's lips pulled into a crooked grin. "You did knock me off my feet when the bride shoved the bouquet into your stomach." He cleared his throat. "All kidding aside, I noticed Jessica's questions were making you tense. Anyway, my explanation worked. She stopped pestering you."

Emily hiked her chin. "That may be true, but you left her with the impression that— I don't want her thinking—"

"…that a proper young lady like you left town with a notorious cowboy?" he finished. "One of likely questionable character?"

"No…that isn't it." Emily was not afraid of Clint McCall—at least not much. She paused to carefully select her next words. "What I meant was, I'd rather she didn't know I left town with a virtual stranger."

He chuckled. "Didn't you?"

She had, but did he have to rub it in? When a lady was left without options, she made the best of the situation. One step at a time. That's exactly what she would do until she could see a clear path before her.

Chapter Five

Clint guided the team down a dirt lane. They rolled another half mile before he pulled them to a stop in front of a sprawling, rustic ranch house. A paddock on Emily's left surrounded a large red barn. What she guessed to be a bunkhouse was attached to it.

A teenage girl dashed out of the house to meet them, a long dark braid flying behind her. "What took you so long?" She asked Clint the question, but her curious gaze slid over Emily.

"Doc was attending a wedding. I hated to interrupt it. How's Ma?"

"Sleeping. I gave her the last of the medicine. It calmed her cough for a while, but now it's started up again."

An intermittent raspy cough came through an open window. The poor woman must be suffering. Emily swallowed hard. She had watched her mother die with a weakened heart. The girl nodded toward Emily. "Who's this?"

"Oh, just some pretty lady who knocked me off my feet." When the girl's eyes narrowed, he paused to scratch his chin "I should clarify. Miss Hammons fell into me and knocked us both off the church porch."

The girl giggled. "I wish I'd been there to see it. How did it happen?"

Clint tugged on her braid. "I'll tell you about it later. The doctor will be here any minute." He nodded toward Emily. "After he sees to Ma, he will look at her foot." He glanced from Emily to the girl. "Oh. Where are my manners? "Emily, this is Alissia, my little sister. Alissia, this is Emily Hammons."

Alissia tossed her head. "He still calls me his 'little sister,' even though I'll turn sixteen in October."

"Only a child," Clint replied with a sigh.

Alissia's eyes narrowed but before she could counter him, a buggy pulled into the yard and the doctor hopped out with his black bag. He appeared to be familiar with his surroundings because he stepped up on the porch, nodded at them, traipsed past, and into the house.

Clint held the screen door open for Emily and slid his arm around her waist. "I'll help you to the kitchen and get you seated. Then Alissia will fix you a glass of lemonade."

Alissia glared at her brother's back. Tension crackled in the evening air. She pranced past them and entered the kitchen first. Was this a sibling spat or was it connected to a deeper issue?

When Clint had settled Emily at the table, he headed down the hall to join the doctor. Emily clasped her hands together and smiled at Alissia. "I hate to put you to any trouble. If I hadn't twisted my ankle, I would pour my own lemonade, plus a glass for you."

"I'm sorry for the way I acted, Miss Hammons. I don't mind serving you. It's my brother spitting out orders that riles me. I was about to ask if you wanted refreshment when he beat me to it. He doesn't think I have enough sense to offer a guest a cool drink after a hot, dusty ride."

She doubted Clint realized he had barked orders at his sister. She figured it was just his way. "Alissia, I don't think he meant to use that tone. He's worried about your mother. And, you can call me Emily."

Alissia pulled four glasses from the cupboard and set them on the table. She twisted the lid off a gallon glass jug of lemonade filled with lemons and began to fill two glasses. "I suppose. But Clint's been acting like that for a while."

"He has a lot on his mind. How long has your mother been sick?"

"She's had a hacking cough for nearly two weeks. I've been praying for her, but it hasn't done much good. I wonder if God is even listening."

Emily had recently had the same thoughts about her own situation. Alissia lowered her gaze to her lap and said, "You know, there's a verse in the Bible that says God won't hear your prayers if you're holding a grudge. I wonder if…"

"Are you?" Emily looked her in the eye.

Alissia sniffed. "Am I what?"

"Holding a grudge?"

Alissia chewed on her lip. "Not exactly…but I get really mad at Clint, over one thing or another, and almost every day."

Emily had gone through those same growing pains as well. The teen years brought a lot of changes in a girl's body. Besides the physical changes, came a host of other things, including emotional outbursts over the least little things.

"Is there any way I can help?"

"My brother is the problem," she huffed. "Clint thinks because he's older, he can nose into my business. He tries to control everything I do, where I go, who I talk to, even how I dress."

Emily nodded her understanding. "That is frustrating. I have an older brother too."

When her father left, Roy appointed himself as head of the Hammons' household. He kept a close eye on Emily, choosing her friends, and enforcing decisions about where she could and could not go. She didn't like it but later realized he'd had her best interest at heart.

"Was your brother as bossy as Clint?"

"I don't know your brother well enough to say, but yes, Roy was very protective where I was concerned." Emily sipped from her glass before setting it on the table. "My, that is refreshing and delicious after the hot ride from town."

"Want some more?"

"Yes, thank you. Emily slid her glass across the table for Alissia to refill. Tilting her head to one side, she studied the girl. "Where's your father? I haven't met him yet."

"My father?" Emily detected the bitter edge in the girl's voice.

She feared she had touched on a sensitive topic. He had deserted them, as her own had?

Alissia slid into a chair across from Emily, clasping her hands together on the table. "I don't have one. Not anymore. Ma left him when I was four. Neither she nor Clint will tell me anything about my pa. It's as if his marriage to Ma is some big secret that I'm not supposed to know. From what I can gather, he was a no-good drunk and a gambler."

She shrugged. "He died last winter in a saloon brawl in Nevada. I only know that from eavesdropping."

Emily regretted bringing up the subject. "I'm sorry. I didn't know."

"Don't be. I was young when we left. I don't remember much about him. At least not much good. The one thing I clearly recall is Pa's voice. He laughed loud when he was happy, but when he was angry, he got louder. Clint toted me to the wood-shed to hide out when Pa started screaming at Ma. The last time they got into an argument, Clint locked me in and left.

"Something must've happened because I was in there a long time before Clint returned. When he did, he had bruises on his arms and face, and he was holding his shoulder."

No wonder Clint was protective over his sister. Alissia had been exposed to things a child should have never seen. Emily shifted in her chair. "Did you find out what happened?"

"I figure Pa walloped Clint when he got between him and Ma. My brother can't stand to see anyone bullied. Especially a woman."

Emily's admiration grew for the cowboy. If the man was drunk and began to hit their mother, Clint should try to intervene. "How old was your brother at the time?"

"Twelve." Alissia sighed. "It was the last we saw Pa. He was galloping away when we came around the house. I remember Ma sitting at the table with her hands over her face, shaking like a leaf. She stayed like that until Clint started bellowing orders. He told us to start packing, that we were heading back to Texas. We loaded everything we could haul on the wagon and left Nevada to come here."

Emily doubted that Clint would approve of his sister revealing family skeletons, but since she'd already waded in this deep, what could it hurt to wade deeper? "What made you come here, to Abilene?"

"Grandpa and Grandma Lawson owned this ranch. They'd told Ma to come home if things didn't turn out for her. Both my grandparents died three years ago from an outbreak of smallpox. I sure do miss them."

Like Emily, this family had had its struggles. She supposed everyone went through hard times. If not financial ones, emotional or spiritual.

Emily shook her head to clear it. She should be planning her next move instead of asking Clint's sister personal questions. Where would she sleep tonight? And, how would she eat? She had enough money for one meal. What after that? Her stomach growled on cue.

Alissia smiled. "Would you like a bowl of peach cobbler? I made it myself."

How could Emily refuse, not knowing when she would eat again? She flashed a smile. "I would love some cobbler. Is there anything I can do to help out in the kitchen?"

"No, I'll get everything. Just stay seated and sip your lemonade. You need to stay off that foot, anyway. Does it hurt much?"

"Some. Only when I move it," Emily admitted.

"We have a good doctor. He will fix you up, once he's through treating Ma."

While Alissia scooped up the cobbler, she caught Emily up on Abilene's history. "The town didn't exist until the railroad came through. That was only three years ago, in '81. My grandparents got to see the buildings going up but didn't live long enough to see the businesses open.

"Before the train came through, we went to Buffalo Gap for our supplies. I'm glad Abilene was formed into a town because it has better shops for ladies, shops that aren't in Buffalo Gap. The shops in Abilene carry the latest fashions. I especially like the selection of hats at two shops. One millinery carries hats shipped all the way from Paris, France. And the mercantile and general stores carry a larger selection of fabrics and notions."

Emily understood. Fashion was important to a girl embarking on womanhood. "Does Clint—?"

"Does Clint what?"

Emily flinched. Clint languished against the door jamb grinning with his arms folded across his chest. How long had he been there, and how much had he heard? Why had they not heard his boots clomp across the wood floor? She would have to be careful about asking Alissia questions.

He swaggered over to the sideboard and picked up the glass of lemonade his sister had poured for him. Clearing her throat, Emily said, "I was about to ask if you ran this ranch singlehandedly."

Clint upended the glass and drained it, plunking it down on the table. "Ah. That was delicious." His gaze caught Emily's.

"The answer would be no. Cowhands Bud and Slim stayed on after our grandparents died."

Alissia sighed. "And now we also have Landon," she added with a lilt to her voice.

"Yeah…Landon," Clint muttered.

If Emily were a gambler, she'd bet Clint did not approve of Landon—whoever he was. Did he have anything to do with the dreamy look in Alissia's eyes?

Curiosity got the best of her. "Who is Landon?" she dared to ask.

"Landon Reilly is a kid still wet behind the ears," Clint stated matter-of-factly. "The Reillys live down the road a few miles. They have a passel of young'uns. Poor folks."

"Landon's the oldest," Alissia explained. "He's eighteen and really smart. He graduated Valedictorian in May. Landon plans to become a doctor."

Clint clicked his tongue. "A big dream for a boy without two copper pennies to rub together."

Alissia shot her brother a cold glare before turning to Emily. "Landon is going to Dallas in a few weeks, to take a medical exam. If he makes a high score, he will be accepted into the University of Arkansas to study medicine. It'll be too late to start this semester. He will have to wait until the first of the year. If he makes the highest grade, he will be awarded a full scholarship."

Ignoring his sister, Clint turned to Emily. "I hired the boy to help with spring roundup. Landon and his folks live in a little hovel on the way to town. There are six children. I figured they could use the extra money, so I kept Landon on the payroll. He tries, but he has a lot to learn about ranching."

Alissia flung her braid over her shoulder. "Landon's a fast learner. In April, he helped you deliver a calf coming breech. Whatever a person puts his mind to, he can do it. You said it yourself, Clint. Doctoring is Landon's gift. Not everyone has to be a rancher."

Clint groaned. "You made your point, Sis, but delivering a calf, doesn't prove he can deliver a baby."

Alissia glared at him. "It's not much different." She turned to Emily. "Landon's pa lost a leg in the War Between The States. They came here from Arkansas, two years ago."

Clint tugged on his sister's braid. "As long as Landon sticks to ranch work while he's here, you won't hear me complain."

Alissia's mouth gaped as if she intended to argue. She noticed Emily and closed it. Picking up the dishrag, she scrubbed the oilcloth with a vengeance. Without looking up, she asked, "What did Doc Simmons say about Ma?"

Clint blew out a breath. "He's still in there. Just as I thought, he says it's pneumonia. It could be weeks before she's up and about. She'll need constant care. Even after she's on her feet, she won't be doing much around the house for a good while."

Alissia raised her chin. "Tell me what to do, and I'll do it. I can cook, clean, and whatever else needs doing."

"No, not you. School starts back next week. You need to concentrate on your studies, getting your education. I'll figure out something. Maybe I can hire the Widow Allen to look after Ma. She's been known to tend sick folks."

"She caught the train to Dallas on Monday, to visit her kids," Alissia piped in. "Won't be back until November."

Clint raked a hand through his coppery hair. "Oh, that's right. I guess that's out. She mentioned it at church, Sunday." He propped his backside against the sideboard and stretched his lanky legs out before him. "There must be somebody we haven't thought of."

Alissia nodded toward Emily. "What about her?"

"Me?" Emily squeaked. Two sets of eyes sized her up. Clint's probing gaze made her heart flutter. Whether from fear or something else, she wasn't sure.

He finally shook his head. "No. I'm sure Miss Hammons has other plans."

Alissia slapped her hands together. "Oh, come on, Clint, you could at least ask her."

Clint graced Emily with a winsome smile. She was sure it worked on the ladies. But she had always been leery of men who used their charm as a method of persuasion.

"Miss Hammons, do you have other plans?"

Emily pulled her gaze from his and focused on the empty glass in her hands. Her first impulse was to say, "Yes, I do."

She didn't mind attending to their sick mother, but Clint McCall had made his disdain of mail-order brides, very clear. How could she accept his offer? What if he discovered she had come to Abilene through one of those ads?

On the other hand, what other option did she have? She had to be practical. Accepting this job could be a temporary solution. She had little money and nowhere to go. When Clint and Alissia's mother was up and about, Emily would find a job in town. Surely, in that short time, Clint wouldn't discover her secret.

Emily swallowed her pride. "I have no other plans at this time. I accept your offer."

Alissia sighed. Clint's green eyes twinkled. At the same time, they seemed to plead. "Are you sure?" he asked. His next words gave Emily an out. "I hate to impose on your kind nature."

"I don't have a job as of yet. I can attend to your mother until she recuperates."

Clint's shoulders relaxed. "Thank you. I appreciate it, Miss Hammons." He twisted his head to one side as if listening. "Ma's cough has quieted. The medicine worked."

Footsteps clomped on the wood floor before the doctor appeared in the kitchen doorway. He tipped his hat at Emily and Alissia before turning to Clint. "Your mother may sleep for a while. You should consider hiring a woman to attend to her and do housework until she's better, one who can also administer your mother medicine as needed." He shook his head. "Not Alissia. Don't pull her out of school."

Clint waved a hand toward Emily. "We were just discussing the matter, Doc. Miss Hammons here, has offered to stay on as long as we need her."

"Good." The doctor grinned. "I think she will make a fine nursemaid."

Emily wasn't sure about that. She thought of herself as a caring person, but nursing wasn't a job she wanted to spend her life doing. Holding onto a chair back, she limped toward the doctor. "Show me what to do."

He patted her shoulder. "With that gimpy foot, you won't be much help for a couple of days. By the time Monday rolls around, you should be fine." He motioned for her to follow him.

Clint slid an arm around Emily to support her. Holding to him, they reached his mother's bedroom. Emily leaned into him as she listened to the doctor explain how to administer his mother's medicine. The pretty, blonde woman lying in bed, snored softly. She looked to be in her early forties. Her pale complexion was surrounded by strawberry-blonde curls.

Clint exhaled. "You don't know how relieved I am to see my ma this peaceful. She's coughed so long and hard, I thought she would burst a blood vessel."

"Pneumonia is hard on a body. The medicine should keep the cough quieted for a time," Doc Simmons confirmed.

"I appreciate all you've done for her, Doc."

"No thanks needed, Clint. I would have come by sooner, but several others are suffering from it too."

The doctor smiled at Emily. "Now, young lady, I'll take a look at your foot. Clint, get her settled in that chair. Then you need to leave."

"As you request, Doc, but just so you know, I've already seen her ankles and more." He winked at Emily, who gasped.

The doctor coughed to conceal a chuckle. "Pay him no mind, Miss Hammons. Clint lives to aggravate." He inclined his head toward the young man in question. "That may be true,

Clint, but it's still not proper. Now, get out. I'll call you if I need you."

"You don't need me to help wrap her ankle?" Clint teased.

The doctor's eyes narrowed in mock sternness. "I said, get out."

"Yes, sir!" Clint saluted before turning to leave. "I'll be in the kitchen. Just give a holler."

The doctor knelt before Emily and pressed the top of her foot. "Does it hurt here?"

Emily flinched. "Yes, a little. But I think it will be all right."

He probed the sides of her ankle. "What about here…and here?"

"Ouch!" She yanked her foot from his grip.

"Hold still," he admonished, setting the injured foot gently on the floor. "Well, it's sprained, for certain. Swelled too but doesn't appear to be broken. I'll leave some gauze. First, soak your foot in a pan of warm Epsom Salts, then wrap it with gauze. Wrap it tight. It should be better in a couple of days. You'll still need to go easy on it for a little while longer. Clint probably has a crutch around here somewhere. Use it to help keep the pressure off."

He rose and walked to the doorway, sticking his head through it. "Clint, do you still have that crutch your Grandpa used when he injured his foot? The young lady will need it for a few days."

Clint said something inaudible before his boots clomped across the wood floor and the screen door popped behind him. Emily watched the tall cowboy through the window as he swaggered toward the barn. Muscular shoulders and a broad chest narrowed to a small waist. My, he was handsome. She pulled her gaze back to Clint's mother as Doc Simmons returned to her bedside.

"Now, about Vera…uh, Mrs. James." He held up two bottles of liquid and a package of powders. After repeating the instructions regarding the patient's medicines, he patted Emily's hand.

"I'll be back in a few days to check on her, and on your foot. She's a fighter, but she needs our prayers. Pneumonia is tough on a body. Not everybody pulls through."

He rubbed the back of his neck and smiled. "About Clint— he's not the ladies' man he appears to be. He just jokes around a lot. Sometimes he takes it too far."

Emily returned his smile. "Thank you for everything, Doctor Simmons."

As soon as the doctor left the room, she whispered, "Lord, help me."

What had she done? If something awful happened to Mrs. James while under her care, everyone would blame her. She took a calming breath, admonishing herself for letting her thoughts run amok. Because Emily's mother had not recuperated under her care, it did not mean Mrs. James wouldn't.

Tears pooled in her eyes. Things could be worse. If she'd arrived on time, she could be wearing that three-timing dentist's wedding band. And this could be her wedding night.

Emily's stomach churned. She hadn't considered all the implications when she'd replied to the ad. Truth be known, she hadn't thought ahead at all. She had been desperate to leave a chaotic home life. And because of her decision, she had almost jumped from the frying pan and landed in the fire. She thanked God for her brother's appointment with the banker. The delay was a blessing in disguise.

Tears trickled down her cheeks. She dried them on her dress sleeve. How long before Clint discovered her shameful secret? Emily wrapped her arms around her waist and shivered despite the Texas heat. She deserved whatever happened. She'd gotten herself into this mess, and she would get herself out.

Chapter Six

Clint found the homemade crutch hanging on a hook behind the barn door. He pulled a bandana from his pocket and rubbed off the excess dirt. Grandpa had carved the crutch from a white oak tree limb after he'd broken his foot when the wagon wheel ran over it. He grumbled that if he'd set the brake, he'd be walking on two good feet.

Clint's thoughts drifted to the young woman inside the house. Emily was an enigma. What young woman in her right mind took a train from West Memphis to Abilene without the promise of a job, or at least a beau, waiting at the end of the line? It made no sense. Memphis was only a short distance from Emily's hometown. If she needed a job, why hadn't she looked there?

He needed to mind his own business instead of Emily's. He hoped, besides nursing their mother back to health, she would be a good companion for his little sister. Maybe she could talk Alissia out of her infatuation with the young hired hand. It didn't take a genius to see she was smitten. Clint had other plans for his little sister, and they did not include Landon Reilly, who didn't have a nickel to his name.

Alissia wouldn't be sixteen until October, too young to

become enamored with a boy. She should be concentrating on her education. Clint would see about enrolling her in some kind of women's college after she earned a high school diploma. Furthering her education would give his sister a certain amount of independence. She wouldn't be at the mercy of a man, like Ma was.

He would do everything within his power to see that Alissia did not end up marrying a silver-tongued brute who spent his free time gambling, drinking, and carousing.

A woman had to be careful. Clint learned it firsthand when his ma married Alissia's pa.

Clint could not count the times the louse had beaten his mother. It would not happen to Alissia. He would intercept any boy who tried to court her. He wanted his little sister to have a better life than the one his mother experienced.

Clint dipped the handkerchief in the water trough and ran it down the length of the crutch, giving it one last inspection. "It'll have to do," he muttered, tucking the crutch under one arm and traipsing toward the house.

Soft voices drifted from Ma's bedroom. He stuck his head through the door and found Emily coaxing her into taking a little broth. She hadn't eaten enough to keep a cat alive over the past two weeks.

Clint slipped into the kitchen where Alissia bustled about setting the table. The aroma of beef roast and vegetables tantalized his nostrils. His little sister's cooking skills equaled their ma's. Someday she'd make somebody a good— No! Alissia would further her education if he had any say in the matter.

"Supper will be ready in five minutes." Alissia's chin had a stubborn jut. She'd come by it honestly from their Ma. And Clint had inherited a generous dose too.

She was still out of sorts with him over that Reilly kid. Well, that couldn't be helped. He hadn't said a thing that wasn't true and did not aim to apologize.

"Thanks, Sis. Everything looks and smells delicious."

He hadn't eaten since breakfast, what with fence-mending, and afterward taking the trip to town to fetch the doctor and Miss Hammons.

"We need to set up the cot for Emily, in Ma's room," Alissia said.

Clint stroked his chin. "I'll do it after supper." He hadn't thought about where Emily would sleep. Her overnight bag sat by the front door where he'd dropped it.

Clint picked up the crutch and started back toward Ma's bedroom. Emily's voice drifted out as he reached the door. "There, there, doesn't that feel better?"

Emily had laid a wet cloth over his mother's forehead. Clint cleared his throat to make his presence known. She looked up at him. My, those bluebonnet eyes were gorgeous.

"Supper will be ready soon." He held up the crutch. "I brought this for you. I wiped it down. You can use it as long as you need to."

Emily averted her gaze to her patient. "Thank you."

"After we eat, I'll move the cot in here. It's not the most comfortable bed, but it's not bad." He had relinquished his room and slept on the cot when company came.

"I appreciate it, and the crutch," she said.

"And we appreciate your willingness to stay here and take care of our ma."

She raised her head and smiled. "I'm glad to be of help."

Clint's heart sank when he caught sight of her flushed cheeks and red-rimmed eyes. Had the doctor said something more about Ma's condition that he hadn't told Clint? No, the doctor would have told him first.

Before Clint blurted out questions that were none of his business, he propped the crutch against Emily's chair and left.

~

Clint had left abruptly. Why? Emily pressed a hand to her chest where her heart drummed against her ribcage. He must have seen evidence that she'd been crying. She didn't want him to think she was a crybaby. Emily wished she had kept better control over her emotions.

Why had she taken Clint up on his offer to nurse his mother back to health? Seeing the pale woman lying in bed, reminded her of her own mother, and filled her with an overwhelming sense of guilt. Emily's mother had died despite her prayers and everything else she'd attempted.

Reality struck the day the doctor told them that Mama's weakened heart would be lucky to last three months. Emily realized that day, her mother's health was out of her hands.

Their mother lived exactly ninety-one days after the prognosis. Until the day she passed, Emily clung to the hope that God would make her well again. She'd been wrong.

Dead wrong. God had failed her. Could she have done more? Or was Emily a jinx? Did God even listen to her prayers? He was probably too busy with everyone else's problems.

Answering the dentist's ad was supposed to solve her brother's financial problems. Emily thought leaving home would make her brother's life easier, and that it was God's will She had prayed about it, but when He hadn't answered, she'd decided on her own. Look how that had turned out. What a mess she was in!

Emily picked up the tortoise-shell mirror from the bedside table to check her reflection. It was too late to remedy her tell-tale eyes, but she could tame her curls. She pulled a comb from her purse and tugged it through her tangled tresses. Emily grimaced at her reflection and dropped the comb inside her purse. She was not satisfied with the results, but at least she'd made an effort. After shaking the wrinkles from her skirt, she stood and propped the crutch under her arm.

Clint sat at the table eyeing her when she clomped into the

kitchen. His gaze slid over her, lingering on her face before he jumped up and helped her over to the table.

Alissia set a bowl of sliced tomatoes on the table. "Supper is served." Seating herself in a chair at the far end, the girl patted the chair to her right. "Sit here, Emily."

Clint helped Emily settle in the chair. When he'd sat across the table, he extended one hand toward her and the other toward his sister. Emily realized he wanted to join hands to say grace. His strong warm fingers wrapped around hers. A warm tingle skittered up her arm. She exhaled a ragged breath and tried to appear calm.

Blessing the food had been a tradition at her house while their mother was alive. It had flown out the window after Mama died. Roy made no mention of praying at meals. Neither had she. It reminded them of the empty chair at the table.

Clint bowed his head and thanked the Lord for their food, adding a request for his mother's speedy recovery. All the while he stroked the back of Emily's hand with his thumb. Whether the gesture was from habit or his attempt to comfort her, she could not tell. Before he closed, he added, "And thank you, Lord, for bringing Miss Hammons into our home to care for Ma."

He released Emily's hand and reached for the platter of beef roast, offering it to her. "I forgot to ask about your trip, Miss Hammons. I hope it was tolerable. Train rides can be uncomfortable. When they start to rock going around curves, you think the cars may tip over."

"That's true," Emily replied. "The soot blowing through the window was even worse. But it couldn't be helped. The train would have been unbearably hot with the window closed."

"I've never been on a train," Alissia interjected, "but Clint takes it sometimes".

"It was my first time," Emily admitted, forking roast beef and carrots onto her plate.

~

CLINT NOTICED Emily's puffy eyes, although she kept them downcast, and avoided looking up. He'd caught her wiping them when he came into Ma's bedroom. Was she homesick already, or had seeing his mother's weakened condition upset her? Maybe the long trip had taken its toll. A good night's sleep should remedy that.

Clint took the bowl of sliced tomatoes from his sister and extended it to Emily. She thanked him and lowered her head again.

"I take the train to Kansas on cattle business," Clint explained. "Since the railroad came through, we drive the herds eight miles into town, load them on the cattle cars, and ship them to wherever the current prices are best. After that, the cattle belong to the railroad. It's better than the old way of driving the herd up to the Kansas stockyards."

Emily raised her head. "You must be relieved. I've read about those long cattle drives. They are hard on the drovers and the cattle."

Clint took in Emily's long, dark lashes and red-rimmed eyes before she focused on her plate. She must have learned something about ranching from those wild west stories. He hoped she wasn't thinking of leaving soon.

Where had that thought come from? He washed down a bite of roast with a gulp from his glass. "Driving the herd north took time and was tedious work. The drive took weight off the cattle, meaning ranchers lost a lot of money. The railroad makes the job easier and faster. I help load the cattle then take the same train to Kansas to dicker over prices and to pick up the check."

Emily's fork trembled on the way to her mouth. Clint couldn't stop staring at the woman. Shimmering raven locks cascaded down her back halfway to her waist. She possessed an ethereal beauty as no woman he'd ever seen.

"Miss Hammons, I hope you will be comfortable here. If you need anything, let me or Alissia know."

She looked up and her blue gaze locked with his. "Just my trunk from the depot," she reminded him. I only have one change of clothes in my overnight bag."

"I need to go into town for supplies, in the morning. You can ride along, and we'll pick it up. Alissia can sit with Ma."

His sister huffed. "I hope that's all right with you, Alissia. Emily needs to get her trunk, and the doctor wants someone with Ma at all times. At least until her fever breaks."

"Of course." Alissia slid her chair back from the table and rose. Picking up her plate and eating utensils, she walked to the dishpan.

Clint understood his sister's frustration. Since their mother had taken sick, she had taken on an extra workload, leaving her little or no free time. It was too much for a fifteen-year-old girl, but what could he do? It was a busy time at the ranch. On the bright side, Emily's presence would lighten Alissia's burden.

"Alissia, do you have a grocery list ready? I'll drop Miss Hammons off at the general store. She can collect the items while I make a couple of other stops. It'll save time."

"It's ready," Alissia answered coolly while raking scraps from her plate into the pan they used to feed their coon dog. "Do you have anything to add to the list?"

"No, but Miss Hammons may."

Emily sipped from her glass before setting it down. "I can't think of a thing."

A beautiful lady should have pretty things. He would love to shower Emily Hammons with gifts. His gaze slid over her outfit. The dark fabric didn't suit her, and the style looked a little outdated. But what did he know about ladies' fashions?

Clint couldn't stop staring. She must think him a Casanova. "If you see anything you want at the store, let me know."

~

EMILY RAISED HER CHIN. "Thank you for the kind offer, Mr. McCall," she replied. But she would not mention one thing she might need. Clint had done more than enough by taking her in when she had no place to light. He had given her a roof over her head and provided her with a delicious meal, prepared by his sister.

He did not know she was down to her last two dollars and too proud to admit it. She planned to hold onto the money as long as possible.

Clint's scrutiny made her uncomfortable. She felt him taking in her hair, face, and dress. Did she not measure up to his standards? Was something wrong with her outfit? She would do her best to ensure that he had no regrets about surrendering his mother to her care.

Emily's family had gone through hard times since her pa left. They hadn't the money for frivolous things. She learned to sew at an early age and began making her own clothes. The dark traveling suit she wore now, belonged to her mother. It fit her well but was out of style. Emily had diminished the bustle to bring it up to date.

She'd only worn it because she'd heard stories of soot blowing in through train windows. The dark color concealed the black specks. She hoped Clint was not judging her by her outfit. The dresses in her trunk were more stylish, and better suited to the Texas climate.

Emily watched Alissia pour steaming water in a dishpan. The girl's around-the-house dress looked light and comfortable. Rose-pink flowers adorned a baby-blue background. She assumed it had once been her Sunday-go-to-meeting dress. She also preferred pastels over drab, earth colors which tended to depress her. Enough musing. Emily concentrated on finishing her supper. She hadn't eaten since breakfast and everything tasted delicious.

Clint extended the cornbread plate toward her. "Want more?"

"Thank you." She reached for a second slice. "This is delicious and very moist, Alissia." Emily fanned herself. How did the girl stand the heat in the kitchen?

Alissia blushed. "Thank you. Ma has a special recipe."

Emily broke off another piece and inspected it. "You must share it with me."

"Gladly. It's easy."

While Alissia explained the trick to making moist cornbread, Clint slid his chair away from the table. "If you ladies will excuse me, I'll leave you to your girl talk. I'll move the cot in Ma's room, Miss Hammons, after I go to the barn and mend the harness."

"Thank you." Emily took her last bite as Clint clomped across the plank floor toward the door. When the screen door slapped to, she rose and stacked the remaining dirty dishes. When a pain stabbed through her foot, she bit her lip to stifle a yelp.

"Alissia, I'd like to do the dishes. You've already outdone yourself cooking this meal."

The girl poured soap flakes into the dishwater and swished them around. "No. You have an injured foot. You need to sit and rest."

"What if I lean against the counter to take the pressure off it?" Emily offered.

"Tell you what—you can sit at the table and dry the dishes as I hand them to you. I need to familiarize you with the kitchen, anyway, show you where things are stored."

Emily let out a long breath and sat down in the chair closest to her. Alissia pulled a dishtowel from the sideboard drawer and tossed it to her.

The girl seemed a little sad. "How long has your mother been sick?"

Alissia handed her a dripping plate, pausing before she picked up another dish. "A week. Her coughing got a lot worse today. It scared me."

Fear showed in her eyes. The girl carried too much responsibility. Emily was determined to lighten her load.

Alissia's curious gaze studied her. "Where did Clint find the doctor? He was gone a while."

Emily paused for fear she'd reveal too much. "The doctor was attending a wedding at the Methodist church. With the church so crowded, many of us were forced to stand outside on the porch and look in the best way we could."

"Oh, I forgot!" Alissia's eyes lit up. "Our town dentist was scheduled to get married today. How did it go? It's been the main gossip for months."

"Why is that?" Emily feigned disinterest as she wiped dry a serving bowl.

Alissia whistled under her breath. "You haven't heard?"

"Heard what?" Yes, she had heard the story from Clint, but she wanted to hear Alissia's version.

"While I sat at the depot, the church bell started to peal. Because I had wearied of sitting, I walked down there."

The girl's eyes widened. You didn't know Oliver Clemons was getting married? That he'd ordered three brides? That's according to Adella Payne who owns the general store."

"Three?" Hearing it spoken aloud still unnerved Emily. Of course, stories could get exaggerated when passed from one mouth to the next.

"Yes. He really did."

Alissia called the dentist Oliver, as had the older ladies on the church porch. On her letter, he'd penned Wendell O. Clemons. Apparently, he answered to his middle name.

Alissia handed her a dripping bowl. "You'd think one proposal would be enough. My guess is Oliver figured two women would change their minds. You can't blame him. He's no prize."

Emily could no longer hold her tongue. "The bride did change her mind. She threw the ring at him and fled the church while they were repeating their vows."

"Fled the church?" Alissia gasped. "What did Clemons do?"

"He looked to be in shock when the ring bounced off him and landed at the reverend's feet."

"I'll bet." Alissia giggled before a frown crossed her face. "How did you happen to be at the wedding? I thought you didn't know anybody in Abilene."

"I knew the bride's sister." Relief flooded Emily that she had a plausible excuse. "Jessica and I met on the train. We shared a seat. She gave me directions to the church. It wasn't far from the depot. I heard the bell pealing and thought it might be announcing the wedding. I walked down the street to see for myself."

Emily hoped Alissia would accept her explanation and not delve deeper. She'd told Clint that she'd come to Abilene in search of work. Clint's sister was too perceptive. The girl's questions made her uncomfortable.

"Wait until Clint hears this. He thinks Oliver Clemons is arrogant." To Emily's relief, Clint's sister seemed more interested in the wedding than questioning her. Alissia frowned. "You didn't say where you met my brother."

"At the wedding. Clint came to look for the doctor. He stood on the porch behind me. Your brother is partly responsible for my injured foot. When the bride rushed out, she shoved the bouquet at me and knocked me into him. When I lost my balance, your brother grabbed for me, and we fell off the porch together. I'm embarrassed to admit I landed on him."

Alissia giggled. "That must have been a sight. And I missed everything."

Emily clucked her tongue. "It was awful. People were staring. My skirt had flipped up, and my calves and petticoats were showing."

Alissia's eyes glowed. "This gets more interesting by the minute. Like the beginning of a fairytale romance."

"I wouldn't say that." Emily lowered her gaze and slid the dishtowel over a bowl.

Alissia was too quick to get false notions. Clint had already expressed his opinion about mail-order brides. Why?

Curiosity got the best of her. "Your brother gave me the impression he doesn't have much use for mail-order brides. Do you have any idea why?"

Alissia's eyes dulled. She sloshed a spoon around in the rinse water before passing it to Emily. "I'm surprised he didn't tell you." She wiped the spoon and laid it down, sensing Alissia's hesitation.

"Our mother was a mail-order bride."

Emily gasped. "I'm sorry I brought it up. I didn't know."

Alissia slung the water off a serving bowl. "It's all right. At least it is now."

"From what you said, I gathered the marriage didn't work out."

"The man was my pa. He'd placed an ad in a newspaper, and Ma replied to it. As I said, he treated her something awful, although I have little memory of it. I was only three when Ma left him. Clint calls him a miscreant. The mention of my pa's name puts my brother in a foul mood. I wish I knew more of the story, but when I ask Ma, she says, 'Best to let sleeping dogs lie.'"

It made sense now. Clint scorned mail-order brides because his mother replied to an ad and married an abusive man. The revelation fortified Emily's decision to keep her secret under wraps.

Clint and Alissia must never know that the dentist's ad lured her to Abilene.

Chapter Seven

The sun spread its golden rays across the rugged Texas landscape as Clint and Emily left for town. She was glad she'd worn the light-weight gingham dress, the one she'd tucked into her overnight bag. She checked her purse again to ensure her baggage claims stub was safely tucked inside. Yes, it was there. Clint promised they would retrieve her trunk before going anywhere else.

Emily guessed the doctor's visit and his mother's suppressed cough was responsible for Clint's lighter mood. He pointed out trees and wide-open pastures where cattle grazed. Houses were few and far between. They passed two in five miles. Clint explained that the Kirbys lived in one, the Mabrys in the other. A few miles farther down the road, they reached a shack where a middle-aged blonde woman tossed feed from a battered pan to a dozen clucking chickens.

Clint tugged on the reins. "Whoa!" When the horses stopped, he yelled, "Good morning, Mrs. Reilly. You need anything from town? We're headed that way."

A light breeze tousled strands of the woman's hair that escaped from her otherwise neat bun. She tucked the hair behind her ears as she walked toward the buckboard, the pan in her grasp. Her friendly gaze raked Emily.

"As a matter of fact, Clint, I'm down to one measure of flour. Not enough to fry a batch of chicken for my hungry bunch. I hate to put you to any trouble."

"No trouble, Mrs. Reilly. We'll pick up a bag and drop it by on the way back." Clint tilted his head toward Emily. This is Emily Hammons. She will be caring for Ma until she's up and around again. The doctor came by last night. He says Ma needs around-the-clock care."

"Emily smiled at the woman. "Nice to meet you, Mrs. Reilly."

The woman extended her hand and Emily took it. "My pleasure. I expect you'll be attending our church."

Emily looked to Clint, who cleared his throat. "Emily and Alissia will work out a schedule. My sister could use a break. Ma has been down with this sickness for two weeks."

The older woman sighed. "Alissia is a fine young lady. She's taken on a lot for her age. Is your ma any better this morning? Landon said she was coughing her head off, yesterday."

Clint pulled off his hat and raked through his hair. "Doc Simmons says it's pneumonia. He gave her some strong cough medicine. It quieted her last night, but it will be a while before she's on her feet again. We're praying the fever breaks soon."

Mrs. Reilly wiped the perspiration from her brow. "Poor woman. It's hard enough to stay cool in this heat without having a fever. Tell your ma, we're praying for all of y'all. I'll be by to visit, once she's better. Maybe bring a peach pie."

Clint nodded. "I'll tell her. All prayers are appreciated."

Worry lines creased the older woman's forehead. "Tell Adella Payne, we'll be in to pay our bill as soon as we're able."

Clint replaced his hat. "Will do. How is Mr. Reilly, today?"

"Oh, his leg's hurting him some. Swears he can still feel the pain below his knee, even though it's been amputated. He even claims it itches sometimes. It's all a mystery to me."

"The doctors call it Phantom Limb pain. It sometimes happens to those who've returned from the war." Clint picked up the reins and waved. "We'd better mosey along, if we want to get back by supper. Have a nice day, Mrs. Reilly." He clicked his tongue and the horses began to move.

Emily admired Clint's rugged profile, straight nose, and chiseled jaw while he faced straight ahead. The cowboy had a big heart. It touched her that Clint cared about families in need. Her pa had been like that, lending a helping hand to those less fortunate.

She swallowed around the lump in her throat. All Pa's charity didn't make up for the fact that he'd left them to make his fortune in the silver mines and had not sent for them. Emily clenched her hands, digging in her nails. How could he have made a promise that important and not honored it? They had waited and waited for a letter. They had received only one, and it came a month after he left. The letter stated he'd staked a claim and was sure he had struck it rich. When he had it assayed, he would send money for them to come West.

"Are you okay, Miss Hammons? You look pale. Is our Texas heat too much?"

Clint's voice jolted Emily back to the present. "I'm fine." She forced a smile and began to fan herself, glad she'd brought the fan along. "It is a little warmer than I'm used to."

"I can imagine. Texas is known for its heat. Your dress is a lighter weight material than the one you wore yesterday." He patted her arm. "We're almost there."

Ten minutes later, Abilene loomed ahead. Wagons rolled along at an urgent pace, flinging up dust, while horses carrying riders trotted up and down the busy street. Everyone seemed to be desperate to reach their destination. The sound of hammers and saws reached her ears. The town was expanding.

When they pulled into the train station, Clint hopped off the buckboard and helped Emily down. He gently set her on the ground and reached into the wagon for her crutch. Circling her waist with one arm, he helped her up on the boardwalk and stayed nearby to open the depot door. He let her precede him inside.

When Emily told the station master her name and showed her claims ticket, he scratched his head. "You'll have to wait until I can get somebody to load the trunk. I'm short on help today."

Clint stepped up to the window. "Mr. Ward tell me where it is."

"I can point it out to him," Emily added.

"Miss Hammons, you say?" The wiry little man pointed to a corner where trunks of various sizes sat, small ones stacked on top of large ones.

Emily pointed out the trunk that belonged to her. After moving a smaller one on top, Clint knelt and wrapped his arms around Emily's trunk. He heaved it up to rest on one shoulder and rose to his feet without so much as a grunt.

"I hope you don't mind me loading it, sir. We are in a hurry."

Mr. Ward waved him on. "Not at all. I appreciate it, Clint. Have a nice day. How is your mother? Heard she was sick."

"She has pneumonia." Nodding toward Emily, he added, "Miss Hammons here, will be taking good care of her."

The station master narrowed his eyes at Emily "Ah, yes. Now, I remember. You're the young lady who got off the train yesterday. You asked about—"

Emily's heart hitched. *Lord, please don't let him say it!*

"As I said, Mr. Ward," Clint interjected. "We're in a rush. I don't like leaving Ma alone for long. Miss Hammons, are you ready?"

"Yes." Emily released a breath.

The station master's gaze followed her as they left. Emily ducked her head in shame. If Clint discovered she'd come to town as a mail-order bride, what would happen to her? She dared not consider it. Clint's interrupting the station master had bought her more time. Hopefully, by the time he learned the truth, she would have a job in town and a rented room.

Emily tapped her crutch on the boardwalk behind Clint, careful to hold to the railing as she descended the steps. Her trunk must weigh seventy-five pounds, but Clint carried it on one shoulder as if it were a sack of feathers. Emily could not pull her gaze from his broad shoulders and muscular biceps, and the way they strained against his green shirt. The shirt that matched his eyes.

When they rolled up to Payne's General Store, Clint lifted Emily out of the buckboard and helped her up the steps. Handing her the crutch and the grocery basket, he announced, "I'm going to the feed store. "I won't be long."

His brow furrowed. "I hate to leave you alone. You don't know anyone. Will you be alright?" He rubbed his bristly chin. "Mrs. Payne speaks her mind and a lot of it. Don't let her upset you."

Emily waved him on. "I'll be fine." She couldn't be any worse than Emily's sister-in-law.

"Do you have the grocery list?" he asked.

Emily pulled it from her purse. "Yes."

Clint walked down the steps, but turned to say, "Add Mrs. Reilly's flour to my bill."

Emily nodded. With the aid of the crutch, she swung herself through the open door of the general store. The overhead chimes tinkled before a tall, gaunt woman with graying-red hair turned from stocking shelves behind the counter. She sashayed up to Emily, raking her with a narrowed gaze "May I help you?"

"I have a list of items to pick up for Clint McCall's family. Put everything on his account."

"I'm Adella Payne. Looks like you've hurt yourself." The woman raised a bushy eyebrow."

"I twisted my ankle. It should be well in a day or two." She decided not to go into detail.

"I'm sorry, but I don't know you. I can't give credit to every Tom, Dick, and Harry who come through my door." She stroked her chin. "Although, you do look a mite familiar."

"I'm Emily Hammons. Mr. McCall hired me to attend to his mother until she recuperates."

Mrs. Payne stared down her nose at Emily. "Oh-h… I see. What is ailing Vera? I heard she was feeling poorly."

"Pneumonia. The doctor gave her medicine to stop the cough, and more to help her rest."

The woman threw up both hands. "Pneumonia? Well, I declare. Keep her away from town. Can't have half the people here infected." Raising her chin, she added, "Vera James is a fine lady. I wish there were more like her. With all she's been through, it's a wonder she's survived. You don't find many virtuous women in these parts. Too many are enticed into lives they soon regret."

When Emily did not respond, the woman's gaze slid from her sunbonnet down to her shoes. "I've been the sole owner of this business since my husband died from the pox, four years ago. Harvey and I ran the store together." She chewed her bottom lip. "Have you been in town long? I can't recall where I've seen you."

The only place the woman could have seen her was on the church porch, and Emily did not plan to fuel her gossipy tongue by mentioning it. If Mrs. Payne knew she'd attended the dentist's wedding, she would draw her own conclusions. And that might not fare well for Emily. She waved the grocery list to distract the woman.

"Do you have time to fill this order, Mrs. Payne? I don't mind helping, but as you can see, I'm on a crutch, and Mr. McCall wants me to have it ready by the time he returns. Oh, and add a sack of flour to Mr. McCall's account. Mrs. Reilly asked us to pick one up for her."

"That's the only way she'll get it," Mrs. Payne groused, dropping a box of canned goods on the floor. "The Reillys have overextended their credit here. I told their son that I couldn't give them any more until their bill was paid."

The store owner took the list and basket from Emily. "I'll fill it. Can't have you trying to, what with you hobbling around on that crutch. It would take you twice as long. Maybe longer since you don't know where anything is."

Mrs. Payne bustled down an aisle stopping to say, "Feel free to browse. Something might catch your eye. We have a nice selection of yard goods, along with lace, notions, perfume and hair ribbons."

Emily thanked her and swung herself to the back of the store to peruse the colorful bolts of fabric. She inhaled their musky scents. While she imagined a dress fashioned from a bolt of shiny yellow fabric, the chime over the door jangled and a petite, blonde woman walked in. Her face glowed. She looked to be a little older than Emily.

Mrs. Payne called out. "Be with you in a minute, Mrs. Kramer."

"The young woman replied, "Don't bother, Mrs. Payne. I'm going to browse the yard goods."

The young woman Adella Payne called Mrs. Kramer, joined Emily in the fabric section and began to stroke a bolt of soft, blue material. She eyed Emily with friendly curiosity. "Are you new in town? I haven't seen you around." She extended her hand. "I'm sorry. I'm Carrie Kramer."

Emily squeezed her warm hand. The lady's exuberant smile put her at ease. "I only arrived, yesterday. Nice to meet you, Mrs. Kramer."

"Please call me Carrie. As for being new in town, I know the feeling. I'm from Denton, Texas, 200 miles east. I've only been here a year. I married Josh Kramer. He owns the ranch, a few miles south of town. Our ranch is closer to Buffalo Gap, but since they moved the county seat here last year, Buffalo Gap has lost several of its stores. Some of the businesses rebuilt here in Abilene."

"I saw the Buffalo Gap sign, yesterday on the way to the L&M Ranch," Emily said. "I'm staying there, taking care of Mr. McCall's mother. She has pneumonia."

"You don't mean it. I heard she wasn't well. Pneumonia is not an easy sickness to overcome. We'll be praying for her."

"I appreciate it, and so will Clin—Mr. McCall." Emily must remember not to call her boss by his given name. What would Carrie think?

Carrie tapped her chin. "Hmm… Not meaning anything by it, since my Josh could make any woman swoon, but Clint's a handsome man. And he's also a God-fearing one." Her narrowed gaze studied Emily. "I hope he finds a God-fearing wife."

Emily ducked her head, fingering the yellow fabric. "I don't think he's looking for one."

Carrie patted her arm. "Oh, I wasn't suggesting anything like that. But things can change in the blink of an eye. I know that, from experience."

Emily kept silent, watching Carrie stroke the soft blue material. Carrie leaned in and whispered, "Feel this. It's soft enough for a baby's skin."

Emily rubbed the material between her fingers, raising her gaze to meet Carrie's. "Are you saying—?"

Carrie whispered again. "We are having a baby in March."

"Really?" Emily squealed.

"Sh-h-h!" Carrie put a finger to her lips. "I don't want anyone to know. Especially Mrs. Payne. She couldn't keep a secret if her life depended on it. Besides, she'd be marking days off the calendar to see if we've been married the proper amount of time. If you know what I mean."

Emily scrunched up her nose. "I know."

"I'm looking for material to make baby gowns. Something soft. No flannel, since it will be spring before it's needed." She mulled over the bolts before looking up at Emily again.

"How did you happen to come to Abilene? Do you have relatives here?"

"No," Emily replied.

Carrie held her gaze, waiting for her to explain. If only Emily could confide in her.

"You wouldn't believe the circumstances that brought me here," Carrie said.

"Do tell."

Adella popped up from behind the pickle barrel and raised her bushy eyebrows. "Your order is ready, dearie." Both ladies flinched. How much had the woman heard? Emily exhaled, relieved she had not spilled her sordid story to Carrie.

The store owner slid her gaze to Carrie. "Have you found anything that interests you, young lady? We got in a new shipment of fabric last week."

Carrie picked up the bolt of soft blue material. "I'll take two yards of this."

"Two yards isn't enough to make a—" Adella's eyes widened.

When Carrie stared at her without responding, the store owner clamped her lips together and began to unwrap the bolt. "Two yards, you say?"

Carrie nodded. Mrs. Payne spread the material on the table, picked up her scissors and began to cut. "This is nice and soft. I think it will be perfect."

Meanwhile, Emily compared several bolts of fabric, trying to decide which ones she would prefer for a dress. A lightweight material with tiny blue flowers sprinkled on a cream-colored background, caught her eye. With baby-blue lace at the collar and sleeves, plus matching buttons, it would make a lovely summer dress. She stroked it, knowing she didn't have the money to buy enough yardage.

Carrie followed Mrs. Payne to the counter and waited while the store owner wrapped her bundle. She picked it up and waved at Emily. "It was nice meeting you. I hope I see you again."

Emily waved back. "Same here."

When the door jangled announcing Carrie's departure, Mrs. Payne walked back to where Emily stood. "I'll bet you didn't know that young woman came here as a mail-order bride. Why any woman would advertise herself to catch a man, I'll never understand."

Emily bit her bottom lip. Was this what Carrie almost disclosed when Mrs. Payne interrupted?

The store owner studied Emily. "Did you come to town to attend the big wedding?"

Emily's cheeks burned. She turned away, pretending to peruse the goods, and squeaked, "Wedding?"

"Yes. Don't tell me you haven't heard about our eligible young dentist's farce of a wedding. It was supposed to be the biggest event this town had ever seen. I said, supposed because it never happened. The bride ran out of the church as if her dress was on fire." The store owner paused and waited for her reaction. Emily's tongue clung to the roof of her mouth, paralyzing her speech. Even if she could speak, she didn't know how to reply without incriminating herself.

Mrs. Payne seemed not to notice the lull in their conversation and took up the slack. "Wendell Oliver Clemons—I call him Ollie—was set to marry a mail-order bride he had never laid eyes on." She wagged a finger. "Why he placed that ad, I will never understand. With the money his family has, he could have his pick of any single lady in Abilene. I can't imagine why any of them wouldn't be interested in marrying a dentist." The woman rambled on. "Whatever Ollie lacks in comeliness a young lady could overlook considering all she stands to gain. Young women are too nit-picky. Prestige and security are worth a lot. If she can overlook his voice. I've heard sick bullfrogs that croak in tune better than he does. Our church choir voted him out last year. His sour notes were throwing us off-key."

Emily tried not to laugh, but it erupted anyway. She coughed and made a show of clearing her throat, pointing to her neck. "I'm sorry. I had a slight tickle."

Mrs. Payne was not easily fooled. The older woman's bushy eyebrows drew together in a frown. "Hmph. If you need something for it, I have an elixir—"

Emily threw up a hand. "No, thank you. I'll be fine."

"As you please. Now, as I was saying—when Ollie's father got wind of our plan to throw him out of the choir, he called a town meeting and reminded them how the Clemons had made large donations toward the building of our church. That was the end of the matter."

"But that didn't solve the choir's problem," Emily said.

"Not at all. I sing in the choir and stand next to Ollie. I have to endure his croaking in my right ear every Sunday. I've tried singing louder, but it's no use. That will be the day when a soprano can overpower a bullfrog's croak. He ruins the experience for the rest of us. I wish we could find a way of dismissing him while making him think it was his decision."

Mrs. Payne was a tall, gaunt woman compared to a short and rotund Oliver Clemons. Emily could imagine the dentist's mouth bellowing sour notes into her ear.

The urge to laugh struck Emily again. She moved across the floor aided by her crutch and hoped the clunking sound covered her laughter. Stopping in front of a stack of canned goods, she picked up a can of peaches and pretended to read the label.

When the urge to laugh subsided, she said, "I'm sorry you have to endure Dr. Clemons's off-key singing. It must be awful."

Mrs. Payne stacked the bolts of fabric. "Never mind that. I shouldn't have gotten off on a rabbit trail. We were discussing the wedding. The entire town turned out for it. The church was so packed you couldn't have stuffed another fly in there. Folks crowded outside on the porch just to get a peek at the bride. Out of curiosity, I'm sure. She was a pretty thing. I managed to get a pew near the front, but only because I closed the store early and arrived an hour before the ceremony."

Everything Mrs. Payne said was true, but Emily wanted to wash the memory from her mind.

Now she remembered where she'd seen Adella Payne. She was one of the two women ranting about "Poor Ollie" while Emily sat on the church porch nursing her sprained ankle.

She wished the woman would drop the subject. If only Clint would rescue her. No, she could not count on Clint. He had a couple of stops to make before he returned.

Emily disagreed with Adella Payne on one thing. The dentist might not easily find a local bride. After one look, she would have fled too. Even without his treachery, no amount of money could have persuaded her to marry him. She slid her fingers across a strand of lace, making an effort to change the subject. "How much is this?"

"I'm running a special this week. One yard is free when you buy five yards of material."

Emily dropped the lace, letting it dangle from the bolt. "Thank you. Maybe another time."

"It will be on sale until the end of next week, in case you change your mind," Mrs. Payne chirped.

The bell over the door jangled. Wendell Oliver Clemons pranced in wearing a three-piece suit and a derby hat. Emily froze as his gaze slid over her. He tipped his hat.

When she could get the crutch in the proper position, she ducked behind a rack of canned goods and hid in the shadows. Her heart drummed against her ribcage.

What would she do if he sought her out and asked her name? The last thing she wanted was for him to discover she was one of his mail-order brides. Oh, no! The store owner knew her name.

Emily closed her eyes. Maybe the store owner's memory would lapse. Wiping clammy palms down the sides of her dress, she whispered, "Please, Lord, let him leave before Clint returns."

Taking a deep breath, she stuck her head out and strained to hear the conversation between the dentist and Mrs. Payne.

"How do you do, Adella?" he croaked. "I guess you heard about my sham of a wedding."

If that was Clemons's normal voice, Mrs. Payne was right. He sounded like a sick bullfrog.

"I was there, Ollie, on the second pew from the front." Mrs. Payne sighed. "I wouldn't have missed it for the world. I—I didn't mean it like it sounded. I hate what happened. I just meant—well, your family has always patronized Payne's General store. The young woman humiliated both you and your family. I was shocked to see her take off at a run. She disgraced you, as far as I'm concerned. The way she bolted out of the church you'd have thought her dress tail was afire."

Adella Payne clicked her tongue before she added, "And then that rude young woman stood and clapped. Did the bride say why she ran?"

"I couldn't locate her to ask," the dentist said. "But I'm not worried in the least." He scratched his chest. "I have backup insurance. As the saying goes, 'There's more than one fish in the sea.' I talked to old Ward at the depot. He said my runaway bride caught the eastbound train this morning headed home with her troublemaker sister, no doubt. She's the one who clapped."

Did the dentist call Jessica a troublemaker? Emily felt anger rise, but she bit her tongue.

He leaned against the counter. "My next bride should arrive at any time."

"What do you mean by 'next bride'?" Mrs. Payne laid a hand on her throat. "You didn't."

"Let's just say, a wise man always has a backup plan."

Emily shuddered. "Wise man" was not the description of the dentist that came to mind. Her ankle started itching around the bandage. When she bent to scratch it, her crutch slipped, knocking three cans off the rack. They clattered to the floor and rolled into the aisle. She held her breath and ducked down another aisle, dreading her fate.

"What was that racket?" Clemons asked.

"Oh, just a couple of cans falling off the shelf," Mrs. Payne explained. "It happens all the time if they aren't balanced just right."

"Who was the young lady I saw back there? I've not seen her around town."

Mrs. Payne hesitated. "Ollie, you know how bad I am with names. Seems like she said, Evelyn. I don't recall her last name. She's staying at the L & M ranch to help out with Mrs. James until the woman recuperates. If she does."

Emily peeked from behind the canned goods to see and hear more clearly.

"She's a pretty thing," Clemons commented. Emily jerked her head back behind the stack when he swerved to look in her direction. Another can fell off the shelf, this time on her good foot, and rolled out into the aisle. She stifled a moan. Her high-topped shoe took most of the brunt, muffling the noise. Apparently, neither heard it. While she waited to hear more of their conversation, she prayed the dentist would not seek her out.

The store owner cleared her throat. "Mrs. James has pneumonia in case you haven't heard."

"No, I haven't. That's a terrible disease, and it's highly contagious. It would be awful if the other family members, including Miss Evelyn, contracted it."

Adella turned the conversation back to the wedding. "What are you going to do if that other bride doesn't show up? It was inconsiderate of this one to pull a stunt like that. And of all times, while you were exchanging vows."

Emily peeked out again. Mrs. Payne gave the dentist's hand a consoling pat.

Clemons jerked his hand off the counter and gripped the lapels on his jacket. "Just a minor setback, Adella. As I said, a wise man has more than one backup plan. Old Ward told me something very interesting." He clamped his lips together.

"Please, do tell." Adella Payne's voice became giddy with anticipation.

Clemons reached into his pocket and pulled out two coins. "Hand me a can of snuff, and I'll be on my way. We have a patient due in ten minutes. We could use help to hold old Garvey in the chair while I extract his rotten tooth. I think the roots reach halfway to his knees. If my bride hadn't fled, she'd be helping me today."

Mrs. Payne snickered. The coins clinked on the counter. Clemons stuffed the metal container in his vest pocket and pranced toward the door.

Mrs. Payne called after him, "You didn't say what Mr. Ward told you."

Clemons didn't bother to turn around. He threw up a hand and kept walking. "Good day, Adella."

The storekeeper exhaled an exasperated sigh before the bell jangled. "I don't know why he wouldn't tell me. What harm would there be?" she muttered to herself.

Emily would also like to know the dentist's information, especially if it involved her. She stepped out of hiding. Leaning on her crutch, she clopped up the aisle.

Adella pinned her with a curious gaze. "I'll have your order ready in a minute. I had to wait on Ollie Clemons. He was in a hurry to get back to his dental practice. Had a patient waiting."

"I understand," Emily said with a sigh.

While she waited, she browsed the dress patterns, noting this year's fashions called for a smaller bustle. If bustles continued to shrink, they would become a thing of the past. She would miss them. They added finesse to an outfit.

Adella mumbled while stuffing grocery items into the basket. "I wonder what Mr. Ward told Ollie. I'll bet he has another bride up his sleeve."

Emily swallowed around the constriction in her throat. The dentist could marry the Queen of England, for all she cared, as long as his plans did not involve her. His looks were bad enough, but even if she could get past those, he had deceived her—made her believe she was the only woman he had proposed to.

Why was she kidding herself? It wasn't only his deception that changed her mind. She had begun to regret her decision during the long, bumpy train ride. Surely, she could have found another way to relieve her brother's burden. Why hadn't she looked for a job in Memphis? She would have been close to home and could have visited now and then.

No use worrying over what had already been done. What if Clemons's backup plan did include her? Clint made no bones about how he felt about mail-order brides. He would throw her out on her backside if he knew she was Clemons's second option.

Emily could kick herself for giving the station master her name and disclosing that she was waiting for Dr. Clemons. If only she'd kept her mouth shut.

Mama often warned her about revealing too much to strangers. Her favorite saying was, "The less folks know about your business, the better off you'll be."

Keeping quiet came naturally for her introverted Mama. Not so for Emily. She enjoyed chatting with folks. This way she learned interesting things like where they were from, where they had traveled and discovered interests in common. Mama predicted that Emily's friendly ways might become her downfall. She hoped it didn't happen in this situation with the dentist.

At least gossipy old Mrs. Payne had forgotten her name, if she hadn't forgotten where she was staying. How Emily wished she had changed the subject to avoid answering the woman. The weather was always a good topic, but what was done was done.

As it stood, when Clemons returned to the store, the two would strike up another conversation and her name would come up again.

Would he seek her out—force her to keep their agreement? He had paid for her train ticket. Would he use her debt as leverage? Who knew train fare would be so expensive?

She exhaled slowly, determined to keep her bearings and plan her next step. What would happen if the dentist discovered she was indeed one of his other mail-order brides?

"Miss, I told Ollie Clemons that your given name was Evelyn," Mrs. Payne studied her, waiting for an answer "…but I don't recall your last name."

"Uh…it's—it's—" she stalled, not correcting the store owner in regard to her first name.

The bell over the door clanged once again and in walked Clint. Emily was so relieved, she wanted to fling herself into his arms.

Chapter Eight

Clint stepped through the door of the general store, and Emily appeared to relax. What had that busybody Adella been up to while he was gone? Emily limped up to the counter and stood next to him.

Mrs. Payne spread a cloth over the basket of goods and swept her gaze from him to Emily. "I understand you have taken in this young woman to assist with your mother's recuperation."

"That is true." He nodded toward the basket. "Is everything in there?"

"Yes, your order is ready." Mrs. Payne ducked her chin. "Evelyn says your ma's a little better."

"Who?" Clint frowned and Emily squeezed his arm. He was sure it was to silence him. But why?

Mrs. Payne pointed to Emily. "This young lady who will be caring for her."

"Oh." Clint scratched his chin. For whatever reason, Emily didn't want Mrs. Payne to know her name. He would respect her wishes. "Ma's not out of the woods yet. The coughing quieted last night, but she still has a fever."

"It's best you keep her out of town until she's well. We don't need an epidemic, for sure."

Clint gripped both sides of the basket. A burn crept up from his neck and flooded his face. Sarcasm laced his reply. "I appreciate your deep concern for my mother, Mrs. Payne." He left it at that and heaved the basket upon his shoulder.

"Clint, I just meant— Well, you know the pox took my Harvey from me. He contracted it from old Lambert at the Livery stable. We don't know who Lambert got it from."

Clint tipped his hat. "Good day, Mrs. Payne."

"You young folks have a nice day," she called after them.

With the aid of her crutch, Emily kept up with his long strides. When they reached the wagon, he set the basket in the back. When he lifted her to the wagon seat, his fingers almost met around her waist. My, she was tiny. Did the girl eat enough? Last night, she'd devoured her supper like a starving dog.

Emily frowned at him. Maybe she would explain the peculiar way she'd behaved in the store. He pulled his lips into a thin line and asked, "What was that about?"

Emily hesitated a little too long but finally answered. "Mrs. Payne is overly inquisitive. She seems to know everyone and voices her opinion about everything."

Clint shook the reins. "Giddy-up! That's a nice way of saying she's a busybody. Is that why you told her your name was Evelyn?"

"I didn't. I introduced myself as Emily when I came into the store, but she must have forgotten."

"You didn't correct her. I think I understand. You'd prefer she didn't know your business. Adella is the one everyone comes to, to catch up on the latest gossip. Who needs a telegraph office with her in town?"

Emily nodded her agreement but added nothing.

"I suppose she gave you the details on Clemons's wedding disaster?"

"She did mention it." Emily pointed to the flowers growing alongside the road. "Aren't they beautiful? What are they called? I haven't seen them where I come from."

"Bluebonnets. They're the same color as your eyes." Clint's cheeks burned. Why had he let that slip? Emily had changed the subject, but he'd get it back on topic.

"Did Mrs. Payne mention a second mail-order bride? Grimes at the blacksmith shop said Clemons's second mail-order-bride may already be in town. Or at least on her way."

"Grimes—said that?" Emily squeaked.

"Yes."

Why was she working herself into a tizzy over this? He could understand why she'd be upset over Jessica's sister and the dentist. But she knew nothing about the second woman Clemons had sent for.

"No, Mrs. Payne didn't mention it." Emily turned her gaze toward the meadow.

"Clemons hasn't located her yet. But he's searching."

Emily's hands, clasped in her lap, shook as Clint continued. "Who knows? She may have arrived yesterday and left this morning. The same as Jessica's sister."

Another thought occurred to him. "You didn't by chance, notice another young lady about your age, get off the train, yesterday?"

"No." Emily's answer was firm. She tugged at her skirt before smoothing it across her lap. "Just Jessica, the sister of the bride who fled."

"Hmm." They rode in silence until he pulled up to the Reilly place. Mrs. Reilly hung out the wash while three giggling children and a dog ran around the yard. Diapers and clothes of all sizes were pinned to the line. Clint hopped down and reached into the back of the wagon. Hefting the flour sack to his shoulder, he started toward the house.

The dog barked. The children froze and stared at him. Mrs.

Reilly turned around, her mouth stuffed with clothespins. She pulled them out and pointed to the rickety porch. "Just set it over there, Clint. I'll get it after I finish hangin' the clothes."

Clint propped the sack against the porch post, tipping his hat at the older woman on his way back to the wagon. She flashed him a smile. "I truly appreciate your kindness. Tell your ma, I'm praying for her."

Clint didn't mind helping the family. Mr. Reilly was the victim of a terrible war. Would the country ever fully recuperate from it? He climbed up to his seat and shook the reins while Mrs. Reilly waved at Emily, who smiled and waved back.

CLINT MCCALL HAD A BIG HEART. Emily doubted that Mrs. Reilly knew he had added the flour to his account. What other surprises were lurking beneath the surface?

He appeared to have slipped into deep thought. Emily admired Clint's profile. She worried when his lips pulled into a frown. He made no attempt to converse again until they rolled into the yard and he set the brake on the wagon.

"I hope Ma's better today," he said. "I don't know how much more her body could've stood. She coughed hard enough yesterday, to bust a gut."

This explained why he went into town after the doctor. "Surely, the fever will break soon. I'll keep applying a cool cloth to her forehead to help bring it down."

"I appreciate it, and I'm sure she will too. I'll keep you supplied with cool water." His green eyes softened. "Thank you for accepting my offer to care for Ma. I didn't know where else to turn. Everybody around here is either busy with their own families or they're scared they'll catch something by being around Ma."

Emily laid a hand on his arm. "I'm happy to take care of her.

I appreciate your letting me stay here until I can find a job. After your mother is on her feet again, of course."

Clint hopped to the ground and circled the wagon, reaching up for Emily. "No thanks needed. Call it trading favors." His large hands encircled her waist, setting her feet on the ground. "I need someone to nurse Ma back to health, and you need a place to stay."

Emily was relieved to see the sparkle had returned to his eyes.

CLINT UNHITCHED the horses from the buckboard. After they had slaked their thirst from the water trough, he led them to the barn and pulled out a brush. He found it relaxing to confide in his horses while he groomed them. Brushing the tangles from Penny's mane, he said, "That opinionated Mrs. Payne riles me to no end. She probably doesn't realize half the hurtful things that fly out of her mouth. Whatever she says about me, I just let it roll off like water from a duck's back. But I won't stand for her insulting folks I care about."

The horse nudged Clint's arm when he paused the brush. "I knew you'd agree, Penny. That's why I like talking to you." He chuckled. "Or are you telling me to get on with the brushing?"

He slid the brush to the horse's withers. "What do you think about Emily Hammons? Isn't she the prettiest lady you ever laid eyes on?"

Penny nickered. "Sorry, girl. I meant, besides you. I shouldn't have told her that her eyes were as blue as Texas blue-bonnets. But being around Miss Emily addles me. The words just popped out." Clint groaned. "I hate admitting that Adella Payne and I have something in common.

When the horse shuddered, Clint resumed stroking. "Yeah, it

is a terrible thought. Could be I'm edgy because Ma's sick. We're all praying she gets better, and soon."

Finished with Penny, he led her to a stall and brought Copper out.

As Clint stroked the second horse, he let his breath out slowly. "Copper, I have a problem with Alissia. She doesn't understand that I only want what's best for her. That's where Miss Hammons could help. I hope she will set a good example for my little sister, teach her things a young lady ought to know. Things about how a proper lady should act. And maybe she'll talk some sense into Alissia. She thinks she's grown up, that I should let her do whatever she wants. I can't. Not for a long while. She's not even sixteen, yet."

He ran a comb through the horse's mane. "Ma made some bad decisions after Pa died, and she was already in her twenties." Patting the horse's shoulder, he added, "She should never have answered that ad and took off to meet a man she didn't know. Hank James was big trouble."

Clint mentally shook himself. Dwelling on the past fueled his anger. He should show a little respect for Hank, since the man was dead. And because he was Alissia's father.

He continued. "It's all water under the bridge. I need to let sleeping dogs lie. We can't go back and change anything. The only good that came from his and Ma's marriage was Alissia. And I aim to see that no man ever takes advantage of her."

Folks claimed that being born with red hair and an Irish temper brought grief, and that one born with red hair couldn't do a thing about controlling his temper. Clint didn't put much stock in what folks said. A man could control his actions if he took a notion. Especially, if he sought the Lord before acting on his impulses. With the Lord as His guide, no one would ever trample Clint into the dirt again, like his stepfather had.

A shadow fell across Copper's back before a female voice said, "Alissia said to be ready to eat in ten minutes."

Heat flooded Clint's face. How long had Emily been standing there? Had she heard him talking to his horses? How many more times would he embarrass himself around her?

He looked at her hoping the color had subsided from his burning cheeks. "I'll be right there. I've finished with Penny and am almost through with Copper. I still need to brush Bowie, but it can wait until later. He hasn't had a workout for a couple of days."

Bowie was Clint's pride and joy—a golden Palomino named after one of the great heroes of the Alamo, Jim Bowie. He never hooked Bowie to a wagon. He kept this horse for pleasure riding.

"Bowie? Which one is he?" Emily glanced around the big barn.

Clint pointed to his right. "Over in the far stall. Bowie's a special horse. Sad to say, I haven't ridden him nearly enough lately. He loves to run like the wind."

Emily walked over to the stall and began stroking Bowie's forehead. "He is beautiful. I'd love to ride him sometime."

Clint winked at her. "That might be arranged."

"Really? Promise?" She flashed him a smile, her blue eyes shimmering with excitement.

"We'll see." With effort, Clint dragged his gaze from her face. "Right now, I need to finish brushing Copper, go eat, then get back to fence mending. Bud and Slim, are waiting for me in the north pasture."

"Do you think Copper will allow me to brush him?"

"Sure," Clint replied while applying long, smooth strokes to the horse's neck. "This is the way he likes to be brushed." As he handed the brush to Emily, the sunlight glinted off her raven hair, giving it a sheen.

"How's Ma?" he asked fighting the urge to reach up and caress the shiny tresses cascading down Emily's back.

"Alissia said she was awake about two hours while we were gone and took some broth. Soon after she swallowed it, she fell asleep. I think her fever's down a bit. I just laid another cool cloth on her forehead."

"I'm happy to hear some good news," Clint said.

Emily applied the brush to Copper's withers with slow, easy strokes. "Copper, you're a handsome boy," she oozed. "Does your master ever tell you that?" The horse nickered, appearing to relax under her touch.

Clint cleared his throat. "No. We menfolk don't normally lavish each other with compliments. It wouldn't be manly. Besides, Copper might get conceited."

Copper used his nose to nudge Clint's shoulder. He frowned at the horse. "Hey, boy, I was just joshing you. I'm the one who takes care of you every day. Remember? Wouldn't you rather I brushed you than this pretty lady?"

When Copper shook his mane in what appeared to be a negative answer, Emily giggled. In a mock apology, she said, "I'm sorry. I didn't come out here to cause discord between you and your horse."

Clint could get lost in her eyes. He refocused his thoughts and feigned a remorseful expression. "It's not your fault. Looks like I lost out all the way around. You made a loyal friend of Copper."

Emily fluttered her eyelashes. "It's my southern charm." She continued brushing the horse while Clint pitched hay into their troughs.

When Clint set the pitchfork down, she handed him the brush. "I think he's relaxed now." Emily's hand brushed against his when he took the brush from her. He couldn't help thinking how soft her skin felt despite the work she'd been accustomed to on a farm. He hoped she would be happy at the ranch, and never want to leave.

Ridiculous. What was wrong with him? He couldn't have developed feelings for her already. He'd known her less than twenty-four hours. It must be concern for her welfare. Yeah, that was it. Where would she go when his mother was up and about? Back to Tennessee?

Clint wracked his brain to come up with a business in town that might offer her a job. No, it was no use planning weeks ahead. He could not foresee the future. Anything could happen between now and the time his mother was well enough to take care of herself. Besides, the idea of Emily moving into town didn't set well with him.

Color tinged Emily's cheeks when she caught him staring. My, she was beautiful. He could look at her all day. She lowered her gaze and Clint caught sight of long, dark-fringed lashes.

Emily cleared her throat. "We'd better go inside. Alissia is holding supper for us."

"Probably so." Clint led Copper to a stall and hung the brush on a nail, before they walked to the house.

EMILY FIRST CHECKED on her patient and found her sleeping peacefully. Alissia had administered a dose of cough medicine earlier. Emily joined Clint and Alissia at the table. She hoped to find Mrs. James alert soon and become acquainted with her.

The midday meal consisted of the previous night's beef roast with all the trimmings. It tasted delicious. Alissia had prepared skillet-fried cornbread to go with the roast and vegetables.

"Did you buy anything at the general store besides groceries?" Alissia directed the question at Emily.

"No, but I looked at the fabric and notions. Mrs. Payne carries a nice selection."

Alissia lowered her gaze. "She does, but personally, I'd rather patronize the mercantile."

Emily looked at Clint. His poker face revealed nothing as he wiped a napkin across his mouth. She could guess his sister's reasoning. Adella Payne asked too many questions.

Alissia continued. "Mrs. Payne is a busybody. She tries to meddle in everybody's business."

Clint grunted and stabbed at a piece of beef roast. He added nothing to the conversation. It was up to Emily to say something constructive. "She did ask me a lot of questions, but it could be that she's lonely. She said she lost her husband a couple of years ago."

Alissia appeared to consider Emily's words. "That doesn't give her the right to spread gossip."

Clint took a sip from his glass and set it down. Obviously in an attempt to change the subject, he asked Emily, "By the way, did you run into our Romeo dentist? I saw him prance out of the store while I was tethering the team. He appeared to be in a big hurry."

The cynical tone to Clint's voice puzzled her. She tried to appear calm while her heart did a rat-a-tat-tat against her chest. "I...I was in the back of the store when the dentist came in. He acknowledged me but didn't speak." She hoped this would be enough to discourage further questions.

Alissia waved her fork. "Emily, how did you know it was him?"

The question took her by surprise. Before she could think of an answer, Clint interjected, "Emily attended the 'almost wedding'. Remember?"

"Oh, that's right. It slipped my mind. That's how you two met." Alissia giggled. "You fell off the church porch into each other's arms."

"Don't go around telling that," Clint warned her. "The last part anyway."

Alissia pressed a hand to her cheek. "Oh, why not? It sounds quite romantic."

"Imagine what Adella Payne could do with that piece of gossip."

Alissia huffed. "I suppose you're right. Before long, you and

Emily would be riding off to a castle on a white horse."

Emily nearly choked on her food. She set her fork down and tried to catch her breath. All she needed was someone spreading gossip about her and this cowboy.

Clint cut her a glance, his eyes twinkling with mischief. "It's true, little sister. Emily did sweep me off my feet and fall into my arms."

Alissia sighed. "Very romantic. But seriously, speaking of Clemons, and I don't mean to be rude… But with those buck teeth, he could eat a pumpkin through a picket fence."

Clint struggled to form a scowl, but Emily saw the corners of his lips quirk upward. He covered his mouth, probably trying to conceal his amusement. "Alissia, that was not nice."

"Well, it's the truth," she asserted. "You'd think, being a dentist, he could figure out a way to straighten them."

Without thinking, Emily blurted, "Jessica said her father had a mule that could pass for his brother. She gasped and clapped a hand over her mouth. "I'm sorry. I shouldn't have said that." Why couldn't she control her wayward tongue?

Alissia hiked her chin. "Well, it's true."

Clint ducked his head and started to shake. Was he having an attack? He pressed his napkin against his mouth. Water spewed out, anyway, soaking his shirt and the tablecloth before him.

After he'd blotted his face and shirt with his napkin, Clint threw his head back and howled. Emily didn't know how to rectify the situation. Was he having some kind of fit? She had been in trouble before, for saying the wrong thing, but never had anyone reacted like this.

Wait a minute. Clint was laughing. Now Alissia was giggling. Emily could no longer contain herself. She joined in the laughter. It took several minutes for the three to calm down.

When the laughter subsided, Alissia slid her chair back from the table. "I haven't laughed so hard since the day our billy goat rammed Clint in the backside."

Clint shook his head as if to silence his sister. "But that was not funny to me."

Emily could not wait to hear the story. "How did it happen?"

Alissia ignored her brother's stern look and continued. "Clint bent over to pick up an armload of firewood when the goat caught sight of him."

Emily tried to suppress a laugh. She even coughed to cover it, but Clint was not fooled. "Go ahead and laugh, Miss Hammons. I'm sure it was funny to everyone else."

Alissia's smirk waned into an innocent smile. She clasped her hands together and laid them on the table. "I yelled out a warning, but it was too late. The goat was already charging for its target. Clint's backside was the bull's eye. The next thing I knew, he was sailing through the air spread-eagle. He landed face down across the woodpile."

"Ooh, I know that hurt," Emily tried to sound sympathetic.

Alissia nodded. "Lucky for him, we kept a bottle of horse liniment for his sore…muscles."

Again, Emily fought the urge to laugh. When she had it under control, she feigned remorse. "Sorry. I didn't mean to cause a commotion."

Clint tossed his soaked napkin on the table. "Don't worry about it. We all needed a good laugh. It would have been funny to me, too, if I hadn't been the goat's target."

"We still have old Billy," Alissia reminded him.

Clint turned up his glass and drained it. "Only because he makes a good guard goat." He nodded at Emily. "Billy chases off critters that try to invade the chicken house. Raccoons, foxes, weasels. He chased off a coyote last week."

Clint scooted his chair back from the table and rose. "Well, the meal was good. Bud and Slim are waiting in the north pasture. We've got a section of fence to mend. I'll see you ladies at suppertime." He yanked on Alissia's braid and winked at Emily, setting her heart aflutter.

When the screen door slapped behind Clint, Emily turned to Alissia. "I'll check on your mother. If she's still asleep, I'll help you with the dishes."

～

THE WOMAN STIRRED as Emily entered the room. Her eyes fluttered open and she offered Emily a weak smile. "I'm hot and thirsty."

Emily dipped a washcloth in the pan and spread it over the woman's forehead. "I'll be right back with a cool glass of water, Mrs. James. Meanwhile, this will cool you some."

Alissia had set a fresh pail of water on the counter when Emily hobbled into the kitchen on her crutch. "Where do you keep the glasses?"

Alissia pointed to a cupboard. "In there. Is Ma awake?"

"Yes, and she is asking for a cool drink. I hope it's a good sign." Emily submerged the dipper in the water bucket before filling the glass.

Alissia poured hot water from the kettle, into the dishpan. "I hope so too. She was awake for some time while you and Clint were gone."

Emily loped back to Mrs. James's room with the water. The woman coughed as she approached the bed and offered her the glass. "Here you go. Need me to hold it?"

Mrs. James tucked her damp, blonde tendrils behind her ears before reaching for the glass. "I can hold it. I'm not completely helpless" She swigged half the water down before extending the glass to Emily. "That should be enough for now."

Her glassy gaze swept over Emily. "Who are you? How long have I been asleep?"

"Most of the morning, according to Alissia." Emily pulled the cane-back chair near the bed and sat in it. When the woman eyed the door, Emily explained, "Alissia is washing dishes, and Clint left with a crimping tool to mend a fence."

"A fence?" Mrs. James raised up on her elbows and tried to peer through the window. She fell back on her pillow, exhausted. "I hope those Javelins ain't at it again."

Emily had read about Javelins, a gang of men who fought for open range by cutting ranchers' fences. Often, shooting was involved. She silently prayed for Clint's protection.

Emily brushed damp hair back from her patient's face and tried to console her. "All Clint said was a section of fence needed mending in the north pasture."

Mrs. James dropped her head back against the pillow, closing her eyes. "You ain't told me who you are."

"Emily Hammons. Your son asked me to take care of you until you are well."

"Em-i-ly. She enunciated each syllable. "It's a pretty name. Are you from around here?"

"No, I'm from a small town near Memphis. Bartlett, Tennessee."

"Goodness gracious! What are you doing this far west? You had to cross the Mississippi."

The kind-faced woman looked like someone a girl could confide in. But because she was Clint's mother, Emily knew to choose her words carefully.

"There weren't any jobs in Bartlett, and I was living with my brother and his wife. His wife made me feel unwelcome. They have a baby on the way, plus money is short. The two-month drought hurt our cotton crop, which didn't help matters."

"So, you struck out on your own? Don't you know it's dangerous for a young lady to travel alone? She has to be cautious, not speak to strangers. Especially men. What made you come all the way to Abilene?"

The woman's searching gaze held compassion, making Emily feel guilty for not spilling the entire story. She pressed a cool, freshly dipped cloth to Mrs. James's forehead. "I felt I had no choice. I will find a job in town, once you've fully recuperated."

The woman grimaced. "Not at a saloon, I hope."

"No, never!" Emily blurted. "I'm sorry. I didn't mean to sound rude."

The feverish woman patted her hand. "I think I understand, dearie. It's no place for ladies."

Emily swallowed hard. No, she didn't understand. How could this woman know what she had lived through? Losing both parents was tough enough but being forced to leave home was something Emily could have never imagined happening.

She patted her patient's hand. "I'll look for work as a clerk, or maybe as a secretary, at one of the businesses. I took shorthand and learned how to type and keep books, while in school."

"Smart girl. You stay away from those saloons and dance halls." Mrs. James chewed her bottom lip. "Girl, I could tell you some stories that would make you blush."

Emily waited for Mrs. James to continue, but she only said, "Never you mind. Best not to dig up painful memories." Her patient had hinted of firsthand knowledge of the wilder side of life. Surely, not this woman whose face glowed like that of an angel. Maybe she had heard stories from a wayward family member or a friend. Most families had a skeleton or two in their closets.

Either way, it was none of Emily's business. It was time to coax her patient to eat. If Mrs. James didn't want to confide in her, she would not press the matter. "Would you like some broth?"

"I've had so much chicken broth, I'm startin' to cluck. Get me some solid food before I lay an egg. Have you got any beef roast and mashed potatoes?"

Emily smiled. "Yes, I can fix you a good plate. Let me help you sit up first." She tucked extra pillows behind the woman's back to prop her upright. "I'll be right back with something to whet your appetite."

Emily fixed a generous plate of food and brought it in on a tray. She watched while her patient devoured half the food. After she'd finished, Mrs. James wiped her mouth. "Thank you. That hit the spot."

She picked up a copy of *Wuthering Heights* from her bedside table. "Emily, will you read to me? I started this book and got halfway through before I got too sick to read. I marked the place."

Emily accepted the book and slid her chair closer to the bed. She opened to where the marker was placed and started to read. Engrossed in the intense story of Heathcliff and Catherine, she didn't notice Mrs. James had fallen asleep until soft snores alerted her.

Emily replaced the marker. She would love to keep reading, but it was time to relieve Alissia. The girl had too much responsibility for her age. Emily wanted to take some of the workload from her. She wished the strained relationship between Alissia and her brother would soon mend. Sometimes it was possible, and sometimes it was not.

She recalled a verse from the twelfth chapter of Romans. "If it be possible, as much as lieth in you, live peaceably with all men."

Acquiring peace depended on the willingness of both parties to listen to one another. How well she knew, from experience, peace was not always possible.

Chapter Nine

Buttery rays of sunlight streamed across Emily's face. The rooster crowed, and her eyes flew open. What time was it? With no clock in the room, she could not tell. She sat up and tied on her cotton robe. Propping the crutch under her arm, she clomped up the hall, stopping to peek in Alissia's room. The girl's bed was empty and neatly made. She was probably in the barn milking. And if Alissia was milking, it meant Clint had left without his breakfast.

The grandfather clock clanged six times telling Emily she had overslept. Adjusting the crutch under her arm, she swung herself back to the bedroom. Her patient was sound asleep. She dressed quickly, headed back to the kitchen, pulled an apron from the sideboard drawer, and tied it on. Someone had started a fire in the cook stove. It was warm enough to start breakfast. Lifting a mixing bowl from the shelf above, she pulled out flour, eggs, and butter, and started on pancakes. Then she remembered the milk was lowered on a rope in the well. Emily brought the jug in and stirred milk into the mix. With less than a pint left, she hoped Alissia was almost finished milking. Before pouring the batter into the skillet, she looked in on Mrs. James again. The woman was still sleeping. By laying a hand on her forehead, she noticed her fever had broken. Butter sizzled in the iron skillets while Emily hummed a merry tune and poured a generous amount of mixture into both. .

She jumped when a baritone voice boomed behind her. "Something sure smells good in here." Embarrassment flamed her cheeks. Clint had caught her humming. "I didn't hear you come in."

He lifted the kettle and poured steaming water into the wash pan. His eyes danced with merriment, making her heart flutter. "I didn't mean to scare you. What are you cooking?"

"Pancakes. I think you call them flapjacks in Texas. I hope you like them."

"Whatever we call them, they'll be delicious soaked in molasses."

"How many do you think you and Alissia will eat? I'll also fix one for your mother. Did you know she ate after you left, yesterday?"

"Yes. Alissia told me. That's a good sign." He walked to the stove to peer over Emily's shoulder. "Depends on the size of the flapjacks, how many I can eat. Hmm…those are big. I can manage two."

The warmth from his body plus his masculine scent made Emily's head reel. She paused to get her breath as she flipped the second pancake onto the platter.

Alissia tramped in lugging a full bucket of milk. "Fresh milk to go with breakfast."

Clint took it from her and set it on the counter. "Miss Emily's making flapjacks. Why don't you wash up?"

Alissia picked up the soap and glared at him. "I'm not a child. You don't have to remind me to wash my hands before I eat."

Emily made an attempt to ease the tension. "How many pancakes do you want, Alissia?"

"I'll just take one." Craning her neck to face Emily, she said, "We go to church on Sundays."

"I wondered if you did." What was Alissia getting at? Seconds later she got her answer.

"Ma would not be happy if we didn't attend." Alissia clasped her hands together in front of her chest. "Why don't you go with Clint? I'll stay home with Ma today."

Emily flipped the last pancake onto the serving plate. "No. You two can go. I'll stay with your ma. That's why I'm here."

"Just for today," Alissia pleaded. "You need to get acquainted with folks, make a few friends, if you aim to stay in Abilene. Anyway, I start back to school, tomorrow. Let me spend this last Sunday with my ma."

The girl arched her eyebrows at Clint. "If it's all right with you, of course."

Clint set the plate of pancakes on the table. "Whatever you ladies decide is fine with me."

"All right," Emily said. "Let me feed your mother first. She was still asleep when I peeked in a few minutes ago."

They sat down to scrambled eggs and flapjacks. Very little was said during the meal. When the flapjacks were gone, Alissia jumped up and began stacking the plates. "I'll wash the dishes, Emily. You need to feed Ma and get yourself dressed for church."

Emily nodded and dished up eggs and a flapjack onto a plate. Her ankle was not as tender this morning. She wouldn't need the crutch if she was careful not to bear too much weight on it. If she didn't feel an occasional throb and have a slight limp, she might forget her injury. As she started down the hall with the tray, she almost ran into Clint. Tossing a bar of soap in the air and with a towel draped over one shoulder, he whistled a tune as he headed out the back door. When the screen door popped to behind him, Emily turned to Alissia. "Where is he going?"

"The creek, to take a bath. I guess you haven't noticed that

Elm Creek runs behind our house." She pointed out the kitchen window. "Past that grove of trees over there. The water's clear and only waist-high this time of year. When you need to cool off, it's a good place to try."

"I'll remember that." After the long trip on the train, Emily longed for more water than the pitcher and washbowl supplied. To plunge beneath the cool waters of Elm Creek sounded like heaven. But she would have to wait until another time to indulge herself.

Mrs. James stirred when she entered the bedroom. "I brought your breakfast."

The woman's eyes popped open. She smiled when she saw Emily bearing the tray. "Thank you, young lady."

After propping pillows behind her patient, the woman wasted no time stabbing a bite of pancake with her fork and sopping it in the molasses. She popped it into her mouth and chewed. "Mmm, this is delicious. It's been two weeks since I've had real food. Forgot how good it tasted."

She sipped her coffee then set the cup on the tray. "Did you brew this coffee? It's better than what either Alissia or I make. It don't have a bitter taste. What did you do to it?"

Emily pressed a finger against her lips. "Sh-h-h! It's a family secret."

"Well, as long as it stays this good, I won't be tellin'."

Emily winked. "A pinch of baking soda takes the bite out. My mother taught me the trick."

"I'll remember that. She gazed at the calendar on the wall. "Is this Sunday?"

"Yes, it is."

"Are you going to church with Clint and Alissia?"

"Alissia wants to stay home with you. She urged me to go in her place. She said I needed to meet some new people. That is, unless you'd rather I stayed with you."

"Nonsense. Tell Alissia to go, too. I'm not an invalid. I'll be fine. I can read a while. I'll take a nap if I get tired."

"I can see you are better, this morning, but I think someone should be here with you. At least for a few more days."

"Ma, Emily is right." Clint's broad shoulders filled the door frame, his hair still damp from a dip in in the creek. You need someone here in case you have another coughing spell. Alissia will stay with you." He walked over to his mother's bedside.

Emily hid a grin behind her hand. Clint's shirt hung askew because he'd buttoned it wrong, and his copper-colored hair hung in disarray. An unruly lock dangled across his forehead.

Mrs. James sighed. "All right. No sense wasting my time arguing with you. You're every bit as stubborn as your Pa was. But mind you, I will be gettin' out of this bed, and soon."

Clint folded his arms across his chest and winked. "I don't doubt it. I didn't get my stubborn streak only from Pa."

Ma swatted at him, but he dodged, and she missed. She sent him a mock glare. "You came by it honest, all right. Got it from both sides." She pointed at his shirt. "Now, button that shirt up right before you leave for church."

Clint glanced down at it. "What's wrong with my—?" Color flushed his face. "I'll fix it." He turned abruptly and marched out of the room.

EMILY BOUNCED when the buggy hit a rut. The rough road didn't seem to bother her. She exclaimed over the bluebonnets in one field as they rolled past. Her eyes sparkled like those of a child taking in a new world. Watching her exclaim over wildflowers and scenery warmed Clint's heart.

She pointed to a grove of cottonwood and hackberry trees. "In Tennessee, the woods are so thick, you can get lost in them. From what I've seen, trees grow mostly in small clusters here."

Clint shook the reins to get the horse to trot. "We call the clusters of trees a grove or copse. I've never been to Tennessee. I've been as far east as Texarkana, where the woods are dense. If Tennessee is anything like that area, trees here are sparse in comparison."

"I noticed from the train that Texarkana's terrain and forests were similar to where I came from. The farther west I traveled, the scarcer the trees became." Her beautiful eyes glowed. "How did your family happen to come to Texas?"

Clint adjusted his hat. "They came by covered wagon from Missouri. I hope I don't bore you with the story. I've heard it from Grandpa Lawson so many times, I feel like I was there."

Emily squeezed his arm. "It won't bore me. I enjoy stories about people migrating west."

Clint's heart throbbed against his ribs as he studied her face. Her flushed cheeks made her even prettier. The blue flowers in the white straw hat matched her eyes and the tiny flowers in her print dress. She must have realized her hand was still on his arm because she pulled it away.

He refocused his thoughts to begin his grandparent's migration story. "Grandpa Lawson settled here in '49. He and Grandma set out from Haiti, Missouri, to seek their fortune. They joined a wagon train in Saint Louis, headed to the California gold mines.

"Soon after the wagon train hit the trail, Grandpa became friends with Jack Whitley, a man from Illinois who expounded about the glories of Texas. According to Mr. Whitley, land in Texas was untamed, had thousands of acres of wide-open range, and was there for the taking. At least it could be bought dirt cheap and was perfect for raising cattle. Mr. Whitley planned to break off and head south once the wagon train reached central Kansas."

Emily's eyes flickered with excitement. "It sounds like an adventure."

"It was, and by the time the covered wagons reached the Kansas border, Grandpa had changed his mind about going to California. Instead, he followed Whitley here to Texas." Clint shrugged. "The rest is history.

"The Whitleys are still our closest neighbors, at three miles north. Jack contracted malaria and passed away several years ago when the epidemic spread through this area. Lucky for his widow, their two eldest sons were in their mid to late teens and sturdy enough to run the ranch. Their father trained them well. Mrs. Whitley is up in years now, but she gets around with the aid of a cane. You'll meet her at church."

"The Whitleys attend the church where we're going?"

"That's right. Mrs. Whitley, her children, and her grandchildren. When my grandparents came to Texas, buffalo still roamed. That's how Buffalo Gap, the next town south, got its name."

"Buffalo Gap? That's an interesting name. What happened to the buffalo?"

"Sadly, the buffalo hunters thinned them out, killed them for their hides. The few buffalo left migrated farther west."

Emily's eyes narrowed. "I think it's cruel to kill animals just to profit from their hides."

"So do I. The lure of money entices some folks to do things they wouldn't do otherwise."

EMILY SWALLOWED the lump forming in her throat. Clint might be talking about her. It was as if he saw through her facade. She wouldn't be sitting beside him if she had not been lured by a newspaper ad. She'd come at the invitation of Dr. Clemons, who had offered her, not money, but a job and a roof over her head. Security.

Look how that had turned out. Her reason for leaving wasn't because she wanted to accept the dentist's proposal. She hadn't fully made up her mind until her sister-in-law's scathing words pierced through the screen. "We'll be hard-pressed to feed another mouth once the baby comes."

As a result of the long drought, Roy stood to lose the family farm. She hoped her departure helped his financial situation. He'd met with the banker the day before she left, but never revealed the outcome. Emily prayed the banker had taken mercy on Roy and extended his loan.

It was not the lust for money that had enticed her to answer Dr. Clemons's ad. Emily's was a sacrificial act. Her conscience twinged. Even if she labeled her decision as an unselfish act, money, or rather security, was still at the root. Did that put her in the same class as men who left their families to rush to the gold fields? Men like her father?

How odd that the same need for security led her to Clint McCall's ranch. Emily recalled the tears her mother had shed, the times she'd flown to the window when a wagon pulled into the yard, and the disappointment when it wasn't Papa. Mama had held onto the hope that he would return for them until the very end. But he didn't.

If Mama could see Emily now, she'd tan her hide. If it wasn't for Jessica's sister, she might be on her honeymoon. Her face burned. What respectable woman agreed to marry a man she had never laid eyes on, one from whom she'd received only two brief replies? And to think Emily might have married him. She would not marry Dr. Wendell O. Clemons now, if he was the last man on earth. She never wanted to in the first place, but it galled her that the lout had two replacement brides lined up. A shudder shook her body.

Mistaking her shudder for a shiver, Clint's jolted her out of her reverie. "Are you cold?"

Emily smoothed her skirt. "No, I'm fine. Although it's a rather warm day."

Clint's brow creased. "You shivered, yet your cheeks are flushed. Are you sure you feel all right?

"I feel fine." She hiked her shoulders. Was he worried she had caught his mother's illness? She'd hoped he wouldn't notice her flaming face. The last thing she wanted was to be bombarded with questions.

Clint shook the reins, urging the horse to a canter. To her relief, he stopped asking questions.

Chapter Ten

Emily froze when the white, clapboard church came into view, the same church the dentist's ill-fated ceremony had taken place. The same porch she'd fallen off, taking Clint with her. Her hands clenched into fists. Would Dr. Clemons be at the service?

Buggies and wagons were parked in the shade of cottonwoods and pin oaks. A group of men stood on the porch puffing on cigarettes.

Clint pulled his pocket watch from his vest. "We're a few minutes early. You'll have time to get acquainted with some of the church folks." He hopped down and circled the buggy reaching up for her.

"I don't know, Clint." Emily pressed a hand to her temple. I think I feel a headache coming on." She wasn't making it up. Since discovering this was the same church where Clemons had his ceremony, her head had started throbbing.

"Come on," he urged. "You'll be fine once we get you out of the sun. Besides, I want you to meet someone special."

Emily's breath caught. Not Wendell Clemons! She placed her hands on Clint's broad shoulders before he swung her to the ground. An elderly silver-haired woman leaning on a cane stood in a huddle with two others.

Clint pointed to the women dressed in their fashionable hats and finery. "There's Mrs. Whitley, Jack Whitley's widow, the ones I told you about." He took Emily by the arm and ushered her toward the woman. "Mrs. Whitley?" he called out.

Emily drew back. "Will you slow down, please? My foot hurts each time I place it on the ground." Neither was she in a hurry to discover who might be inside the clapboard church.

Embarrassed, Clint stopped and rubbed the back of his neck. "I'm sorry, Miss Emily. I forgot about your foot. We should've brought your crutch along."

She forced a smile. "I'll be all right if we move at a slower pace."

Clint slid an arm around her waist for support. As they neared the steps, the elderly woman waved. "Good morning, Clint. Who is this pretty young lady hanging onto you? Don't tell me you're getting hitched and didn't tell me."

Emily smothered a giggle when Clint stammered, "Uh…no, ma'am. She's staying at the ranch to help out with Ma."

"Well, do introduce us." The gray-haired lady clasped Emily's hand between hers.

Clint drew a breath to regain his composure. "Mrs. Whitley, I would like you to meet Miss Emily Hammons."

The older woman's gaze swept over her. "You aren't from these parts, are you, dear? Most folks aren't. Our town is young, but it's growin' so fast that I stopped counting."

"I'm from Tennessee." She hoped Mrs. Whitley wouldn't ask too many questions. Jessica had assumed Emily had come to Abilene to visit a relative, and she had not corrected her. Later, telling Jessica the truth was too daunting. Emily could not tell Jessica the truth when her sister stood at the altar with the same man who had proposed to Emily.

Emily realized now, that she had been the dentist's second

choice. Or had he rushed Margie Dawson to the altar because she had not shown up on the appointed date? Where was Dr. Clemons's third choice for a bride? Would she show up too?

Mrs. Whitley nudged a young woman forward who looked to be about Emily's age. The dainty brunette clamped onto Clint's free arm, gazing up at him with adoring eyes." Miss Hammons, this is my daughter, Stella."

Emily nodded. Was Clint courting this woman? "Nice to meet you, Stella."

Stella smiled sweetly as her gaze slid over Emily. The smile did not quite reach her eyes. "Same here," she replied. "Who are you visiting?"

Visiting? From her tone Emily gathered that Stella hoped she would make her stay in Abilene a brief one. While she thought of a proper reply a gaunt, middle-aged man stuck his head through the open door and announced, "Almost time for the service to begin, dear flock."

Mrs. Whitley caught his coat sleeve. "Reverend Cole, this is Emily Hammons. Miss Hammons, meet Reverend James Cole."

The thin-faced man smiled revealing a set of gleaming teeth. He offered Emily his hand. "How do you do, Miss Hammons?"

Scanning the churchyard for Dr. Clemons, Emily gripped the reverend's long, knotty fingers. "Very well, thank you." She could breathe easier if she knew Wendell O. Clemons would not show up for the service.

Mrs. Whitley patted her shoulder as Clint escorted her inside. Her eyes flitted over the congregation as he led her to the third pew from the front. To Emily's relief, Dr. Clemons was not among the congregates. If the door opened during the service, she vowed not to turn around to look. A proper lady did nothing of the sort. She admired the art glass windows which splayed a rainbow of diffused light across the pew she and Clint occupied. While she basked in their beauty, someone slipped into the pew behind them.

A finger tapped Emily's shoulder, and she froze. A friendly voice said, "It's good to see you're still in town."

Emily twisted her neck and found her traveling companion smiling at her. "Jessica! Yes, I'm still here, but I thought you went home with your sister."

Jessica's presence could jeopardize her stay at the L&M ranch. The longer Jessica remained in Abilene the more likely Clint would discover Emily's secret.

"Margie did, but I—"

"Open your hymn books to number one-twenty-nine." a voice boomed from the pulpit. The reverend motioned for them to stand.

The pianist struck the first chords and the congregation sang with gusto, "Tis so sweet to trust in Jesus..." Clint's smooth baritone reverberated through the little church blending with her soprano. Emily hardly noticed because her worries over Jessica distracted her. Why had the young woman prolonged her stay?

When the hymn ended, the congregation sat. Pews screeched and slid across the wood floor. Emily shifted in her seat, impatient to talk to Jessica. Determined to focus on the sermon, Emily opened her Bible to Ephesians, Chapter three as the reverend instructed.

"We will read verses 9 through 10, he announced. 'Lie not one to another, see that ye have put off the old man with his deeds; and have put on the new man which is renewed in knowledge after the image of Him that created him.'"

Emily swallowed hard. Why was Reverend Cole studying her? She folded her arms across her chest as he continued.

"Have you been guilty of dealing treacherously with another through lies or deception?"

Was withholding information the same as deception? Suddenly the church felt much hotter. Emily picked up a fan someone had left on the pew and waved it frantically.

She had not outright lied, only let Jessica think what she

wanted without elaborating on the matter. Jessica had jumped to her own conclusions. Emily just hadn't corrected her. As for Clint, she hadn't misled him. She had wanted to come to Texas after reading adventures of the wild west in novels. Was that wrong?

The reverend continued. "Maybe you didn't intentionally deceive the person. Sometimes we get ensnared in a web of deceit before we realize it. Soon the web wraps itself around us, entwining us in a stranglehold from which we cannot free ourselves. Galatians, Chapter 6, verse 7 reads, 'Do not be deceived; God is not mocked: For whatsoever a man soweth, that shall he also reap.'

"Let me warn you, sister or brother. One seemingly harmless lie can lead to a dozen in an effort to cover the original one. Because after you tell the first one, it is difficult to admit you were not completely honest. Pride gets in the way. The original white lie, which seemed no larger than a mole hill, grows into a mountain.

"How many of you, for example, have borrowed a hay rake or a team of mules and promised to return them on a certain day? But when that day came, something else seemed more important, and you did not honor your promise. We've all experienced unforeseen circumstances that prevent us from keeping our promises. But, when they occur, let your neighbor know. It will save a lot of misunderstandings and keep your relationships with others from becoming strained."

A male voice from near the back of the church interrupted the message. "Reverend, may I interject at this point? I have something to say to the congregation."

Emily felt relief at the interruption until she looked behind her and saw who had spoken. Wendell Oliver Clemons stood in the second pew from the back. She quickly turned around and inched down in her pew. How could she walk past the man without him seeing her?

Wait. Dr. Clemons didn't know she was one of his other mail-order brides. But if he started asking questions, he would surely find out. Emily closed her eyes and silently prayed, *Lord, get me out of this mess, please.*

The reverend sighed. "Yes, Dr. Clemons, before we continue, what is it you would like to say to this congregation?"

Jessica whooshed out a breath and whispered a little too loudly, "This should be interesting."

Clemons continued his tirade. "First, I would like to thank all of you who attended my ill-fated wedding. Secondly, I would like to apologize for bringing you out of your comfortable homes only to waste your time. It seems the woman I intended to marry was spoiled. Being from Eastland, Miss Dawson was not accustomed to frontier life such as we have in Abilene. Furthermore, as you spoke of deception and lying, I could not help thinking of how she spurned me. She made a promise and did not keep it. It will be a struggle for me to forgive her."

"Why, that dirty scoundrel," Jessica hissed between clenched teeth, loud enough to receive a cool glare from the reverend.

Emily frowned. The church service was not the place to vent frustrations. She hoped her friend would simmer down, as would Dr. Clemons.

Clint grunted and shifted in his seat. He quirked an eyebrow and leaned over to whisper in Emily's ear. "I don't know what Clemons is up to, but this is not the place to air one's woes."

Emily nodded and returned her gaze to the pulpit. If Clint knew what she had done, what would he say about it?

"Oliver, the Lord instructs us to forgive one another," Reverend Cole advised.

Clemons's raspy voice reached a high pitch. "That woman made a fool out of me. And I'm supposed to forgive her at the drop of a hat? I don't think so."

The reverend groaned. "The young lady must have had her reasons. Remember, there are two sides to every story. Now, please sit down and hold your peace, Oliver. We are in the Lord's house."

A pew groaned as Clemons obeyed. The reverend cleared his throat. "Now, let us return to the message."

A man near the back of the church chuckled. "Maybe it wasn't our way of life here, that was the bride's problem."

Snorts sounded among the male congregates, and a few ladies tittered.

"The groom's high and mighty attitude had more to do with it," Jessica said loud enough to invoke another glare from Reverend Cole.

Emily wished Jessica would keep quiet until they were outside the church. The last thing she wanted was having Clemons's attention drawn to her. Neither would it bode well for Jessica if he discovered the sister of his runaway bride among the congregates. Even if the dentist didn't know Emily's identity, he might ask to be introduced.

Clemons did not take the insult from the male congregate as such, but the man complied with the reverend's plea. "Very well. Out of respect for you, I will remain silent."

The reverend finished his message quickly and instructed, "Turn your hymnals to page 163, and we will sing, 'Take Me As I Am.'"

"Maybe his bride didn't like the way he was," the same deep voice jested.

An uproar spread across the congregation until Reverend Cole raised his hands to invoke silence. "Please, Mr. Evans, let's not forget we are in the Lord's house. We must show reverence."

The man cleared his throat, "Sorry, Preacher, I was just thinkin' out loud. I still think the bride made a smart move."

"Please…see that it doesn't happen again," the reverend admonished.

"Yes, sir."

Following the invitational hymn and dismissal prayer, people gathered outside the church building in small clusters. Some laughed while others appeared to be in a stir.

Clint slid his arm around Emily's waist and helped her walk toward the buggy. "I'm trying to slow down," he said.

Emily twisted to check Clemons's whereabouts. "I appreciate it." She relaxed when she did not see him.

Clint helped her into the buggy. While Emily arranged her skirt, a voice rasped, "Hello, again."

Wendell Oliver Clemons stood next to their buggy, gawking at her. He doffed his derby hat and demurely bowed his head. "We meet again, fair lady." His thick lips parted as he grinned, revealing buck teeth. "Nice to see you again, Miss Evelyn. If you will remember, we met at Payne's General Store."

He held up his index finger. "But we were not properly introduced."

Emily forced a smile while her heart pounded inside her chest. She offered no reply. Clint settled beside her in the buggy and tipped his hat at the dentist. "Have a nice day, Dr. Clemons. We must be on our way."

"Of course, Mr. McCall. I understand your mother is sickly. You have my sincere sympathy." He pressed his hat against his chest. "I just wanted to make this young lady's acquaintance, if you don't mind. I hear she is taking care of your mother. Do you have any idea when your mother will be fully recuperated?"

"It may be a while. Thank you for your concern. I'm sure you understand why we must be going." Clint shook the reins to get the horse moving.

"Wait!" Clemons ran after them calling, "Evelyn, I didn't get your last name." The horse took off at a trot leaving the dentist behind, his mouth gaped open.

~

IRRITATION STUNG CLINT. Had Clemons intentionally parked his buggy next to theirs? He knew it belonged to the L&M, because the emblem was on the side. What did the forward man hope to gain by introducing himself to Emily?

He sucked in a deep breath, drawing his lips into a tight line. Clemons had his hat set for Emily. Clint was sure of it. Asking when Ma would be "fully recuperated" was the dentist's way of finding out when he could begin courting Emily. He hoped she had better sense than to let that odious man anywhere near her.

Clint cut his eyes toward Emily, who picked at her skirt. The dentist made her nervous. Understandable, but why had he called her Evelyn? It was the same name Adella Payne had used when addressing her.

He reached over and patted her hands now clasped in her lap. "Calm down, Miss Hammons. We left Clemons a half mile-back with his jaw dropped. He's not following us."

She exhaled a slow breath. "Thank you for intervening. And please, call me Emily."

He winked at her. "And you can call me Clint. He tugged on his hat brim, clearing his throat. "I'm curious about something. Why did Clemons call you Evelyn?"

Emily bit her lip before she spoke. "Do you remember me telling you Mrs. Payne thought my name was Evelyn? When Dr. Clemons walked into the general store, I overheard him ask her my name. She told him she thought it was Evelyn. I decided to keep silent and let him think it. Now, I'm glad I did."

"I don't blame you. Adella Payne is a busybody and quick to spread gossip." Clint wished the obnoxious dentist would find another woman to pester. "Does Clemons know your last name?"

"No. He asked, but to my relief, Mrs. Payne couldn't remember."

"It's probably for the best," Clint grumbled. "The less that man knows about any woman, the better off she will be." Even as he spoke, he was convinced Emily had not seen the last of the dentist. Clemons would not give up easily. He had lost one woman and needed to get married by the end of October to receive his inheritance. The pressure was on. He would see to it that the desperate dentist did not bother Emily. She deserved better than a three-timing, self-appointed Casanova.

The more Clint thought about Clemons, the more incensed he became. He slapped the reins and urged the horse to run faster. Miss Hammons was way above Clemons's class. The man didn't deserve a woman like her. Clemons expected every woman to fall at his feet because he stood to inherit a dental practice.

She was intelligent enough to see through him. Or was she? Surely, she would not give the dentist permission to court her. Not if Clint had any say in the matter. He slapped the reins harder, urging the horse to a run.

Emily squeezed his arm. "Clint! You're scaring me. Can we slow down…please?" Terror filled her eyes.

"Whoa, there." Clint pulled on the reins and slowed the horse to an easy canter. What was he thinking, frightening her like this? He had no excuse for taking his angst out on Emily or his horses. They would get a good rubdown after this. It's the least he could do to make up for running them ragged.

Emily's shoulders visibly relaxed. "That's better. No need to work the horses into a lather to get home. Your mother's health has improved."

Shame burned his face. Why had he allowed that odious Wendell Clemons to enrage him? The man was looking for a woman to wed. Any woman. And only so he'd receive his inheritance. Emily would not fall to the dentist's prey. He would see to it.

Clint cleared his throat. "I'm sorry, Miss Emily. My mind was somewhere else."

~

MRS. WHITLEY WAS the only congregate Emily had met. She would have liked Clint to introduce her to a few more people, but that did not happen. After the service, Clint had urged her toward the door and on to the buggy. The people were huddled outside, probably gossiping about the ridiculous scene Wendell Clemons had caused.

Where had Clint's mind drifted to, to run the horse ragged? She had little time to mull it over before he guided the buggy down the lane that led to the L&M ranch. When he'd pulled up near the house and hopped to the ground, he bowed in mock eloquence, placing his Stetson over his heart. "Well, here you are, Miss Hammons. Delivered all safe and sound."

As his strong hands encircled her waist, she spied a young, blond man riding bareback on a black stallion, slip out from behind the barn and disappear into the adjacent grove of trees.

Was this Landon, the boy who brought stars to Alissia's eyes? It might be best not to mention what she'd seen to Clint. At least not before she talked to Alissia.

THE CHANCE CAME LATER that evening while Emily and Alissia cleared the supper dishes from the table. Clint excused himself to water and feed the livestock.

Alissia picked up the pie plate. "One slice of peach pie left. You want to split it with me?"

"Shouldn't we save it for Clint?" Emily asked.

"It's not big enough. This slice wouldn't make three bites for him."

Emily picked up a knife and divided the narrow slice. Alissia grabbed a fork and began to eat her half. "Mmm...this is delicious."

When they had finished it off, Emily stacked the plates and set them on the counter next to the dishpan. "How did your ma do while we were gone? I felt bad about leaving you here alone. I should have stayed in your place."

A faint flush crept into Alissia's cheeks. She kept her head down as she lifted the kettle off the stove. Still not making eye contact, the girl poured the steaming water in the dishpan. "No, I wanted you to go to meet some of our neighbors. Ma slept most of the time, but she's better. She talked to me for a little while. I fed her some dinner before you and Clint came in."

"She seems to be improving by the day. It probably won't be long before your mother can join us for meals," Emily added. How long should she wait before looking for a job in town?

But Alissia's mother was not the main topic on Emily's mind. "Did you have company while we were at church?"

Alissia's head jerked up. Her eyes widened as she stared at Emily, chewing her bottom lip. "Why do you ask?"

Emily touched her arm. "Don't worry, I didn't tell Clint about the boy on a black horse I saw coming out from behind the barn and disappearing into the grove of cottonwoods. A nice-looking young man with straw-colored hair. Was that Landon?"

Alissia whooshed out a breath. "Yes. Thank you for not telling Clint."

"I wanted to hear what you had to say first, so as not to jump to conclusions."

Alissia shrugged. "Landon showed up, and I invited him to join me on the porch to sit a spell. Ma was asleep. We talked a few minutes, that's all. Is there anything wrong with that?"

Their meeting was no coincidence. It explained why Alissia volunteered to sit with her mother, urging Emily to go to church in her stead. "Not that I can tell. Still, you are meeting him behind Clint's back. What would he say if he found out?"

Alissia plunked a pot in the dishpan, splashing water onto the floor. "I don't care what Clint says! I am not a child." She puckered her lips, making herself appear every bit a four-year-old, and added, "Neither is he my pa."

"We both know that, Alissia. But try to see this from Clint's angle. He feels responsible for you because you are his younger sister. He worries about you because he cares."

Alissia flung her hair over her shoulder. "Well, he needs to let me grow up and make my own decisions. I'm not stupid, you know. Clint thinks he's the only one in this family with a brain. Sometimes, I'm not sure he has one."

Emily stifled a chuckle. How could she advise Alissia, when she sadly lacked in matters of love? The only boys she'd known were the few who attended her school the entire twelve years. She'd grown up with these boys. They'd played together as children. They were like brothers to her. No quickened heartbeat or sparks had occurred. Unlike when Clint's green gaze locked with hers and her heart melted.

She should be ashamed for having such thoughts. Here she was trying to encourage Alissia to act responsibly and, her own thoughts had strayed onto a dangerous path. How could she instruct the girl in the proper ways to act with a young man when her thoughts were running wild?

Drawing in a breath, she hesitated. Should she try to convince Alissia that her feelings for Landon would fade, that what she felt was merely a passing crush? But crushes often blossomed into true love. At least it was what she believed.

"Promise me you won't tell Clint," Alissia pleaded.

Emily swallowed hard. "You don't want me to mention Landon coming for a visit?"

Alissa nodded, her eyes cast downward. "Please keep it a secret."

That secret could jeopardize Emily's job if Clint found out. Was she willing to take the risk? She did not want to take sides, although she felt that Clint held the reins too tightly where his teenage sister was concerned.

Yes, he had his reasons, reasons Emily didn't fully understand. And who was she to question them? Still, she didn't want to stir up more trouble between Clint and his sister.

"We'll see. I need time to think about it."

Alissia threw her arms around Emily. "Thank you! I knew you wouldn't snitch on me. You, being a woman like me, I knew you'd understand about being in love."

Emily chewed her lip. The girl was wrong about two things. She knew nothing about love, and Alissia was not yet a woman. "Love?" This was worse than she'd thought.

Alissia's eyes took on a dreamy look. "Yes. Landon and I are in love. Can't you tell?"

Emily gripped Alissia's shoulders, forcing the girl to look her in the eye. "I wouldn't tell Clint that."

"Oh, I won't."

"Tell Clint what?"

Emily flinched and dropped her hands while Alissia gasped at the booming voice. Neither had heard Clint come in. As far as Emily had known, he was feeding the livestock. Not listening in on her conversation with his sister. She searched her mind for a reply that would avert the impending interrogation.

Before she could come up with a plausible answer, Alissia blurted, "Don't go sneaking up on people, big brother. You scared us out of a year's growth."

Clint's eyes narrowed. "Got a guilty conscience, have you, little sister?"

Grasping at straws, Emily blurted, "I may as well confess. Alissia and I finished off the pie."

Clint rolled his eyes and groaned. "So that's what y'all wanted to keep from me. Like I wouldn't find out." He thumbed toward the empty pie dish on the table. "Next time hide the evidence. All the while I was brushing burs from Penny's mane, I was tasting that peach pie."

"I'm sorry," Emily offered.

Clint wagged a finger, feigning hurt. "I'll forgive you this time. Don't let it happen again.

"Oh, it won't," his sister blurted.

Emily's conscience twinged at the white lie that had slipped from her lips. True, the pie was gone, because she and Alissia had divided the last slice. But they had not been discussing Clint's disappointment at finding it gone. Covering for his sister was wrong, even if she had halfway promised Alissia she would keep her secret.

Emily rubbed her stomach and moaned. "I wish I hadn't eaten it."

"Emily, you look green. Did that stolen pie make you sick?" Clint teased.

Chapter Eleven

Over the next two weeks, the household fell into the new routine. School started for Alissia. A neighbor who lived two miles up the road stopped by mornings with a wagon load of children, to give Alissia a ride. Mr. Baxter worked at the lumberyard in town. He assured Clint it was on his way and no inconvenience to let his sister hop on the wagon with the other kids.

On the first day of school, Alissia argued that she could ride Copper to school. Clint refused to let her. Alissia climbed up into the back of the wagon, in a huff. He figured he'd interfered with her plan to meet up with Landon. The lad would be on his way to the ranch about the same time.

Emily no longer needed the crutch. Her foot was still tender, but the limp was gone. While Clint sipped his second cup of coffee, he watched her float about the kitchen checking for items to add to the grocery list that Alissia had made up. She moved with grace. How would she feel in his arms gliding across the dance floor? The Coopers' harvest celebration party was set for the first Saturday of October. Maybe he'd ask her to accompany him. Since Ma was getting stronger by the day, the dilemma was how to keep her at the ranch until that time.

He hated to think of her leaving. Emily's cheerful disposition added a bright spot to their lives. Was that as far as it went? Or had he developed feelings for her?

Clint shifted his thoughts back to the grocery list in her hand. He'd seen it on the table earlier. Alissia wrote down staples, last night. Emily added more items as she opened and closed cupboards. Studying the list, she placed it on the table before him.

"I think this will do. I hope it's not too much."

Clint picked it up and saw she'd penciled in a few spices his Ma didn't normally use. He wondered if he might become the recipient of delicious dishes Emily concocted. His mouth watered at the imagery. Ma admitted she wasn't the most creative cook. The food she served was tasty enough, but nothing out of the ordinary. Clint's taste buds craved something different. Maybe Emily would create dishes that would satiate his appetite.

Clint stood and rubbed his bristly chin. He should have shaved this morning but had overslept and didn't want to take the time. He wished he could accompany Emily to town, but someone needed to stay within hollering distance of Ma. The only hand he could spare was Landon. Clint wouldn't have to worry about impropriety, because the boy was polite and practiced good manners, unlike the other cowhands. Would Emily feel comfortable making the trip with him?

Clearing his throat, Clint asked, "Do you mind riding into town with Landon? He should be showing up any minute. I have a long list of things for him to do after you return replacing hinges on the paddock gate and mucking out stalls."

"WHAT ABOUT YOUR MOTHER? She needs someone to be with her."

Mrs. James's routine was to sit up in bed and either read or knit until noon. In the early afternoon, she took a long nap.

Clint licked his lips. "That's why I'm sending Landon in my place. You shouldn't be gone too long, and I'll be in and out of the house, checking on her. I'll stay within hearing in case she calls out. It will save time if Landon drops you off at the general store before he heads to the feed and grain and the blacksmith shop. I figured you might want to shop for a few personal items, also."

"I appreciate that. I do need to purchase a few things." A very few, she thought. How much would four coins buy? She needed to be careful with the money she had left.

"Landon seems to be a nice young man. I don't mind riding to town with him. We'll return as soon as possible. I also need to mail a letter. She had promised to telegraph Roy but decided against it when she discovered a telegram was much more expensive than a stamp. If only she could afford a couple of yards of lace to give one of her dresses a fresh look.

Clint dug in his pants pocket and pulled out a roll of bills. "Which reminds me, I haven't paid you for the time you've taken care of Ma."

He peeled off several bills. "The post office is across the street from Payne's General Store, and down two blocks." When she didn't stretch forth her hand, he picked it up and pressed the money into her palm. Warmth spread up her arm, heating her cheeks. What was he doing to her?

Emily shook her head. "Thank you, but this is too much money. I can't accept it. Providing me a place to sleep and food to eat, is enough."

"Take it, and don't argue with me." When Clint closed his hand around hers, Emily's legs turned to jelly. She stiffened her knees to keep her balance. Why did he have this effect on her?

"You've been kind to Ma, even when she was out of sorts.

She can be a handful at times. And you even cooked and cleaned while you were still limping."

"Take some of it back." She peeled off two bills and tried to tuck them into his shirt pocket. He caught her hand and pressed it to his chest. His strong heartbeat thumped beneath her fingers.

Clint's eyes glinted with mischief while Emily's treacherous heart skipped a beat. "Don't mess with me, young lady," he teased. "You won't win." He pulled her close, his gaze mesmerizing her.

Emily had neither the strength nor will to pull away. A lazy smile split Clint's face before he lowered his head. She closed her eyes as his lips brushed against hers. When his warm breath fanned her cheek, her heart melted.

"Emily!" Mrs. James called from the bedroom.

Emily flinched. Clint dropped his hands and stepped back. "I'm on my way, Mrs. James," she called out.

Clint groaned. "Why now, of all times?"

Emily cleared her throat and stuffed the bills into her skirt pocket. "I need to talk to you about your mother."

"What about her?"

"By now she has probably finished her breakfast. She wants to sit in the rocker by the window for a while. She says she feels stronger today. I told her I would ask you."

"LET'S TALK TO HER TOGETHER." Trying to regain his composure after their "almost kiss," Clint tramped down the hall with Emily close behind. He found his mother staring at the wall, wringing the covers between her fingers. "What is it you're wanting, Ma?"

"To get out of this contraption of a bed," she groused. "My backside's numb from layin' flat of my back for so long."

Clint noted some of the mischief had returned to her eyes and color flushed her cheeks. "Ma, do you think you can handle being by yourself for a while? Landon is on his way here. He's taking Emily to town to pick up groceries. I'll be in and out of the house, and around the barn."

"Help me to that chair and I'll be all right. I can see the barn and paddock from my window if I need to holler at you, which I won't."

Clint couldn't argue with his mother's reasoning. Yes, she was perkier. Her sass was back. And he would make sure he glanced toward her bedroom window often.

He slid his arms around her slight frame, half lifting her from the bed while Emily steadied the rocking chair. When he stood his ma in front of the chair, she swayed. He reached out and caught her.

She touched her fingers to her forehead. "Hold on just a minute, boy. My head's swimming, and this room is rolling like a wagon hitched to a team of wild horses."

"Are you sure you are well enough to be sitting up?" Clint asked.

"Yes, yes, I'm fine." She hiked her shoulders "The spinning's stopped now. Help me get settled in the rocker so I can look out the window and see something besides four boring walls."

A horse nickered before a deep voice yelled out. "Whoa, Betsy!"

Clint leaned forward to look through the window. Doc Simmons's buggy stopped in front of the house. "Ma, you may have some explaining to do about why you're out of bed. I wonder who will be in the most trouble—you, me, or Emily."

Doc's boots clomped up on the porch. He pounded the screen door frame before he tramped inside. "Anybody home?"

"In Ma's bedroom, Doc," Clint answered.

Dr. Simmons appeared in the doorway, his eyes narrowing at the sight of his patient reclined in a ladder-back rocker. He propped a shoulder against the door jamb and folded his arms across his chest. "What are you doing out of bed, Vera? Didn't I tell you to rest?"

Clint sent her an "I-told-you-so" look which she ignored. She flapped a hand at the doctor. "Rest, rest, rest. I'm sick and tired of resting. If I stay in that bed a minute longer, I'll have bedsores on my posterior. And I certainly don't want you treating those."

The doctor's face flushed while Emily's cheeks tinged pink. Clint chuckled. He understood why Emily might blush, but shouldn't the doctor be well beyond it?

Doc set his bag on the bed, ignoring Ma's last remark, directing his question at Clint. "Did you have any trouble getting her out of bed?"

Clint cleared his throat. "Ma's coughing spells aren't as often or as bad, so I helped her to the rocker. She feels stronger today, although she got a little dizzy-headed when I set her on her feet."

The doctor sighed. "Understandable. Your mother's been lying in a horizontal position for some time."

"Too long a time, I might add," Ma grumbled. "I aim to remedy that, starting today. And y'all can quit talking about me like I've passed on to glory. I figure I've got a good many more years."

The doctor studied her. "You were dizzy when you first stood?"

"Yes, I was a little dizzy when I first got up, but it went away in the shake of a lamb's tail."

"Vera, that occurred because your blood has been circulating horizontally for weeks. It could take a couple of days to retrain it to circulate vertically."

Ma gave the doctor a curt nod. "I just want it to circulate. And today is as good a day as any to start retrainin' it to circulate in a vertical direction."

Doc pulled a stethoscope from his bag. "We'll see about that. Unbutton the top of your gown, so I can listen to your heart."

When she did, he pressed the stethoscope against her chest.

"Hmm… that sounds better. Now, lean forward so I can listen to your lungs."

He placed the stethoscope on her back beneath a shoulder blade. "Take a deep breath and hold it." Ma did as told without complaint.

Doc set his bag on the bed ignoring Ma's last remark and directing his question at Clint. "Did you have any trouble getting her out of bed?"

Clint. "They sound—"

Ma raised her hand and waved it in front of the doctor's face. "Speak to me, Doc. I'm right here. I'm the patient."

The doctor looked her in the eye and winked. "Vera, your lungs sound a lot clearer. I believe you are on the road to recovery, young lady."

Emily straightened Ma's gown, buttoning it before fluffing a pillow and placing it behind her head. She had become very attentive, and Ma was eating it up. To the point of becoming spoiled.

Emily's nurturing skills seemed to come naturally. She would make someone a wonderful wife. Clint paused to scratch his forehead. Where had that thought come from? Not his wife, but someone's. He pushed away the visual of Emily tucking two small children in bed at night, a dark-haired little girl and a red-headed little boy.

He took a deep breath to refocus, relieved that no one had noticed his strange behavior. Emily held Ma's hands, speaking words of comfort, while Doc Simmons tucked his stethoscope inside his black bag.

Ma smiled when Emily angled the rocker toward the window. "That's better," she said. "Thank you, Emily. Now I can enjoy a nice change of scenery outside of these boring walls and ceiling I've stared at for weeks. And, I can see who's pullin' up in the yard."

The doctor wagged his finger at her. "Vera, it will be a while before you regain your full strength. Don't go getting any big ideas." He fastened his black bag. "Let's get something straight. If I permit you to sit up two hours a day, will you promise me you won't try to take over running the house?"

Ma sent him a blistering look that told them this was exactly what she had in mind. She raised her chin in defiance. "Look here, Floyd Simmons, I don't need your permission to get out of this bed. Why don't you take care of your business, and let me take care of mine?"

He pointed his bony finger at her. "You *are* my business. And as long as you're my patient, you will follow my orders."

Ma raised a hand in surrender. "All right, I'll follow your orders for the time being. But don't think you've gotten the upper hand."

The doctor groaned. "Vera, I pity the man who thinks he has. You are one stubborn woman."

"And you, Floyd, are a nagging, persistent old coot, who doesn't know when to quit talkin'."

Emily giggled, obviously enjoying the banter. Ma and Doc's friendship went back a long way. For as long as Clint could remember, they had thrived on arguing. He wondered if something stronger than friendship might be developing. Ma couldn't ask for a finer gentleman than Floyd Simmons.

Doc hooked his thumbs in his vest pockets. "I wouldn't have to nag if you'd do what I told you. Everything I tell you to do is for your own good."

Ma aimed a crooked finger at him. "If you'd quit nagging me, I might do as I was told. Have you ever thought of that? Put that in your pipe and smoke it."

"I don't smoke a pipe, and you know it. Tobacco, in any form, is harmful to the body. Swallowing all that smoke can't be good. Neither can breathing it. I have middle-aged and elderly patients who indulge. All have respiratory problems. Same goes for dipping snuff. It's not good for a body, either. The only thing tobacco is good for is chewing it up then spitting it out to apply to a wasp sting."

Ma rolled her eyes. "You've got an answer for everything."

"I try to stay on top of medical news. You should appreciate that since I'm your doctor."

She waved a hand. "Be off with you, you old coot. Come back when you've got time to argue."

The doctor flashed her a crooked grin and patted her hand. "I know when you're trying to get rid of me." He picked up his medical bag. "I'll be back in a few days. I won't tell you when, but I'd better not catch you bustling about in that kitchen."

Ma folded her arms across her chest. "Floyd, two can play that game. I'll have Emily on the lookout for your buggy. When it pulls into the yard, I'll jump into bed, yank the covers up around my neck, and moan like a dyin' calf. 'Cause I'd hate for you to waste a trip coming out here."

Doc Simmons threw up his hands. As he left the room he muttered, "Vera, you're the orneriest woman I was ever pleased to meet."

Clint and Emily followed Doc out to the porch. He turned and nodded at Emily "You're doing a great job with Mrs. James. Since she's improved, I suggest you move to the guest room, so you can rest better at night."

Emily searched Clint's face for his approval. He turned to the doctor. "That can be arranged this very day. Thank you for coming by. Ma gets a kick out of arguing with you."

Doc chuckled. "Same here. Trying to come up with clever replies to her sassy remarks, keeps my mind sharp."

~

CLINT HELPED Emily step up to the buckboard where Landon waited, the reins in his hand. "You take care of Miss Hammons. Don't dawdle. I have chores for you when you get back."

Landon gave a quick nod. "Yes, sir."

Emily appreciated the extra money Clint had given her. The pay was more than she had expected, since she was already receiving free board and meals. She would save most of her pay until she had the prospect of a job and enough for a month's rent at a boarding house. Mrs. James would soon be up and running the household again.

Her heart ached at the thought of leaving the ranch. She'd grown attached to Mrs. James, formed a bond with Alissia, and, if she would admit it, had grown quite fond of Clint. Each day, at the sound of approaching hoofbeats or a wagon pulling into the yard, she caught herself running to the window, only to be disappointed when it was Alissia coming in from school, or a hired hand riding in to get a tool from the barn.

Landon sat erect, focusing on the road. He chewed his bottom lip, obviously in deep thought. Emily noticed the patches on the knees of his denim pants and the scuffed toes of his work boots.

Seated beside her, the young man remained silent except for the occasional clucking sound he made to get the horses moving faster. A red hawk circled overhead and emitted a loud screech. Its red-tipped wings spread wide as it glided, searching for prey.

She finally broke the silence. "Landon, how long have you worked for Mr. McCall?"

He shrugged. "Since spring. Why?"

"I heard you graduated at the top of your class and plan to become a doctor."

He studied her as if trying to discern if she were friend or foe. "Where did you hear that? The only one I told was—"

"Alissia?" Emily suppressed a smile when he clammed up and faced forward.

"Yeah, well—"

"Well…what?"

"I'd rather it didn't get out about me wanting to go to medical school. Who else knows?"

"Clint."

"Mr. McCall?" He groaned. "I asked her not to say anything yet."

"Why do you want to keep it a secret?"

"Because it's a dream that doesn't have much chance of coming true. And, because Mr. McCall doesn't like me."

She understood how he'd reached that conclusion but asked anyway. "Why do you think that?"

"He gives me a stern look every time Alissia's around." Lance pointed to the sky. "See that red-winged hawk? Mr. McCall is like him, and I'm a field mouse. He stands over me making me nervous while I work. Watches my every move. Then I mess up, even if I know how to do the job. I can't do it correctly, with him hovering."

Emily smoothed her skirt. "Have you given him a good reason to watch you closely?"

"No." Landon answered a little too quickly. Color rushed to his face, turning it rosy pink.

Her digging for the truth, made him uncomfortable. "Could the way Clint watches you have anything to do with Alissia? He's as protective as a mother hen when it comes to his sister."

When Landon didn't answer, she added, "I don't think it's you. It's about keeping his little sister safe."

Landon raised his chin and faced her. "I would never do anything to hurt Alissia. You have to believe me."

Emily patted his arm. "I do. It's Clint who needs convincing."

"And how would I do that when he won't even give me a chance?"

"The only advice I can give is to do everything he tells you to the best of your ability, and without complaining. Show him you're reliable."

Landon worried his bottom lip. "Are you sure the way he treats me only has to do with his protective nature? My family doesn't have much in the way of worldly goods. I wonder if Mr. McCall wants Alissia to marry a rich man. Like a banker's son."

The lad was probably ninety-percent right, but a romantic at heart, Emily didn't want Landon to give up his pursuit of Alissia. "That may be part of it, but I think Clint prefers honor and respectability above wealth."

Landon's eyes widened. "I hope so. Do you think, if I won the scholarship and got accepted into medical school, Mr. McCall would change his opinion about me?"

"I couldn't say for sure, but it would be well worth the effort."

Landon seemed to sit taller on the seat. "I'm going to study like the dickens to win that scholarship. Not just for me, but for Alissia too. For our future."

Emily paused not sure how much more to say. "Alissia isn't sixteen yet. She has two more years of schooling. Don't rush into anything."

"We won't. We're too young to consider marriage if I want to become a doctor. After I get through medical school, we'll be old enough. Doc Simmons says I have what it takes to be a good doctor because I care about people. He's invited me to go along with him on his rounds. When Mr. McCall doesn't need me, of course," he added. "Doc said it would be good experience, good training."

"I think that's a great idea. You could learn a lot from an established doctor. Things that will help you as you go through medical school."

Chapter Twelve

Landon helped Emily out of the buckboard in front of the general store. The lad assured her he would return as soon as he'd completed his errands. The sunbonnet Emily wore provided a shield from the blazing sun. Swinging the wicker basket Alissia had set out this morning, she stepped up on the boardwalk and entered Payne's General Store.

Adella Payne fanned herself from behind the counter where several bolts of fabric were stacked. "Come in, dearie. It's a powerful hot day to be outside and bareheaded. Be glad you're wearing a bonnet."

Emily nodded. "The bonnet makes a difference. It's warmer here than in Tennessee, although the humidity isn't nearly as high." She glanced around the store, perusing the shelves stacked with canned goods, the sacks of flour and sugar, a barrel of pickles, and inhaling the scents of fabric, peppermint candy, leather, and pipe tobacco.

Mrs. Payne stroked a bolt of fabric on the counter and began to unroll a section of the green and gold print. "How may I help you, today?" She pressed the swath to her throat. "These bolts just came in. Wouldn't this one make a pretty dress? What do you think, considering my coloring?"

Emily studied her a moment. "Yes, it would be flattering." The green print complemented Mrs. Payne's red hair, although it could not rectify her pointed nose and beady, close-set eyes.

"Thank you." The store owner blushed, rewinding the fabric around the bolt. "Enough of that. I see you have a list. Let me have it and I'll start filling your order."

Emily handed her the list. "I don't mind gathering the items. I'm sure you're busy."

"Nonsense. I know where everything is. And before I forget to ask, how is Vera?"

"Much better. She's sitting up for the first time, today."

Adella clucked her tongue. "I hope you didn't go off and leave the poor dear sitting in a chair."

"She's not alone. Clint…uh…Mr. McCall is within yelling distance. And I plan to return as quickly as possible."

"Clint, you say?" Adella gave Emily a sly grin at the slip of his given name. "I suppose Alissia has started back to school. That leaves you and Mr. McCall alone, to care for Vera."

Adella's pause on "alone" was not lost on Emily. The woman's insinuations infuriated her. How dare she imply something improper had developed between her and Clint.

She held the store owner's gaze. "To the contrary, Mrs. James and I are the ones who spend a lot of time…alone." She enunciated alone, clearing her throat.

Adella pretended to study the list Emily submitted and continued on as if she had not heard Emily's reply. "You must find it awkward at times staying at the ranch, you being an attractive young woman and Clint being quite a handsome young man."

"Not at all," Emily answered a little louder than necessary. "Mr. McCall works outdoors and on his large ranch, checking the cattle, mending fences, daily ranching chores, while I take care of his mother's needs, plus I cook, clean, and hang out the wash."

Emily had heard all she wanted to from this gossipy woman. Another moment and she might say something she would regret. She handed over the basket. "To save time, I'll walk to the post office while you are filling the order. If you don't mind giving me directions."

"Of course." Adella pointed directly across the street. "Cross the street to the barbershop. After you pass it, there's an alley. Keep to the boardwalk and go past a few more businesses. You can't miss the post office." She flapped a hand. "Be off with you now, and I'll be about filling your order."

Emily dipped her head. "Thank you."

She stepped off the boardwalk and crossed the dirt street, careful to look both ways. Even on a Monday, Abilene buzzed with traffic. Buggies and wagons rolled past, kicking up dust. Everyone seemed to be going somewhere, in a hurry. She fanned the dust in front of her face and coughed. A slow, gentle rain would settle it, but Clint told her it didn't rain often in east Texas.

A series of hammers pounded in all directions as she stepped across the street, her shoes covered with dirt. The town was growing. New establishments were popping up on both sides of the street and at both ends. These businesses would provide jobs for a lot of people. Emily hoped one would be hers.

How a town could grow this quickly was beyond her comprehension. Clint had told her how the town was formed in 1881. It did not exist until the Texas-Pacific Railroad laid its tracks three years earlier. In the following two days, 317 plots of land were auctioned off and Abilene was born.

Clint's grandfather had previously traded in Buffalo Gap. With Abilene nine miles to the north, the L & M ranch lay halfway between the towns. According to Alissia, Abilene boasted a larger variety of stores and better-quality women's fashions.

Emily hiked her skirts above her ankles and stepped up on the boardwalk. A sign above a red-and-white-striped pole read Cal's Barber Shop. A stocky cowboy stepped out of the barbershop, blocking her path. He smelled of soap, whiskey, and sickly-sweet aftershave. His lecherous gaze raked Emily from her head to bare ankles. She quickly dropped her hiked skirt.

"Well, looky here what I found." He doffed his hat. "Haven't seen you around these parts, purty lady. You need help findin' your way?"

He was overly friendly, and the gleam in his eye frightened Emily. "No, thank you. I know where I'm going." He leaned against the barber pole, grinning at her, blocking her path and not bothering to move. "Sir, if you will be so kind as to let me pass, I'll be on my way."

The cowboy ignored her request, offering his arm instead. His broad grin revealed two missing upper teeth. She figured he'd lost them in a saloon brawl.

"I don't mind helpin' at all. I'll escort you, just to keep you safe," he persisted. "You never know what kind of ruffians you might run into."

The only ruffian she'd run into was this half-drunk cowboy. Emily bit her tongue to prevent speaking it aloud. She should have waited until Landon returned, and asked him to accompany her to the post office. Abilene was nothing like her hometown. A lady could walk all over Bartlett without fear of being accosted.

"No thank you and good day, sir." She tried to pass, which was a mistake.

He grabbed her arm, pulling her to his side. "Let me walk with you. For your protection."

The pushy cowboy may have enjoyed a shave and been doused with aftershave, but his body reeked of sweat and cow manure. She almost wretched from the odor, and her heart pounded against her ribcage.

As Emily debated how to free herself from the bully's clutches, a wiry middle-aged man stepped through the doorway of the barber shop. She guessed him to be the barber since he was clad in a white apron. He waved a straight razor at the brutish cowboy.

"Joe, leave the young lady alone and be on your way."

The barber ducked his chin. "I apologize, Miss. Joe is usually harmless. He's just had a little too much drink."

This early in the day? It wasn't even noon. Emily had learned from the novels she'd read, that Western towns did not come to life until after sundown. She smiled her gratitude to the barber.

The cowboy dropped her arm, but stood his ground, and argued with the barber. "Looky here, Cal. I was having a nice chat with this purty lady. Why don't you stay out of it?"

Emily looked down the boardwalk, saw a means of escape, and seized it. She hiked her skirts and hurried away as fast as was ladylike. When she'd scrambled past several places of business, including a dress shop, a newspaper office, and a hardware store, she slowed her pace. Surely, she'd lost the inebriated cowboy now.

She turned to look. He still argued with the barber. When he pointed down the boardwalk, Emily's breath caught. "Lord, please help me find a hiding place," she prayed.

Ducking into an alcove, she strove to calm her ragged breathing. When she saw the door was open, she dashed through it and moved to a corner away from the window. The spartan room contained only a desk and a filing cabinet near the back wall with two framed documents hanging on the wall above it.

This should hide her until the drunk cowboy gave up his pursuit. Emily spied a back door and wondered where it led. She had turned back to peek through the window when a shadow fell across her.

"Hello, Miss Evelyn. It's a pleasure to see you again," the raspy voice oozed. She whirled around and found Wendell O. Clemons standing a few steps behind her. His lewd gaze sent tremors through her. He grinned. "I haven't been able to get you off my mind since we met."

Emily suppressed a scream. What rotten luck! Of all the businesses, she had ducked inside Clemons's Dental Practice. If only she'd walked a few steps farther.

Wendell's thick lips bared to expose his protruding incisors. Alissia was right. As a dentist, didn't he have the means to straighten them? He must not think the procedure necessary.

As he strutted up to her, the glint in his eyes made her cringe. Before Emily could move or speak, he snatched up her hand and bent to kiss it, leaving it wet with saliva. She fought the urge to yank her fingers from his grip and scrub her hand down her skirt to rid it of his touch. When he looked the other way, she would.

Her chances might have been better with the overzealous cowboy. Swallowing hard, she deliberated the best way to graciously excuse herself. Good etiquette required that much of a lady. She slipped her hand from his grip. "Hello, Dr. Clemons. Sorry to intrude on you. I was headed to the post office. Seems I chose the wrong door. I'll be going now. Good day." She took two steps before the dentist blocked her.

"Not so fast." His face contorted to form a scowl. Had she offended him? It lasted one second before he flashed another smile. Had she imagined the scowl?

"I want you to meet someone," he insisted, gripping Emily's wrist. He twisted his neck and yelled toward the door in the back. "Father! Can you come out here?"

A voice boomed in response. "Get in here, Son! I need help with this patient."

Emily exhaled a sigh of relief when the dentist's shoulders sagged in defeat. For the second time, she'd been rescued from a bully. She silently thanked God for delivering her.

Dr. Clemons rolled his eyes. "Evelyn, I would escort you to the post office, but it seems Father needs my help. Perhaps we could get together soon? Maybe a picnic? Yes?" His bushy eyebrows jiggled as he anticipated her answer.

Not if she could help it, Emily thought. Ignoring his invitation, she tried free her hand. His grip tightened. "I should go now, Dr. Clemons."

"But—" He frowned toward the door in the back before returning his attention to her.

"Get back here, now!" the older male voice ordered.

The dentist dropped her hand as if it were a hot potato. "I have to go. My father is not a patient man." Sashaying toward the back room, he announced, "Coming, Father."

Emily stepped out into the sunlight and scanned the boardwalk. Head down, the cowboy tramped toward her. She slipped back into the alcove, holding her breath and praying he would walk by, looking neither right nor left. When after a moment, he did not pass, she peeked out.

Her pursuer had become enraptured by an attractive brunette. They stood in front of the dress shop three doors up. While his back was turned, Emily ducked around the corner of Clemons's Dental Practice and stepped into the alley. She spied a stack of wooden barrels that would provide a sturdy barricade and conceal her. Crouching behind them, she waited.

When a few moments had passed, she slipped out of hiding to peek around the corner. One arm linked through that of his newly found prey, the cowboy escorted her across the street toward Corabelle's Diner.

As Emily released her breath, a familiar raspy voice drifted through the open window above her. She strained to hear what the dentist would say.

"Father, why didn't you come out to meet Evelyn? She's the young woman I mentioned—the one I saw at the general store and later at church. I don't know her last name, but I plan to find out."

"No!" Emily blurted and clapped a hand over her mouth. It would be the last straw. She held her breath, waiting.

What was surely the older Clemons's voice echoed her worries. "How will you find out?"

"Mrs. Payne said Evelyn was staying at the L & M ranch to help out with McCall's mother. I don't recall what kind of disease she has, only that it's contagious."

"Pneumonia," his father replied. "I talked to Doc Simmons the other day. Go on."

"Yes, that was it. I did discover that Evelyn arrived the very day of my disastrous wedding. It makes me wonder—"

"Wonder what?" The older Clemons asked. "Wait! Did you send off for two brides?" A long pause. "No wonder you asked for an exorbitant amount of cash to pay for train fare. I calculated it, and knew the cost was way too much for one ticket from Eastland."

"I'd rather not divulge the details, Father, if you don't mind."

"I understand why. Oliver, I'm disappointed in you. What made you do such a thing?"

Oliver huffed. "You know what they say: 'Better to have it and not need it than to need it and not have it' or 'A bird in the bush is worth two in the hand'. I wanted to ensure I had enough birds in my hand." A long sigh. "As it turns out, I'm bereft."

Emily wanted to laugh. Good enough for him. Clemons's father knew about the second bride, but he had yet to learn that his son had sent for a third one.

"Do you know anything about the second bride?" his father asked.

"Only that she was traveling from Memphis. I'll ask old Ward at the train station if a young lady by the name of Emily Hammons, got off the train on August 15th or 16th. I did receive a telegram a day late, stating she was on her way. She is probably hiding in town. Evelyn looks a lot like her, by comparing her to the tintype Miss Hammons sent."

Emily gasped. She'd forgotten about the tintype. If he questioned Mr. Ward, she didn't stand a chance. Her only hope was that the station master's memory was sluggish

"Oliver, I did not approve of your placing that ad," his father admonished. "Now, you've made yourself a laughingstock in town. It's bad for business. A man ought to be able to find a bride without stooping to such measures."

"I thought these measures would weed out the undesirables. I asked questions to ensure each woman was easy on the eyes, had good credentials, and physical stamina."

"And for all your efforts, you have no promise of marriage. My decision remains firm. Before your next birthday, find a woman willing to be courted—one who is open to marriage, or I will not sign this practice over to you." Silence then, "I will sell it first."

"Father be reasonable," Oliver whined.

"I have been. And I will allow you a reasonable time of courtship. But before I retire and relinquish this practice, I want a grandchild on the way. I want to ensure my practice is passed on to the third generation. And don't argue. I think I am being lenient. I am giving you time to court, marry, and give me the promise of an heir. I did not invest forty years in my dental practice, thirty-seven years in Dallas, and three here in Abilene, to let it fall by the wayside."

The younger Clemons asserted, "I will not let you down, Father."

"Do you think this young woman whom you call Evelyn, is willing to be courted?"

"Of course. Why wouldn't she be? I have a lot to offer her."

The older Clemons groaned. "Yes, and you thought your first choice for a bride was the perfect one. But she made a fool out of you, Son. The entire town is snickering behind your back. Tell me, did you send these ladies tintypes of yourself when you replied to their letters?"

"No, Father. I considered it but decided against it. Why? Should I have?"

"Son, a woman prefers to know what she is getting in the deal."

"The only reason I didn't was, I didn't want any woman marrying me for my looks."

A loud groan emanated from the older Clemons. When Emily tried to suppress the laughter gurgling in her throat, it erupted as a loud snort. She clamped her hands over her nose and mouth too late.

"Father, did you hear that hideous noise?" the younger Clemons asked.

Emily held her breath. If he found her in the alley, what excuse could she use? That she'd dropped a coin and it rolled behind the barrels. But that would be an outright lie.

"I didn't hear anything, Son."

"I'm sure I heard a hog snort," the younger Clemons asserted. "If old man Stiles has parked his hog wagon outside again, I'll demand he move it. Even if it means involving the sheriff."

Emily flattened her back against the building as footsteps clomped out to the boardwalk. Holding her breath and praying for what seemed like five minutes, she waited until his footfalls sounded above her again.

"I didn't see anything that resembled a hog. Old Harley's mule is tethered in front of the hardware store next door. It could have snorted."

If Emily hadn't been so relieved, she would have taken offense at being compared to a hog or mule. She started to slip out of hiding when the senior Clemons said, "Back to our discussion, Son. If you are counting on looks to snag a bride, you may want to try a different method."

Oliver had either not taken his father's words as an insult or ignored them, because he replied, "Evelyn is pretty to look at, and I believe she is intelligent. Also, I believe she is sturdy enough to stand on her feet all day. If I could lure her away from that insolent McCall, I would court her. The imbecile hovers over her as if he owns her. He whisked her away from the church while I was trying to introduce myself. The ignorant cow punch is the epitome of rudeness."

"Is he now? I've always considered Clint McCall to be an intelligent and polite young man."

A muffled voice called out. "Dr. Clemons, I'm going to be sick!"

The shuffle of feet sounded above Emily and faded away. She stepped out of hiding and hurried along the boardwalk until she came to a wooden structure with a sign hanging above an open window that read, Abilene Post Office. A round-faced middle-aged woman with pert features stepped up to the window and eyed her curiously. "Good afternoon, Miss. How may I help you?"

Emily pulled the letter from her purse, scooping up a few pennies that had settled to the bottom. "Three stamps, please. One for this letter, plus two extras." Postage was much cheaper than a telegram. After attaching the stamp to the letter, she handed it to the postmistress.

The letter to her brother was brief and vague. In it, she'd let Roy know she had found a nice place to stay and was well taken care of. Also, she told him she'd changed her mind about marrying the dentist. Emily did not reveal the reason, intentionally omitting that she'd been duped.

Telling Roy the entire story would only make him worry, and she would appear gullible. Thankfully, she had found out about Clemons before it was too late. Imagine being married to that man.

Emily had her pride. She would admit her mistake to her

brother if she was sure he wouldn't tell Louise. Even now, she could imagine her sister-in-law's scornful laugh.

The postmistress stamped the letter. "Will there be anything else?"

Emily envisioned loose tendrils around the woman's face that would give a more youthful appearance. The woman's hairstyle was none of her business. She would do well to keep her opinions to herself. The woman would likely become offended if she voiced them. Her mind automatically jumped to ways of improving a person's appearance. It wasn't always the hairstyle or their manner of dress. Sometimes, it was straightening the posture or trimming bushy eyebrows, that made all the difference.

She shook the thoughts from her head. The Bible said, Man looks at the outward appearance, but God looks at the heart. If only she could live by that verse.

In her musings, she'd almost forgotten the postmistress had asked her a question. Emily adjusted her bonnet. "As a matter of fact, I could use some information. Do you know any businesses in town that are hiring women? I type well and am proficient with sums."

The woman laid Emily's letter on the stack beside her before extending a hand through the window. "Let me introduce myself, first. I am Dorothy Miller. You can call me Dorothy. And, who might you be?"

Emily clasped the woman's fleshy hand. "I'm Emily—." She was hesitant to reveal more.

The woman didn't let Emily's pause deter her. She squinted down at the envelope. "Hammons, I see it now. Emily is a pretty name."

Of course, she would know her name. Emily forced a smile. "Thank you." The postmistress knew, as did the man at the depot who had held her trunk overnight. How long before Dr. Clemons discovered her identity?

And what would happen when Clint found out her true reason for coming to Abilene? He had minced no words on his opinion of mail-order brides. And sadly, she agreed with him. It was a stupid idea. How had she gotten herself into this mess?

The postmistress pressed her lips together and squinted against the sun. "I haven't heard of any particular business advertising for a typist or bookkeeper. Usually when a business places a Help Wanted sign in the window, somebody grabs it within the hour. Abilene is a thriving town in case you haven't noticed. If you can't tell it by the wagons rolling down the streets, you can tell it by the hammering all around you. New buildings go up every day. It shouldn't be hard for a body to find work of some kind."

Emily tucked the extra stamps in her purse. She would need a job in a matter of weeks. Because soon, her patient would no longer need her assistance. Returning to Bartlett was not an option.

"Thank you. I plan to look." But not today. Clint had asked them to return as quickly as possible. "Where would you suggest I start?"

The older woman's gaze swept over Emily before she winked. "An attractive girl like you could hire out at any of the saloons. Or, if you can sing, one of the dance halls would take you on. But, as a God-fearing woman, I wouldn't recommend either."

"No, ma'am. I was raised in a Christian home. I won't go near those places."

"Wise girl." Dorothy pointed past Emily's shoulder. "There's a saloon across the street. I'm thankful it doesn't get wild until after I close up. They say it's especially lively on weekends.

"I've asked for help here at the post office. Don't know what the holdup is. Most days it's busy in the mornings and stays that way until early afternoon. As the town's population grows, it will become more than I can handle by myself." She chewed her lip. "Check back in a month."

"Thank you. Perhaps I will."

To avoid passing the dental office and barbershop again, Emily retraced her steps by one block then crossed the street in front of the hotel. As she stepped up on the boardwalk, Jessica Dawson ran down the hotel steps yelling, "Emily! I need to talk to you."

Why was she still in town? Hadn't her sister boarded the train the day after leaving Clemons at the altar? "Hello, Jessica. I thought you had gone back to Eastland."

"No, I got a job as a clerk in the hotel." Shrugging, she added, "Truth is, I only had enough money for one return ticket. I figured Margie needed to get out of town worse than I did."

"I understand," Emily replied.

Jessica raised one eyebrow. "Guess who came by to ask about you."

Emily's heart drummed against her ribs. Was her worst nightmare coming true? "Who?"

"Dr. Clemons, of all people."

Emily clasped her hands together to keep from wringing them. The dentist was already asking questions? "What did he say?'

"Somebody must have told him we came in on the same train." She chuckled. "The man didn't even know your name. He called you Evelyn, and I let him think he had it right." Jessica's eyes narrowed. "I wonder where he got that idea."

Emily swallowed hard. "Mrs. Payne at the general store thinks it's my name. Dr. Clemons came in while I was there. I overheard him ask her my name. She told him it was Evelyn, and I let it stand. She still calls me Evelyn. I didn't want the dentist to get any notions about me. You didn't tell him my last name, I hope?"

Jessica sniffed. "I most certainly did not. I started to tell him you had better sense than to attach yourself to the likes of him. I bit my tongue instead. To my relief, a customer came in before he could persist with his nosy questions."

"Thank you." Jessica couldn't know how appreciative Emily was.

"You're welcome. After the customer left, Clemons asked why Margie stood him up. I didn't have the heart to tell him, she didn't like his looks or his persnickety ways. I excused myself, told him I had work to do. I know I offended him because he tipped his derby hat and said, 'Good day, Miss Dawson. I shall return.'" Jessica clicked her tongue. "All I can say is, heaven forbid!"

Clemons was asking questions about Emily as if he was a Pinkerton agent and she a fugitive. How she wished she had the money to reimburse him for train fare and thereby be rid of him. She would love to stuff the bills in his hand and tell him to, "Get lost."

No, she could not afford to make him angry. He might retaliate by telling Clint everything.

"Jessica, I need to go. I told Mr. McCall I would return as quickly as possible. I'm taking care of his mother, as you know. I left her in his care to pick up a few groceries."

"I understand. Maybe we could have lunch together when you have more time."

Emily nodded. "Yes, maybe. Well, have a nice day."

"Same to you," Jessica flung back as she hiked her skirts and climbed the hotel steps.

It had been an interesting day. Emily had been stalked by a drunk cowboy, detained by Clemons, and now, she'd discovered he was asking questions about her.

If she had more time, she would check with a couple of businesses, ask if they were hiring. Because if Clint discovered why she'd come to Abilene, she could be jobless and homeless.

Chapter Thirteen

Before Landon and Emily turned into the lane that led to the L&M Ranch, a wagon ahead of them loaded with school children, turned down it. Landon urged the horses to move faster. They pulled into the yard as Alissia walked toward the house with a stack of books and a lunch pail.

Landon yanked on the brake and leaped off the buckboard. "Alissia!"

The girl whirled around and yelled back. "Landon!"

He sprinted toward her. "Let me carry those books. They are too heavy for a young lady."

"Thank you." Alissa graced him with a wide smile before relinquishing the books. The couple stepped upon the porch together. While they talked, Landon propped one hand against a porch post. Alissia, laughed, seemingly mesmerized by the lad.

Oh, to be young and in love, Emily thought as she watched from the buckboard. At eighteen, she was young. But, in love? A visual of Clint McCall's teasing green eyes flitted through her mind. She shook her head to dispel it.

"Landon!" A male voice boomed to Emily's left. "Unload that feed so we can start working on the paddock gate." All eyes turned toward Clint, who stood near the paddock, arms folded across his chest.

Landon's countenance fell. "Yes, sir." He passed the stack of books to Alissia. Head held high, he marched toward the buckboard. Clint joined him and lifted Emily, setting her gently to the ground. Even though he was not smiling, his warm hands at Emily's waist set her heart to fluttering. Her breath released as a soft sigh.

Clint picked up the basket of groceries and escorted Emily to the porch while Landon climbed up to the buckboard and turned it toward the barn. Clint set the basket on the porch and scowled at his sister. Alissia refused to look at him and stared after Landon, a mixture of hurt and anger in her eyes.

Clint broke the silence. "Sis, don't you have chores to do?"

Alissia's flushed face said she was more humiliated than angry. Her mouth opened but whatever rebuttal she had planned, didn't come out. Spinning around, she fled inside the house.

Clint's gaze followed his sister until the screen door slapped to behind her. He shuffled his feet, staring down at them. "Hmm… I could've handled that better. That's what you're thinking."

Emily slowly nodded. "Landon is a perfect gentleman from what I've seen. He has big plans, to go to medical school. He's as smart as a whip. I believe he has the drive to reach his aspirations." Clint's narrowed gaze challenged hers. "Seriously, Alissia could do a lot worse."

His jaw clenched. "Landon can keep his high aspirations as long as they don't include Alissia. She's too young to be swept off her feet by a wet-behind-the-ears kid. I'll not let her mess up her life like—"

Emily arched her brows and met Clint's cool gaze. Like your mother did, she silently finished. The first time she had talked to Mrs. James, the woman had hinted at a regretful time in her past.

And she had heard some tales from Alissia the first day. Was this why Clint kept a tight rein on his sister?

Clint clamped his lips together as if he realized he'd said too much. Emily knew not to prod a man who was on the verge of exploding. He needed calming words, not ones to fuel his anger.

She needed to remind herself that this was a family matter and did not involve her. Her job was to attend to Mrs. James's health. Nothing more.

Emily wished she could talk to Clint about his sister. Would he listen, or would he reprimand her for adding her two-cents worth to something that was none of her business? Still, if she learned why Clint was afraid to loosen control over his sister, she would be better equipped to offer sound advice.

She laid a hand on his arm. "I would like to say—"

Clint stepped out of her reach. "I have chores waiting in the barn. Can you handle the basket of groceries?"

"Yes." She nodded as he turned to leave.

Had he intentionally walked away to avoid her forthcoming advice? She admired his broad shoulders and lanky frame as he swaggered away. A sigh escaped Emily's lips. My, he was handsome.

She hoped he wouldn't give Landon a hard time. Although the young people were infatuated with each other, it wasn't a crime for Landon to carry Alissia's books or to talk to her.

Emily stepped up to the porch and picked up the basket of groceries. It was time to check on Mrs. James and start supper. With Alissia and Clint upset, supper could prove to be an ordeal.

CLINT FOUND Landon in the barn unloading feed sacks from the buckboard. The young man remained silent while Clint helped him stack the feed. Neither did he speak to Landon. Guilt niggled at him. The boy had done nothing wrong. A gentleman should assist a young lady if she was carrying a load.

Landon's kind gesture didn't worry him. The lad's ulterior motive did. The kid used any excuse he could find to flirt with Alissia. Clint did not want to consider where that might lead.

He had been harsh with Landon, who was polite, respectful, and a hard worker, even if he didn't have the makings of a rancher. Emily was right. Landon's smarts came from books, not experience. The lad's dream was to become a doctor and his talents leaned in that direction.

Two months ago, cowhand Duke's horse got tangled in a barbed-wire fence. Landon mixed up a poultice from clay and who-knew-what-else and smeared it on the animal's leg before wrapping it. The wound healed nicely and left no noticeable scars. Duke still talked about it and encouraged Landon to become a veterinarian. He didn't know the boy's aspirations went higher.

A medical doctor? Clint shook his head. What was the probability of Landon achieving such a goal? With his background, it was like reaching for the stars and hoping to grab one. He came from an impoverished family whose father struggled to breathe and walk after an injury in the War Between The States.

Some men weren't cut out for ranching and Landon was one. Still, he needed to learn to perform everyday tasks, to prepare him for life. And Clint was happy to teach him. He didn't care what occupation Landon chose, as long as it didn't involve his little sister.

Emily's words reverberated through his head. "Alissia could do a lot worse."

Clint groaned. This might be true, but Alissia was too young to make life-altering decisions. He was her older brother, and ensuring she made good choices was his job. He grudgingly admitted that Landon did his best at every chore assigned him, and without complaining. Unlike ranch hands Bud and Slim, who constantly grumbled about something. Clint mostly tuned them out. It was their way.

Clint tossed the last bag on the stack while Landon rubbed the dust off his hands. "Did you get the hinges?"

"Yes, sir." The young man pulled a bag from beneath the wagon seat and handed it to him. Clint looked inside. "Good job, Landon. You remembered the screws." He patted the lad's shoulder. "After you give the horses a rub-down, meet me at the paddock, we'll replace the hinges on the gate."

Clint hoped the pat on the shoulder would lessen the sting of his harsh words directed at Landon earlier. The boy was no stranger to humiliation. Clint should be encouraging him, not berating him. If Landon had not shown an undue interest in Alissa, that would be easy. Landon needed to understand that his little sister was off-limits. Clint had plans for her future, and they did not include marrying at a young age and having a passel of young'uns.

A twinge of shame swept over Clint. Hadn't he been taught by his mother and grandfather that a man's worth wasn't measured by what he owned, but by what was in his heart? Had he so soon forgotten he had been in a similar place when Ma married Hank James? The first few years of the marriage had been tolerable, although Clint's stepfather made it plain that he was not welcome. Mostly the man snubbed him.

If Ma had let Hank know she had a son, would the man have treated him better? Or maybe his anger was because he'd discovered Ma had been working at a saloon. Would they have been spared the fear and pain his stepfather inflicted if his mother had been forthright? Or would Hank have reneged on the marriage offer? At least that would have spared Clint and his mother years of agony, plus the suppressed anger he'd dealt with since.

During the first years of their marriage, Hank treated his mother respectfully enough. Clint was eleven when the vein at the silver mine dried up and his stepfather became an angry, disillusioned man who squandered his pay from odd jobs on drinking and gambling. Those were lean years for Clint and his mother, who did without.

By then, Clint had become a fair marksman with a rifle. He used his skill to hunt wild game for their supper. Sometimes, he trekked two miles with a fishing pole, to snag a mess of fish from Washoe Lake. It was a difficult time, but they managed to eat. God must have been looking out for them, even if he hadn't stopped the abuse.

Clint wanted to say that nothing good had come from his mother marrying Hank, but he couldn't. Their union had brought sweet, giggling Alissia into the world, the only bright spot for the endurance of the marriage. Clint wouldn't take anything for his little sister, even if she had become moody as of late. He supposed it was all part of growing up.

If only she would try to see his point of view. Alissia was infatuated with this farm boy down the road. That was it, only infatuation. She was young and vulnerable. He, as her older brother, was the obvious one to protect her.

Clint reached the paddock, the hinges in his hand. After he and Landon replaced them, he would have to face Alissia. Dread engulfed him.

If it wasn't one thing, it was another. At least Ma was better. She would be joining them at the table tonight.

Regardless, supper would be a strained affair with Alissia doling out the silent treatment. What could he expect from Emily? Would she keep the conversation flowing, keep the topics light? She was a natural peacemaker. He figured she wanted to say more on the topic of Alissia and Landon. Well, he didn't need her input, no matter how well-intended. Alissia was his little sister, his responsibility.

～

CLINT HEARD voices before he let the screen door slap to behind him. As he tramped toward the kitchen. Ma said, "I think I heard your brother come in, Alissia. Fill the glasses."

"I'll do it," Emily answered before a chair scraped across the floor.

When Clint reached the doorway, Emily was filling the glasses. She looked up at him and smiled as he picked up the soap and started washing his hands. "Did you and Landon get the hinges replaced?"

"Yep." He'd prefer not to mention the boy's name, considering what had transpired earlier.

"Did he do a good job?" Alissia challenged, her eyebrows arched.

Too late to keep Landon out of the conversation. Clint dried his hands and hung up the towel "Yes, he did. He'll make some young lady a good husband. But he won't make a good rancher or a farmer."

The lad lacked roping skills and even cringed when his hired hand Bud, stuck the branding iron to a calf. Roping and branding were required to be a cattle rancher.

Alissia plunked the pitcher on the counter and turned to face him. "You won't need to worry about that. Landon will never be a farmer or a rancher. He's going to become a doctor."

After a measure of strained silence, Emily spoke. "Let's eat, folks. Supper's on the table."

Ma's curious gaze swept from Alissia to Clint. "Land sakes! What's going on? Can't a body eat supper in peace?"

Silence prevailed. Clint sat down, surprised to see his little sister seated at the far end of the table. Alissia did not want to hold his hand for the blessing.

Alissia lowered her head. "It's nothing, Ma."

Her avoidance of eye contact told Clint their conversation was not finished. And judging by Ma's frown, she was not fooled by what was transpiring.

He cleared his throat and ignored Alissia, reaching for Ma's and Emily's hands. "Let's bow our heads and bless the food."

He would let Alissia be until she came down off her high horse. As he bowed his head, Emily squeezed his hand. Was she reassuring him that everything would work out? Or was she warning him to hold his tongue?

He would, for Ma's sake. Closing his eyes, Clint mumbled, "We thank thee, O Lord, for this food and for the hands which prepared it. Amen."

When they had placed their napkins in their laps, Ma's gaze lingered on first one and then the other around the table. Clint hoped she wouldn't say anything to rile Alissia.

He let out a sigh when she said, "Pass the cornbread, please."

The topic turned to the dry weather and how the vegetable garden could use a long soaking rain. Ma turned to Emily, changing the subject. "How was your trip to town? Did you find the post office without much trouble?"

Emily dropped her gaze to her lap. "Mrs. Payne at the general store gave me directions. I had no trouble finding it."

Something had scared Emily. Her fork shook as she raised it to her mouth. Clint would ask her about it later when they were alone.

EMILY EXHALED SLOWLY and looked up. Alissia appeared to be lost in her thoughts while she stabbed at the meat in her plate. Clint and his mother studied Emily as if they expected her to elaborate. She would not reveal the trouble she'd had with the overzealous cowboy or the altercation with the obnoxious dentist. If she did, Clint might refuse to let her return to town. And she certainly couldn't tell them about her conversation with Jessica and what the young woman had disclosed.

Someone needed to break the silence and at the same time,

change the subject. Emily turned to Alissia. "How was school today? Do you need help with your homework?"

The girl lifted her gaze to Emily. "It was fine. No, I can handle it," she said before refocusing on her plate.

As Alissia lowered her head again, Ma slapped the table. The silverware pinged next to her plate. "All right. Out with it! What's wrong, Alissia?

Alissia slanted her gaze to Clint. "Ask him."

"I'd rather hear your side first."

The girl raised her head and sniffed. "I was having a perfectly innocent conversation with Landon. Until he stomped out of the barn and started yelling."

"I hired Landon to work. Not dilly-dally," Clint interjected.

Ma raised a hand. "Wait your turn, Son. I'm talking to Alissia right now." She turned back to her daughter. "Tell me the whole story."

Emily felt she was intruding on a private family discussion. "May I be excused?"

"No, finish your supper," Ma spoke in her no-nonsense voice.

Emily casually picked up her fork and knife and sliced off a piece of beef as Alissia elaborated.

"The school wagon pulled out of the yard at the same time Landon and Emily pulled up in the buckboard. All Landon did was offer to carry my books to the porch. Like a gentleman is supposed to do." She glared at Clint. "And I let him do it."

Emily was sure Alissia's reference to gentleman was meant to slur her brother. Clint's lips tightened into a thin line.

Alissia grinned when he squirmed. "Well, Landon was talking to me when a loud voice boomed. We both jumped and Landon was scared out of a year's growth."

Clint snickered. "I think he's grown tall enough. He's almost six feet.

Alissia's eyes narrowed. "That's not the point." The girl

sucked in air before she mimicked her brother's stern tone. "Clint yelled, 'Landon, unload that feed!'"

Clint winked at his sister. "Did I really sound that mean?"

His sister slapped her napkin on the table. "Yes, you did."

Emily coughed to cover a giggle, but Ma's glare sobered her.

Ma turned her scrutiny to her son. "Clint, is this true? Did you raise your voice at that boy?"

Clint crossed his arms over his chest. "Ma, I hired him to muck stalls and repair fences. He doesn't have time to lollygag with my little sister."

"That isn't what I asked."

"Maybe I did…a little."

Alissia opened her mouth to argue, but her mother raised her hand. "Wait. I'll handle this. Clint, you know the good Lord says that a soft answer turns away wrath. Don't you think you could've handled this a little better?"

Clint scratched the nape of his neck. "I suppose. But, have you seen the way …?

"We will not discuss this any further at the supper table. Your sister and I will have a little talk. Meanwhile, I want you to do your part to keep peace in this house. There ain't nothing that sours the stomach worse than a dispute at the eatin' table." She picked up her knife and sawed through a slice of beef roast. "Now. Let's finish our supper."

Emily's glance bounced from Clint to Alissia. Clint drew in a slow breath before he stabbed a potato with unnecessary force. His sister pressed her lips together. Emily could tell this discussion was a long way from over.

At least the topic was steered away from Emily's trip to town. She decided to talk to Clint about Alissia and Landon. Not that she'd had any experience in matters of the heart. At eighteen, she'd never had a real date unless she counted her classmate Johnny Grogan, who escorted her home from a high school dance last year. The only man Emily had kissed was her pa.

Still, she could give Clint the female perspective he lacked on love. How could he, being a man, understand the workings of a young woman's mind?

After helping Alissia tidy up the kitchen, Emily went to the barn in search of Clint. The musty scent of hay, leather, and horseflesh invaded her nostrils as she stepped through the door. He had his back to her, brushing Bowie's golden mane. A glowing lantern hung above the stall.

Clint sighed. "I don't know if I'll ever understand females, Bowie. They're too complicated for my pea-sized brain." He paused the brush as the horse looked him in the eye. "Think you could you give me a few pointers?"

Emily swallowed a giggle when the horse snorted. Clint pulled the brush through Bowie's mane. "Just as I thought. They've got you bumfuzzled too."

Emily stepped out of the shadows to make her presence known. Clint whirled around when hay crunched beneath her foot. She walked over and stroked the horse's mane. "He's beautiful."

"Bowie's a Palomino." Clint cleared his throat. "It's a beautiful night too. Did you see the sky?" He laid down the brush and took her hand, leading her outside. Pointing to the moon resting above the horizon, he said, "It's bright enough to read by. There must be a gazillion stars out. I see the Big Dipper. Have you ever wondered why God made so many planets and stars?"

"Yes, and I've wondered if there's intelligent life on any of them. It seems a waste, if not."

"Sometimes I wonder if there's intelligent life on earth," Clint mumbled.

His reference must have been to Alissia and Landon. Emily had to make him understand that forbidding them to see one another could backfire. Two couples in Bartlett had eloped because their parents forbade them to court. One of those marriages ended in disaster.

"Do you dance, Miss Emily?" Clint's words broke into her thoughts.

"A little. I haven't had much chance to practice."

"It's easy. Let me show you." Clint placed one of her hands on his shoulder and slid his arm around her waist. Pulling her close, he swept her over the dusty ground, belting, "Rose, Rose, Rose of Killarney, I love you-u."

Spellbound, Emily floated through the motions, letting Clint lead. Was he aware of the words he was singing? Were they a profession of his love for her?

No. She was here to take care of his mother. Not to win this handsome cowboy's heart. A longing for something she could not have, settled in Emily's chest. She mentally shook herself. Clint had chosen this ballad for one reason only—to help her practice the waltz.

She relaxed as his smooth baritone took on an Irish accent and reached a crescendo. "Rose of Killarney, I … love …you!" He laughed and twirled her one last time for the grand finale. When he stopped, both were breathless. "You're pretty good. Just need a little practice."

Emily wished the dance could go on forever. She felt safe and protected in Clint's arms. Imagining an embrace from Dr. Clemons, she shuddered.

Clint gaze searched hers. "Are you cold?"

"No." She'd told him the truth without giving an explanation.

The money Emily owed the dentist dangled above her head like a noose. Reimbursing him for the train ticket would only be right. Even if she had the money, she couldn't offer it to him, because if she did, he would know she was one of his mail-order brides. The first bride fled. If only the third would show up. What a tangled web.

Loud howls pierced the air. Emily flung herself back into Clint's arms. He held her close as she shook. "There, there. It's alright. They won't hurt you. Coyotes howl to alert the rest of the pack that they've caught something for supper. Probably a poor little jackrabbit."

Emily took a step back and looked up at Clint. Bad mistake. His eyes smoldered in the dusk. Mesmerized, she could not pull her gaze away. Slowly, he bent and lightly brushed his lips across hers. His warm breath tickled her ear, making her legs tremble. She closed her eyes and sighed. His lips captured hers in a sweet, gentle kiss. Of their own volition, her arms slid up and encircled his neck, pulling his head down.

As the kiss intensified, Emily's heart pounded in her chest. Only clinging to Clint kept her from slithering to the ground.

Her friend Betsy claimed that a kiss from her beau was like a bit of heaven. Emily could only guess what she meant, until now. She would describe the kiss Clint gave her as alternating between a raging storm and a warm, summer breeze.

After too short of a time, Clint stepped back, breathless. "I— uh— Did you come out to tell me something?"

Her head still reeled, leaving her feeling silly and light-headed. Emily searched her elusive memory.

Oh, yes. Now she remembered. But she dreaded bringing up a topic that would spoil the magical moment. Nevertheless, she must. Her face stung from the rough stubble on his face brushing hers. She looked up at him and braced for a battle. "It's about Alissia."

"What about her?" Clint's gruff voice told her she'd touched a sore spot.

She paused to consider her words. "Maybe, you are a little hard on her?"

Clint folded his arms across his chest and looked down at her. "She's my little sister, and my duty is to protect her."

"From what?" Emily had pushed this far. She wanted an answer.

"From marrying a kid who doesn't have two nickels to rub

together. One who couldn't brand a calf if two cowhands roped and tied it for him."

"That may be true. God gives different talents to different people. Not everyone is meant to be a rancher."

"In these parts, a man had better learn to be a rancher or starve. Because there's not much else that will provide a living."

Emily tapped her finger against her chin. "Let's see. Every town needs a good doctor."

Clint huffed. "Abilene already has a good one, Doc Simmons."

"Doc Simmons is a fine one, but he is getting up in years. He wants to train a young man to take his place. He's seen potential in Landon and even invited him to ride along on his visits to treat his patients."

"And how do you know all this?"

"Landon told me during our trip to town. This way he can get training and see if this is truly the occupation he wants to pursue."

"Even if Landon is inclined to become a doctor, and is smart enough, how will he get the funds to attend medical school? His family is impoverished. I'm doing him a favor by letting him work here on the ranch."

"And I'm sure he appreciates it. Landon will soon leave for Dallas, to take a test. If his score is high enough, he will be awarded a scholarship to the University of Arkansas, to study medicine. Alissia mentioned he graduated valedictorian of his class last year."

"He did. It was a class of ten students." Clint yanked off his hat and raked his fingers through his short, coppery curls. "Alissia is way too young to be thinking about boys. Land sakes! She won't be sixteen until next month."

"I know, but stop and think about it. If they plan to marry, they would need to wait until Landon finishes medical school. Landon would be away for long stretches of time. In the meantime, Alissia could finish high school and enroll in a women's college. She and Landon would only see each other during the summer and on long holidays until he received his degree."

"So far it sounds good. Go on," Clint urged.

"If you encourage Landon to pursue his dream, and it works out, this would take a load off your mind. And the long separation would be a good test to see if their love is the enduring kind, or if it's mere infatuation."

"Love?" Clint growled. "What do those kids know about the responsibilities that go with it?"

"Maybe more than you realize." When he grimaced, she quickly added, "Plenty of girls get married right out of high school. Some even quit to marry at age sixteen."

"That is not happening here, although I see your point. Encouraging Landon to go after his dream might work to my advantage. And to my sister's, even though she won't see it that way."

He toyed with his hat brim. "You really think my easing up on those two will help matters?"

She cleared her throat. He needed to face the facts. "Unless you want them to elope."

"Elope?" Clint's eyes blazed in the moonlight. "Landon had better not try it if he knows what's good for him."

Emily laid a calming hand on Clint's fisted one. "I'm just saying, you know how some kids are. The more you try to control them, the more they rebel. I sense a rebellious spirit in Alissia."

From what Emily had seen, the girl had come by it honestly. Not only from her mother, but also from her brother. Emily's pa had called it "a generous dose of stubborn."

Clint's shoulders drooped. "What do you suggest?"

Instinct told Emily he would not be easily sold on any idea that threw his little sister in with a boy. But she had to try. "You could allow Alissia to go to the dance at Cooper's Barn.

According to her, it's the big event of the year in all of Taylor County."

"Yes. It started as a festival to celebrate the fall harvest. People come from miles around."

"It's set for the first Saturday in October," Emily added. "Alissia will almost be sixteen."

"Her birthday isn't until the following week," Clint mumbled. "And, if she does go, she won't be going with that kid. Not as long as I have a say. She'll go with me. With us."

"Us?" Emily's heart fluttered. Was Clint asking her for a date?

Clint pressed his hat to his chest. "Miss Emily, will you go to Cooper's barn dance with me? Ma shouldn't need constant care by then." He spun around and pointed to the buggy in the shed. "There's plenty of room for the three of us."

Emily's joy dimmed. It wasn't a real date, after all. They would be chaperones for his sister. She swallowed her disappointment, determined to do this for Alissia's sake. "Of course, I'll go."

She ventured another question. "Shall we swing by to pick up Landon? We could make it a double date." She knew she'd said too much when Clint's jaw clenched.

"Double date? That is not going to happen. If Landon wants to go to the dance, he can meet us there. I won't forbid him to dance with my sister, as long as they keep plenty of daylight between them." He ducked his head to look Emily in the eye. "I will be watching them. You can tell her that."

Emily flashed him a smile. Of course he would, and Alissia knew it, too. "Thank you. Alissia will be delighted to hear this. Do you want to tell her, or shall I?"

Clint pulled his lips into a smirk. "You tell her. I think she'd rather hear it from you since we're not on the best of terms."

Clint was right. Any other time, Emily would have suggested he relay the good news to his sister. She would tell

Alissia and hope it applied a soothing balm to her emotional wounds.

"She will be overjoyed. You still need to set things right between you and Alissia. I think your intervention this afternoon, embarrassed her more than anything else. You know how it is when a big brother interrupts while his sister is talking to her friend."

"Her friend? I wish," Clint groused. "I know the gleam a man gets in his eye when he's romantically interested in a young lady. Landon gets that same look when my sister's in sight."

Emily hesitated, mentally searching for words to reassure him.

He exhaled. "What should I say to Alissia? 'I was a pompous fool for yelling at you and Landon this afternoon. Can you please forgive me?'"

Emily nodded slowly. "That would be a good start."

Clint studied her a moment before he groaned. "You're serious, aren't you? Do you think it's really necessary?"

Emily fixed him with an admonishing look. "If you want peace in the house. Alissia may pretend not to accept your apology, but after a good night's sleep, she'll come around. In case you haven't noticed, your ma isn't happy about this tension between you and your sister, either."

"Yeah, and I also noticed she takes Alissia's side most of the time."

"That's because your ma remembers how she felt at sixteen."

"Fifteen. Alissia won't be sixteen until next month. Let's not push it."

"Close enough. Your ma is a pretty woman. I imagine she had a beau or two pursuing her."

"You just proved my point. Look at the trouble Ma got—"

... herself into? Emily silently added, waiting for Clint to continue. She was disappointed when he eyed her like a mouse with its head caught in a trap.

Tugging on his hat brim, he announced, "I have chores to attend to. I'll be in later."

With that, Clint turned to leave. While he swaggered toward the barn, she lifted her eyes toward heaven and breathed, "Dear Lord, please work this out to bring peace between Clint and Alissia."

How far had his mother's desperation driven her? How could the sweet woman she attended have done anything that brought her regrets?

Mrs. James had hinted about a time she wasn't proud of. Emily had a good notion to question her about it. No, she would not pry, but wait until the right opportunity presented itself.

Chapter Fourteen

The wait wasn't long for Emily. While helping Mrs. James into her nightgown, the woman exhaled a long breath. "I wish Clint would use more patience with Alissia. She's got some growin' up to do. His hovering ain't helping matters. Some things a girl has to learn for herself."

She tugged the gown over her patient's head and smoothed it. "He is a bit overly protective. Does he have a good reason, or is it because he's her big brother?"

The older woman sadly shook her head. "I guess he's got a right to be cautious, considerin' the stupid mistakes I've made. He's afraid she'll fall into the same trap."

Plucking the hairpins from Mrs. James's hair, Emily let the shimmering gold mass fall down her back. The woman was still beautiful. By calculating Clint's age, Emily guessed her to be in her early forties. "I can't imagine you making stupid mistakes. You seem to be an intelligent woman."

"If I am, it's because I learned my lessons the hard way." Mrs. James eased down on the edge of the bed, pointing to the rocker. "Sit down, dearie. It's time you knew a few things about my past. And it won't be a pretty story."

Emily settled in the rocker and clasped her hands together. Mrs. James had hinted at a regretful past the first week she had come to the ranch. She found it hard to believe the woman's character was anything besides exemplary.

"Mrs. James, I can't imagine you being anything besides a respectable lady. I would be shocked to learn otherwise. You don't have to tell me anything if it dredges up bad memories."

"I want you to know. Young lady, prepare for a shock. You don't know anything about the woman I once was. I thank God every day, for His grace and forgiveness."

Emily rose and helped her settle in bed. As she fluffed her patient's pillow, the woman began to speak. "Clint was a little tyke when Brady, his pa, died. We were livin' in a lean-to in Kansas. I tried my best to find a job to support us, but there weren't any for women in that dusty little town. It weren't much of a town to begin with. Just a feed store, a rickety diner, a general store, and a couple of filthy saloons. The only place hiring was the Red Slipper. When things started looking bleak, I swallowed my pride and traipsed in. You should've seen the look on the cowboys' faces. They stopped their mugs halfway to their mouths and gawked.

"I was too proud to come back here after the way Pa treated Brady. He'd already told me I was makin' a mistake by takin' off to Kansas with him, and he'd threatened to disown me. We didn't leave here on the best of terms."

"Why didn't your parents approve of Brady?" Emily ventured.

"It wasn't that Pa didn't approve of Brady. Pa had already made him a foreman, had big plans for him to take over the runnin' of this ranch when he retired. But Brady had an independent streak. Always wanted to be his own boss, but he stuck it out seven years, although his heart wasn't in it. He didn't want to be a rancher. Brady wanted a plot of land of his own, to raise a few pigs, cows, and chickens, and a place to plant a vegetable garden.

Apparently, Clint had inherited his independent streak from both parents. Since Emily didn't know Alissia's father, she figured the girl had gotten hers from her mother. Being stuck in the wilderness with a child and no means of support, conjured up all kinds of horrific scenes in her mind. She imagined the woman standing on the street corner in rags, begging for food. Emily shuddered, but her patient paid her no mind.

Mrs. James continued. "When the Homestead Act passed, we loaded our belongings and headed for Kansas in a covered wagon. Clint was eight. We weren't there no more'n two months before Brady and another man got into a feud. The man claimed the land was his. They both had papers to prove it. I don't know if it was a mistake at the claims office, or one of us got hoodwinked.

"Neither Brady nor the man would give an inch. The feud went on for two weeks until the day they got into a fistfight. The other man pulled a gun. They struggled, the gun went off, and Brady was shot in the chest. I reported it to the marshal, but there was nothin' he could do. He called it self-defense because they were fightin'. Kansas was wild in those days. Outlaws hidin' behind every bush."

Emily's jaw dropped. What if the same thing had happened to her own pa? She'd not considered it. "How awful! What did you do? You had a small child."

"Clint's pa left us with a little money. I knew it wouldn't last long. There was the issue of his schooling as well. He was old enough to attend, but we were too far from town. Besides, winter was coming on and we would've frozen to death in that bunch of twigs and sticks called a lean-to. Brady planned to build a real house before winter. It was fall when he died. And I didn't want to stay there near that man who had killed Brady and claimed he owned our land. I figured he would throw us out any day."

"The man must have felt guilty because he gave me some money. I didn't want to take what he offered. It felt like blood money—as if he was trying to pay me for taking my husband's life. I compared it to a man who steals a steer and offers to pay the rancher after he's already slaughtered it.

"I was very angry. As I started to tell him what I thought about his offer, Clint came out of the lean-to and said, 'Mama, I'm hungry.' That stopped me in my tracks. I had to think about what was best for my child and forget my own sense of justice.

"I took the money and we moved into a boarding house at the edge of town. Clint started to school and was doing well. By May, when he was out for summer break, the money was nearly gone. I did what any desperate mama would do. I paraded into that saloon, straight up to the bar, banged my fist on it, and yelled, "I need a job!

"Ol' Sam rubbed his chin whiskers and looked me over. He said, 'You're a little on the skinny side, but you'll do.'"

Emily gasped, her eyes wide. Alissia had mentioned her mother taking a job in a saloon, but she still found it hard to believe.

"It's true," the woman replied. "I was desperate, and Sam was short of help. One of his girls had run off with a card shark the week before. I let him know I would only serve food and drinks, not do any favors for the men. He didn't like that one bit, liked it less when I refused to wear the skimpy outfits the other girls wore.

"He finally hired me on my terms. I guess he figured I'd change my tune about the skimpy dresses and dishing out favors when I saw the money the other girls were making. But it didn't change my mind. Money can't buy a woman's respectability, and that's most important.

"I managed the first month, although, my conscience suffered every time I brought a bottle of alcohol to a table. I detest being around strong drink, much less serving it."

"Your parents raised you with high moral standards, as did mine." Emily smoothed a wisp of hair from Mrs. James's eyes. "What changed after the first month?"

"A rowdy bunch of drovers, fresh off the trail, came in for drinks, carousing, and gambling. They were a loud, foul-mouthed gang. I served them bottle after bottle of whiskey. The more they drank, the louder they got.

"Two of the filthiest ones started making vulgar gestures at the other girls. The one that reeked most of sweat and whiskey grabbed me while I passed his table and pulled me onto his lap. He started scratching my neck with his whiskered face. At the same time, he started runnin' his hands over me like I was some kind of trollop. When I tried to get away, he gripped me tighter. I saw only one way out. I grabbed his whiskey bottle off the table and cracked it over his head."

Emily giggled in spite of herself. "Did you knock him unconscious?"

"Yes. First, his eyes rolled back in his head. Then he fell out of the chair and took me down with him. The place got real quiet. You could've heard a pin drop.

"When ol' Sam got over the shock, he growled at me. 'You apologize to that fine gentleman, or you're fired!'

"Tact never has been one of my traits. I was as mad as a hornet. I pointed down at that dirty drover and said to Sam, 'If he's a fine gentleman, I'm next in line for the convent.'"

Laughter burst from Emily's throat. It took several minutes to subdue her convulsing. When she had, Mrs. James went on with her story.

"Ol' Sam stood there with his narrowed eyes, still waitin' for me to apologize. That's when I asked him, 'How do you suppose a body goes about apologizing to a passed-out drunk?'

"Everybody in the place roared. Everybody except Sam. He didn't think it was a bit funny. His face was red enough to light a match. He slammed his fist on the bar and yelled, 'You're fired!'

I told him my rent was paid up until the end of next week. He said, "Be out by then."

"Where did you go?" Emily asked. This lady's spunk had carried her through tough times. If Clint's ma had been in her situation, Emily's sister-in-law would have been the one looking for a job and a place to move to.

When Clint's ma reached for the glass on the bedside table, Emily handed it to her. When she'd drunk half the contents, she continued her story.

"I had a little money put back. Enough to last us a month, by bein' careful. Before I'd taken the job at that nasty saloon, I'd answered one of those mail-order bride ads. I imagine you've read a few of those."

Emily's throat tightened She nodded and squeaked, "Did you get a reply?"

Mrs. James's story was beginning to sound familiar. With little money, where would Emily be now if she hadn't fallen off the church porch and Clint hadn't offered her this job?

"Yes, I got a reply the same day I was fired. What I did next was a mistake." She shook her finger at Emily. "Don't ever judge another's actions until you've walked in their shoes, young lady. You might think you'd never do a certain thing, but given the right circumstances, you just might. Especially if you had a child to consider and saw no other way out."

If Mrs. James knew a mail-order bride ad had brought her to Abilene, what would she say? How Emily wished she could confide in her.

No, that wasn't a good idea. She needed to consider the consequences and keep her mouth shut. If Mrs. James knew her story, Emily might be out of a job.

On second thought, Clint's ma might show her mercy. But would the same be true for Clint? She thought it best to not take the chance. Folding her hands together to make herself appear relaxed, Emily said "I'm sorry if I appeared to be judging you. I promise I wasn't. Your story took me by surprise."

The woman's searching blue eyes raked her. "I guess you would be surprised, at that. I imagine you've led a pretty sheltered life. So had I, up until I left here with Clint's pa. It didn't take me long to see there was a whole other untamed world out there. That part of Kansas was not a safe place to raise kids. We'd passed through rowdy towns, heard the shoutin', the loud saloon music, even drunken laughter comin' from those places. In Dodge City, we nearly got caught in a shootout. If we hadn't halted our team and high-tailed it inside the local mercantile, one of us might've been killed right there in the middle of that dusty street."

"That is scary. What did you do about the reply from the mail-order bride ad?" Emily didn't want to sound too curious, but she needed to know how the story ended.

Mrs. James shook her head slowly. "Hank James was lookin' for a wife. I figure I did what any woman would've done. His instructions were to join a wagon train in Kansas and meet him in Nevada. If only I'd known what I was gettin' myself into."

After clearing her throat, she said, "I need to back up on somethin' I said earlier. About my marriage to Hank James bein' a big mistake. Because if it wasn't for it, I wouldn't have my Alissia. And I wouldn't take a pretty penny for my sweet girl. I love my boy just as much."

"Was Mr. James mean?" Emily asked. Alissia had mentioned it but she wanted to hear more.

The older woman threw up her hands. "Abusive is puttin' it mildly. At first, Hank was nice enough. Even then, he never took up with Clint, just ignored him. I thought I could live with that. I figured he'd eventually come around.

It never happened. Three years later, the vein in the silver mine dried up. He'd invested everything in that mine. He started drinking nearly every night and comin' in after hanging out at saloons. As oft as not, he'd be sloppy drunk. You could count on him bein' as mad as a hornet when he walked in. Hank went stark-raving mad.

"He'd holler, 'Why is my supper cold?' When I would answer, 'Come home at a decent time and it won't be,' the fight would start. Hank would draw his fist back and threaten to punch me if I didn't shut up. If I spoke, he'd knock me flat on the floor."

Emily's body tensed. "Did Clint know about this?"

"He witnessed it several times. He'd try to get between us and—" A sob tore from the older woman's throat. "I never meant for…for Clint to take a beatin' over…me and my big mouth."

Emily held the woman's hand. "There, there. I'm so sorry. It should never happen to any woman." What if Emily had married the dentist and he was as mean as Hank?

Mrs. James wiped her eyes with a handkerchief. "No, it shouldn't. That's why a woman needs to be mighty careful about responding to those ads. She doesn't know what she's gettin' herself into. I learned my lesson the hard way. I should've swallowed my pride and returned here to the ranch. My pride almost cost me everything."

Emily gazed through the window at the kaleidoscopic sunset, soaking it in to calm her turbulent emotions. Peach, baby blue, yellow, and violet swirled across the sky. She'd seen plenty of pretty sunsets in Tennessee. Why did they appear more vivid in a Texas sky?

Sighing, she pulled her gaze back to her patient. Mrs. James's story could have been hers. She didn't trust Dr. Clemons's high and mighty ways or what he might do if his temper was riled.

Especially if he discovered his second chance at a bride was hiding out at the L&M Ranch. It served him right for proposing to three women.

What had happened to his third bride? She hoped the woman had come to her senses, too.

Mrs. James blew her nose. "Hank slapped Clint around too. I did my best to protect my boy, but I couldn't always." She raised a fisted hand and shook it. "No man is gonna lay a hand on my child, ever again! Not if I can help it. Not when he's only trying to protect his ma."

Emily frowned. "Did you report the abuse to the sheriff?"

Mrs. James nodded. "Yes, for all the good it did. The sheriff plainly told me, he didn't like gettin' in the middle of domestic disputes, that Hank and I needed to work things out.

"If Hank came in drunk enough to fall off his horse, or if I saw him staggering toward the house, I'd tell Clint to grab Alissia and head out back to the woodshed and to stay there until I came for him. Alissia must've been three by then.

"Clint thought he could take his stepfather on by himself. He was itching to get revenge on Hank for slapping me around. Once, I found the rolling pin under Clint's mattress. I hid it where he couldn't find it again. That boy was too big for his britches, even at the age of twelve. Clint didn't want to hide in the woodshed, but when I told him to do it for Alissia's sake, he stopped arguing." Mrs. James sighed. "It was a tryin' time."

Her own home life had been happy until Roy moved Louise in. At least she hadn't feared for her life.

Emily shook her head. "I don't know how you survived with your sanity intact."

"Survived what?" Clint's lanky frame filled the doorway.

Emily's face burned. How long had he been standing there? Caught up in his mother's story, she had not glanced toward the door. Had he heard everything? Maybe not. She had seen the glow from the lantern in the barn, minutes ago.

Clint braced one shoulder against the doorjamb and grinned. "Ma, I wanted to check on you before you fell asleep. Do you need anything?"

"I reckon not. Unless it's to feel well enough to be up and about again. But that's up to the good Lord. I shouldn't be complaining though. Emily's an attentive nurse."

Clint pushed up his hat brim. "I can't argue with that."

He winked at Emily, reigniting the flame in her cheeks. She hoped the dusky room concealed the evidence. Suddenly, she felt warm all over.

"Miss Emily, will you join me on the porch swing?" he asked. "I just drew a fresh bucket of water. Two glasses are filled and waiting on the kitchen table. We'll have to hurry. It won't stay cold long in this heat."

Clint would ask about her conversation with his mother. What Mrs. James had said, she considered confidential. What excuse could she use to avoid him?

She blurted the first thing that came to mind. "I need to settle your mother in for the night."

He arched an eyebrow as if he were onto her tactics. "She looks settled to me."

Mrs. James flapped a hand. "You young'uns go on out on the porch and enjoy the fresh air. I can take it from here. I've got a good mystery book to read." She pointed at Clint. "Light my lantern first. I can't read in the dark."

Well, that strategy had backfired. She was doomed to face Clint's interrogation. Worse, she would have to sit in close proximity to him in the swing. How could she think clearly when his presence made her heart beat wildly, as it did now? Whether from fear of the impending questions, or the after-effects of their kiss, she refused to consider.

Emily moved to the doorway to allow Clint ample room to light the lantern on his mother's bedside table. He struck a match and the soft glow illuminated the room. Crouching by his mother's bed, he kissed her forehead. A feeling of tenderness engulfed Emily at the scene between mother and son.

"Good night, Ma. I'll see you in the morning. If you need anything else tonight, just holler. I'm across the hall, you know."

She patted his face and smiled. "Thanks, Clint. You make your ma proud. Y'all had better get those glasses and go to the porch before the water gets too warm."

Despite the upsetting events of the morning, Emily's heartbeat slowed to a steady rhythm. She'd been harassed by a drunk cowboy and detained by the obnoxious dentist, who was asking questions around town. How much had he learned about her?

How much had Jessica disclosed? At least she hadn't corrected him when he'd called her Evelyn. No longer could Emily deny her feelings for Clint. But how could they build a relationship with secrets between them? One lie or deception could destroy everything they had.

She hadn't exactly lied, only withheld a fact. It's the same as deception, her conscience screamed. She had to tell Clint the truth soon. But how?

His kiss had been her first. As in Emily's imagination, it had come from a handsome cowboy. Never in her wildest dreams did she expect the kiss to be all-consuming. She would cherish the memory forever if he never kissed her again. The sweetness and fervor of it had melted her heart. Even now, Emily resisted the urge to touch her still tingling lips.

Now, Clint wanted her to join him on the porch swing with inches between them. How could she when his mere presence made her yearn for something she might never acquire?

She should have told him the truth on the first day. But if she had, she might not have lasted the night. Clint made no bones about his disdain for mail-order brides.

If he discovered she had come to Abilene to wed Clemons, he might throw her out of the house, even now. Did Clint know the price of a train ticket from Abilene to Memphis? She couldn't earn that kind of money in a year.

If Emily had met Dr. Clemons before agreeing to his

proposal, she would have turned him down flat. Lesson learned. A few words on paper revealed very little about that person.

Returning to Bartlett was not an option. Neither did Emily want to return to the house her sister-in-law had invaded. She'd burned those bridges. Roy could not be happy when his wife and sister were at odds.

She'd find work in Abilene and rent a room in a boarding house, once Mrs. James had recuperated. She should have enough money saved by then.

Chapter Fifteen

⁂

C lint didn't appear upset as he crouched by his mother's bed and answered her questions about his day. It could be a facade for his mother's sake. Emily wracked her brain for questions he might ask and answers she might give that would neither bend the truth nor reveal anything. Disclosing her conversation with his mother would be a breach of confidence.

He rose and patted his mother's hand. "Goodnight, Ma. Sleep well." He turned to Emily and smiled. "Are you ready to head to the porch?

CLINT KEPT the porch swing in motion by rocking the toe of his boot against the plank floor. When he had slaked his thirst, he set the glass on his knee and gazed at the distant hills, breaking the silence. "Nothing refreshes the body like a glorious sunset and a cool glass of water."

When Emily didn't reply, he continued. "Most local ranchers dig cisterns to catch rainwater running off their roofs. In this part of Texas, you normally have to dig very deep to find a good water supply that won't quickly dry up.

"Not here at the L&M ranch. Maybe it's because we're close to Elm Creek. Whatever the reason, Grandpa Lawson struck water on his second try. Without digging too deeply." He looked straight ahead while cutting his eyes toward Emily. She hadn't spoken a word since they'd settled in the swing. Her glass shook as she raised it to her lips. Had he frightened her? He hoped it wasn't their kiss. She hadn't appeared upset when she'd left him.

Shifting in the swing, he propped a booted foot across his knee. Should he take the bull by the horns? He wished folks wouldn't keep secrets. They should come out and say what was on their minds like his mother did. At least, you knew where you stood with her.

"How much did Ma tell you?" he asked.

Emily's eyes widened. She studied her water glass. "Tell me?" Raising her head, she gazed up at the starlit sky. But not before he saw fear in her eyes.

She took her easy time answering, probably gathering her thoughts to come up with a satisfactory answer. He slid his arm along the top of the swing. His fingers brushed against Emily's raven tresses. Were they as silky as they looked? He fought the urge to find out. The warmth of her in his arms lingered.

He shook his head in an attempt to clear his thoughts. No telling what he'd do if he dwelt on their kiss. "Ma was telling you about her past, wasn't she?" he persisted.

Her shoulders rose and fell. "You should ask your Ma. What she says to me is between us. I don't think it would be right to discuss it with anyone else."

"Are you worried that telling me would be a breach of confidence?"

Emily took a deep breath but did not reply.

"I assure you, you aren't the first person Ma's confided in

about her past. She's told a few other folks she trusts. Which means she trusts you, too."

Emily picked at her skirt. "Exactly why I would rather you didn't question me about our conversation. I want your mother to feel she can trust me."

Clint lowered his head to her level and sought her eyes. The moonlight reflected in them, making them shimmer. "Ma's a true lady and don't you think otherwise. She has strict standards she lives by, and nobody can make her bend them."

"I agree with you. Whatever she did was out of love and sacrifice. Because she was thinking of…others."

"Ma was a child when she and my grandparents came here from Missouri in a covered wagon. During the spring roundup of '59, when she was almost seventeen, Grandpa hired my pa, a young Irishman, to help out.

"Grandpa took a liking to Pa because, in his words, 'Brady McCall is honest and reliable'. Grandpa made him ranch foreman. He and Ma soon fell in love. Ma was barely eighteen when they married in the fall of '60. I was born the next August.

"Grandpa wanted Pa to build a house here on the ranch and eventually take over running the ranch. Pa had an independent streak. He didn't want to work for Grandpa for the rest of his life. He didn't like folks saying he'd married Ma to get the ranch. He wanted to own a piece of fertile land to farm. When Lincoln signed the Homestead Act, we headed for Kansas to claim a parcel."

Clint slapped his knee. "That's when everything went downhill. Ma should have come back here after Pa died. I can't, for the life of me, figure out why she answered one of those ridiculous mail-order bride ads, instead."

Emily's voice trembled. "Pride, I suspect. She didn't want to admit she needed your grandfather's help. She thought by answering the ad, she would gain a man to take the place of your pa, who would offer you a good life."

"Good life?" Clint blurted. "By binding herself to a good-for-nothing drunk who got his thrills from abusing women?"

As soon as he'd said it, Clint wished he hadn't. He wanted to let go of his anger and bury the past. Sometimes he thought he had. Then images of his stepfather punching his ma invaded his dreams again. "How could any man who called himself a man, hurt a sweet lady like Ma?"

Her hands clasped the water glass. "I'm sorry. I don't have the answers. You saw things a boy should never see. Replying to a mail-order bride ad involves risks. A woman can't know what she's getting herself into, because she can't truly know the man until she's met him, and he's taken the time to court her. Even with that, it can take months, maybe years, before his dark side emerges. I think a woman has to feel she has no other choice before she answers one of those ads."

CLINT STUDIED HER CLOSELY. "How do you know so much about mail-order brides?"

"I-I just know." Emily fidgeted with her sleeve. "Partly from what your ma told me."

He crooked a finger under her chin, turning her face toward him. His green eyes searched hers. A mischievous spark told her he was teasing. She sighed softly. How much did he suspect?

"You are either a very wise lady, or you are hiding something, Miss Hammons. Do you by chance, know a young woman who got caught up in one of those mail-order bride schemes?"

She stiffened. Had he talked to Mr. Ward at the depot? She had asked the station master about the dentist while she'd waited. Worse, had Dr. Clemons questioned the station master about her? Releasing a ragged breath, she was relieved that Clint had not asked if she'd answered one of those ads. "I know of

Jessica's sister, Margie. We both witnessed the scene at the church."

Guilt tore at her insides, twisting her stomach into knots. If this wasn't deception, it came close. Her conscience twinged. She felt as low as a snake in the grass.

She wanted to tell Clint how she'd become entangled in an obligation she'd quickly regretted. But she couldn't. Not yet. She stood to lose too much.

It surprised her that having Clint's respect and friendship ranked high on her list. Friendship? Who was she kidding after their kiss? She was fooling herself if she didn't admit that her feelings for this handsome cowboy surpassed friendship. They went a lot deeper. The ultimate question was how did Clint feel about her?

Why had that thought entered Emily's mind? She'd be crazy to believe their love could grow. It didn't matter how he felt about her. Because when he discovered she'd deceived him, any chance of a future together would be shattered along with her heart.

Clint gently squeezed her shoulder. "Is something wrong?"

She shook her head and brushed stray tendrils from her face. "Why do you ask?"

He didn't look convinced. "You seem nervous and a little frightened."

Ignoring his observation, Emily clasped her hands together and looked up at him. "I didn't get a chance to tell Alissia that she has your permission to attend the harvest celebration at Cooper's barn. She was already in her room with the door closed when I came in. She's probably studying for the math test she mentioned at supper."

To Emily's relief, her tactic worked. Clint didn't pursue his line of questioning. He pulled off his hat and fiddled with the brim.

"Alissia is at the top of her class. She needs to focus on her studies. I want her to continue her education once she graduates. I don't want her to get stuck in a bad marriage like Ma's."

"Landon is nothing like your stepfather, Clint. And don't forget, it was pride that kept your ma from coming back here after your pa died."

"What are you trying to say?"

How could she word it without putting him on the defensive? "I'm just saying, don't let the wall get any higher between you and Alissia. If it gets too high, it will take a lot more effort to break it down. And, having a barrier between you, might influence your sister to make a rash decision."

Gazing at the full moon on the horizon, he raked his long fingers through his coppery curls. "You're saying I've built a wall between Alissia and myself?"

"I don't know how high it is, but yes. The foundation has certainly been laid. I've felt the mounting tension between you two."

A sheepish look crossed his face. "Guilty as charged." He cleared his throat. "What did you mean by 'influence her to make a rash decision'?"

To best answer the question required her to be bold, but to mix it with as much tact as possible. She wasn't sure how to blend the two. Sometimes you had to lay it out there for the other person's benefit. Otherwise, he might not realize what he was up against.

She cleared her throat. "Alissia has a good head on her shoulders, but I sense that she's the type to rebel if the reins are held too tightly."

"What? You think I have her tied to my apron strings?"

The tall cowboy with a checkered apron tied around his waist would be a funny sight, indeed. "Not exactly, but if you try to shield her from everything risky in this life, she's likely to break loose, do something she'll regret. Don't say or do anything that will drive her away from home or keep her from returning if she does leave."

Clint slapped his Stetson against his knee. "Ma and Pa didn't leave this ranch on good terms. He and Grandpa argued. If it wasn't for that, Ma might have come home sooner."

"That's what I'm saying. Learn from your Ma and Pa's mistake."

He spoke through clenched teeth. "If Alissia's got any notions about running off with that wet-behind-the-ears kid, I'll put a quick stop to it. Landon will rue the day he ever met me."

Had she overstepped her bounds? Clint would now tell her to mind her own business. Couldn't he see his attitude had made matters worse between himself and Alissia? "Showing your disapproval of Landon is driving a wedge between you and your sister. If you stepped back a little and allowed Alissia a bit more freedom, it would ease the tension."

"You think I need to let her see more of Landon?" He jammed his hat back on his head. "It won't work. They'll only become more attached to each other. I've seen the gleam in his eye, and in hers, the way they ogle one another. I already said she could meet him at the dance. Isn't that enough? At least at Cooper's barn, I can keep an eye on them."

"That's it exactly," Emily said. "Maybe, you keep too close an eye on them."

"As I said, she can dance with him as long as they keep daylight between them. And fair warning, if he slips outside with her, I'll be right behind them."

The conversation was going nowhere. "Think of it this way. Landon is traveling to Houston to take a medical test, in two weeks. He may be going away soon."

"Not soon enough," Clint mumbled. "And that's only if he's accepted into medical school."

"He has a very good chance, with his high grades."

CLINT MASSAGED the nape of his neck. How did they get off on the topic of Alissia? He and Emily were talking about Ma and how she was lured into marrying a scoundrel through a mail-order bride ad. Clint was careful not to speak ill of the man in front of his little sister. After all, he was Alissia's father.

Emily hadn't fooled him. She had skillfully steered the conversation in a different direction. The mention of mail-order brides had struck a raw nerve with her. Apparently, his teasing had upset her. Why, he couldn't say.

He kept the swing moving with his foot. A warm breeze lifted wisps of raven hair near Emily's temples. He would let sleeping dogs lie for the time being. He was enjoying her company and asking too many questions would only give her an excuse to flee.

How much did he really know about this pretty woman? She'd lost both parents and had a brother and an overbearing sister-in-law in Tennessee. That was about the size of it.

He understood why Emily would leave a tumultuous home situation. Even the Bible mentioned it was better to dwell on a rooftop than in the same house with a contentious woman. Still, his gut told him there was more to her story. Something she was hiding.

Why would a young lady with secretarial skills and exemplary grades journey 600 miles to find work, when she could have found a job in nearby Memphis? She claimed news about Abilene's growth spurt had lured her here. The untamed Texas town was still growing, but he didn't buy it as her reason for traveling this far on a sooty train. Not striking him as the adventurous type, she would have to be desperate to journey this far with no relatives, and no promise of a job, at the end. Train tickets did not come cheap.

This brought up another question. If her brother was in dire straits, who paid her travel expenses? Her story didn't add up. An important piece of the puzzle was missing. But what?

Shifting in the swing, he uncrossed his lanky legs. Emily must either be running from something or hiding from someone. Had someone lured her to Abilene? If so, who, and for what purpose?

Her bluebonnet eyes spoke of secrets. Secrets he was determined to unveil.

Chapter Sixteen

The silvery moon spilled across the yard, barn, and paddock. The sun had set, but Clint could read a newspaper by its light. On impulse he said, "Let's take Bowie for a run. I know he's anxious to work off some energy. He hasn't been out of the paddock for days. Besides, I promised you a ride."

Emily's eyes sparkled. "Do you mean it?" Her gaze skimmed the horizon; "The sun has gone down. How will we see?"

Her childlike eagerness stirred him. "No worries. The full moon is bright enough to guide us, and Bowie is familiar with the area. He should be since he's been all over it many times. I want to show you something that will take your breath away, and tonight is perfect for it."

Emily tugged at her skirt. "I want to, but I'm not dressed properly." Suddenly her eyes widened. "Wait. I packed a riding skirt in the bottom of my trunk."

Clint stood and doffed his hat. "Great. Why don't you take these glasses inside and change, while I saddle Bowie? Meet me in the barn. Be careful not to wake Ma or alert Alissia."

~

Emily slipped into her bedroom and lit the lantern before lifting the trunk lid. Within minutes, she'd changed into her brown split skirt and tied her hair back with a ribbon.

When she came out, Clint stood outside the barn tightening the cinch on the Palomino's saddle. The moonlight had turned the horse silver. "Are you ready?"

"Oh, yes," she breathed, impatient to feel the wind on her face as they galloped through the night. It had been much too long since Emily had been on a horse. And never past dusk, or never astride a horse this grand.

The full moon gleamed across the landscape giving it a golden shimmer. Clint mounted, reaching down to pull Emily up behind him. She made herself comfortable before clasping her hands together around Clint's waist.

When they reached the road, she asked, "Where are we going?"

"It's a surprise, and well worth the wait." He clucked to the horse, urging him into a trot. After a mile, Clint dug in his knees. Dust billowed behind Bowie's hooves. As they galloped down the dirt road, a light breeze stirred the treetops, casting shadows and flickering light on the path in front of them. He was right. The full moon was bright enough to guide their way.

Clint turned Bowie into a field. They left the road and crossed a shallow creek which led to a meadow surrounded by hills. Emily refrained from asking questions.

"Close your eyes," Clint instructed. "We're almost there. I want you to be surprised. I guarantee it will take your breath away."

When they'd trotted a short distance farther, he said, "Open your eyes."

She did so and gasped. The full moon bathed the rolling hills in silvery moonlight, giving the entire scenery an ethereal glow. "This is beautiful! How did you discover it?"

"One night after coming home late from a town meeting, I took a shortcut through here. It was a full moon that night too."

He walked Bowie over to a copse of cottonwood trees overlooking the hills and shallow valley. "Let's get down and give Bowie a rest and a chance to browse."

Clint dismounted and reached up for her, encircling her waist with his large hands. A tingle skittered up her spine as he set her feet on the ground. She tried to still her erratic heartbeat, taking in the beautiful scene before them. "It's like something out of a fairytale."

In the distance a mourning dove cooed, answered by a lonely whippoorwill. A soft breeze stirred the leaves of the cottonwood tree above them.

Clint stood behind her and touched her shoulder while pointing up at the starlit sky. "Look, there's the Big Dipper. And over there is the Little Dipper."

"I see them," She lowered her gaze to the horizon where a star glowed brightly. "Look over there. That must be Venus, the evening star."

"How do you know?"

Emily gazed at the eastern horizon. "I read the *Farmer's Almanac.* It said Venus would be the evening star through September. Clint, look at the moon cresting above the hills. It's enormous," she whispered. "I wish we never had to leave this place."

He slid his arms around her waist and clasped his hands together. "I know what you mean," he whispered in her ear. His whiskers tickled her neck while his nearness left her breathless.

Clint straightened and cleared his throat. "Do you have a beau back home?"

"No. Our community was small. Everyone knew everyone. There were only five boys in my graduating class. When you go to school with the same boys year after year, they become like brothers to you.

"I spent my time studying, to make good grades. I managed to stay on the honor roll. No one in my family had gone past eighth grade. Roy had to quit after Pa left. Pa only made it to fifth grade, and Mama was made to quit when she finished eighth grade. According to my grandparents, it wasn't proper for a young lady to attend high school.

"After my grandparents passed, Mama instructed me to make good grades and to graduate. She said times were changing, and we couldn't stick to the old ways. A woman can't always depend on a man to support her She needs a proper education to make her own way, if necessary.'"

"Did she say this because your pa left all of you for the silver mines?" Clint asked.

Emily sighed. "I'm sure that was a big part of it. Roy had to quit school to help Mama raise cotton. I offered to quit too, but she wouldn't hear of it. What about you, Clint?" Emily ventured.

"I finished school. My grandma and grandpa insisted I get my education."

"I meant, was there ever a special lady in your life? Is there one now?" Emily held her breath, praying he'd answer with a firm no. If Clint was courting another, he had no business taking her on a moonlight ride, no matter how innocent. She would tell him so, even though learning that he had feelings for another woman, would hurt.

"I've been too busy with the ranch since Grandpa died to court."

A heavy weight lifted from her shoulders. The only barrier between them was the secret she had not revealed. Her heart sank. How could she disclose her secret when the confession could destroy all hope that Clint might ask to court her? She would lose his trust. Instinct told her, if she ever lost Clint's trust, she would have to work hard to regain it.

Clint rubbed the nape of his neck. "Oh, I've taken a couple of young ladies to dinner, to appease Ma. She set everything up with their mothers."

A twinge of jealousy pricked at Emily. "She didn't trust you to make your own choices?"

He chuckled. "I think Ma's afraid I'll wait too long and she'll never have grandchildren." He pulled Emily closer. "The girls were nice enough and not hard on the eyes, but the spark was missing." He rested his chin on her head. "Besides, I like to do my own choosing."

Did he feel that spark with her? She felt it with him. What did a girl need to do to turn Clint's head? The breeze picked up, rustling the leaves and branches in the trees above them. Thunder rumbled in the distance, but neither paid it any mind. Clint turned her to face him, his eyes smoldering in the moonlight. "Emily, I've never met anyone quite like you," he whispered.

While she searched the depths of his eyes, she pressed her hands to his chest and felt his strong heartbeat. She wanted Clint's kiss more than anything. If after she made her confession, he never kissed her again, she would at least have this memory to cherish.

She was not disappointed. Clint lowered his head and lightly brushed his lips against hers. Instead of resisting for her heart's sake, Emily slid her hands up and clasped them together behind his neck.

He needed no further invitation, claiming her lips in a sweet, persistent kiss that melted her heart and made her knees wobble. Her swimming head warned her to pull back, but her treacherous heart rebelled.

The kiss intensified. Her heart sped up like a galloping horse. Suddenly, Clint straightened, loosening his hold. Searching her eyes, he breathed, "Oh Emily, I don't know what's come over me. Over these past weeks, you've come to mean—"

"Sh-h!" She pressed a finger to his lips. "Don't." She couldn't let him say it. Not until he knew the truth about her. "There's something you should—" Lightning slashed across the night sky before thunder boomed. Emily squealed and threw herself into Clint's arms.

~

BOWIE'S HOOVES PRANCED. Clint kept one arm around Emily while clutching the Palomino's reins with his other hand. "There, there boy," he soothed. "Calm down. You just get us home."

He studied the sky. Storm clouds had gathered in the west. They would soon cover the moon. Clint hated to scare Emily, but they needed to head for home. "We're in for a bad storm," he predicted. "They can slip up before you know it. This rain is overdue."

He sniffed the air. "I smell it, and it's close. We'd better head back before the downpour hits."

He swung up into the saddle, pulling Emily up behind him. Thunder crashed behind them as Bowie galloped through the night. Emily flinched when lightning slashed across their path. Clint prayed they would make it back to the ranch, safely, and thanked God that Bowie knew the way.

Emily's hands around his waist gripped Clint tighter with every zigzag of lightning and clap of thunder. Her body trembled against him. He winced each time her nails dug into his flesh. He would have bruises, for sure. She shook so hard he feared she'd fall out of the saddle.

The wind blew his hair back from his face as he craned his neck to say, "Hang on, Emily. We'll be home soon."

"I'm…try-ing," she stammered. "I've…never been fond…of storms."

He wished he could stop and pull her into his arms to whisper comforting words to put her at ease. But there was no time. The wind picked up, whipping at their backs, swirling dust around them. Clint kneed Bowie again, urging the horse forward, praying they would reach home before the heavens opened.

Minutes later, lightning lit the sky, and Clint spied a light just ahead. Lightning flashed again and outlined a slight figure in a white gown, waving a lantern. He galloped toward it, reining in his horse when he reached the porch.

"Ma get back inside! What are you doing out here?"

She propped a hand on one hip and hiked her chin. "Well, I might ask you the same thing."

Not able to think of a sensible answer, he slid off the horse and helped Emily down. The first pelts of rain started to fall.

"I'll see to my horse." He led Bowie to the barn while Emily took his ma by the arm and ushered her inside the house.

WHEN THE LADIES stepped through the door, Mrs. James shook Emily's hand off. "I want to know what in heaven's name is goin' on."

While Emily tried to think of a good reply, the older woman asked, "Where did you two go out in this storm? Don't you know folks have died from lightning strikes?"

"It wasn't storming when we left," Emily meekly replied. "The stars were out, and the moon was full, light enough to see by. The storm came up all of a sudden. Before we realized it."

"Probably had your minds elsewhere," Mrs. James muttered under her breath. Aloud she said, "Summer storms can do that. It's dangerous to be out, especially on a horse. If Bowie had spooked and run off, where would you be now?"

Emily chewed her lip, reluctant to speak. What happened between Clint and herself was private. She wanted to hold the memory of tonight's kiss close to her heart.

Mrs. James chuckled. "You two went for a moonlight ride,

didn't you? Clint's pa used to take me ridin' on a full moon too, weather permitting."

Emily shrieked when thunder clapped, glad for the reprieve from Mrs. James's questions. She patted the older woman's arm. "We'd better get you back into bed."

Mrs. James shook off Emily's hand again. "Not so fast. I got myself out of bed, and I can get myself back in it."

Rain pounded the roof, a few hard drops at first. The drops multiplied before the heavens opened. Clint's mother looked up. "I do believe the good Lord has given us a gully-washer. We needed one."

The door burst open and Clint stepped inside, shivering and drenched. Water ran off his hat brim. His shirt was plastered to his body. "It's coming down hard."

"I see it is." His ma folded her arms across her chest. "Where did you and Miss Emily get off to this time of night, to get caught out in a thunderstorm?"

Clint shrugged. "You could read a paper by moonlight when we left. Not a cloud in sight."

"That's what Emily said. But I asked where you two went?" she persisted.

Clint pulled his soaked shirt away from his body. "Don't you need to be in bed, Ma?"

Mrs. James raised her chin. "Don't try it. Emily already did. It didn't work for her either."

He glanced at Emily, and she shook her head. Clint looked back at his mother. "Bowie hadn't been ridden in days. I thought tonight would be a good time to let him run. I asked Emily if she'd like to ride along. We didn't go that far."

"Uh…huh." Mrs. James's eyes raked Emily before moving to Clint. "Did you show her those hills that turn to silver in the moonlight?"

Emily gasped while Clint's jaw dropped.

Mrs. James chuckled. "I thought so. It's a romantic view for a young couple." With an exaggerated yawn, she stretched her arms above her head. "Well, I'm off to bed, young'uns. Clint, get out of those wet clothes before you catch cold. Hang them near the wood stove. I'll see you both at breakfast."

～

CLINT STAYED busy the next two weeks cutting hay and stringing new fence wire. He came in late at night, ready to drop, and hurried through his supper. After taking a dip in Elm Creek, he would drag himself to bed.

Emily worried that he was working too hard. The dark circles beneath his eyes showed weariness, but when she mentioned it, he said it was all part of running a ranch. Although she missed her alone time with Clint, his absence allowed her to think more clearly about her future.

Mrs. James was now up and about, able to bathe and dress herself. Miraculously, the night of the storm had done her no harm. Her strength was returning. Soon she would need no assistance. As of late, the woman insisted on doing light house-work, including washing dishes.

The dance at Cooper's barn was coming up. Alissia and Emily had gone to town the previous Saturday to buy material for new dresses. Clint insisted on paying for the fabric and the notions. He'd peeled several bills from a roll and insisted the young ladies spend whatever they needed to make their dresses pretty and fashionable, and to not come home until they'd spent the money.

In her spare time, Emily set about stitching Alissia's dress on Ma's treadle machine. The shiny brocade fabric both ladies selected was interwoven with intricate designs. Both young ladies were attracted to its sheen and feel. Emily had never made anything from brocade and was surprised how easily the material slid through the machine and held its shape.

Alissia's dress was burgundy, while Emily had chosen a color called Napoleon Blue. Smaller bustles were the fashion this year, allowing leftover material to adorn the dresses with bows and such. She hoped she'd have enough extra to make them each a matching drawstring purse.

Except for hemming the sleeves and skirt, Alissia's dress was finished. The girl offered to finish it, but Emily turned her down. Alissia had enough to do with her schoolwork and after school chores. With Ma's improved health, Emily was left with some free time.

Landon was on his way to Houston to take the medical school entrance test. Doctor Simmons passed his hat around town and after church services, to garner enough money for the lad's round-trip train ticket. Doc was persistent. When all was said and done, he'd collected the train fare, plus enough extra for Landon's meals and a two-night's stay in a Houston hotel.

The benevolent doctor's fund-raising kept Landon from hitching horses to a wagon and making the long journey, which would have taken several days. Emily suspected Clint had made a generous donation toward the travel fund. Not so much out of a benevolent heart, but to put distance between the lad and Alissia. She did not ask him about it. He would never admit it anyway.

In Landon's absence, Alissia moped around the house sighing. Only the mention of the harvest party at Cooper's barn, and the new dress she would wear, cheered her. Clint's permission to let Alissia attend had brought calm to the household, if only temporarily. If the contention between brother and sister returned tomorrow, at least she would have a short reprieve.

Emily hadn't decided where she would look for work when Mrs. James had fully recovered. Out of the nine girls who graduated from her class, six married. Of the remaining two, one was set to get her teaching certificate in Memphis. The other had applied to nursing school.

Nursing was not Emily's cup of tea. She gagged at the sight

of blood, and offensive odors made her nauseous. Even the thought of sticking people with needles, made her cringe.

Emily enjoyed teaching the Sunday School class of youngsters at Bartlett Baptist Church, but she feared she lacked the stamina and patience to control an entire classroom of children.

Most of the listings for women in *The Commercial Appeal*, were for waitresses. Emily didn't mind the grueling work, but she preferred a bookkeeping or secretarial job. Although she'd been an exemplary student throughout school, she lacked experience, which could disqualify her from securing the type of work she desired.

It was time to begin her search for employment. Clint's mother grew stronger and more independent by the day. Emily needed to prepare herself for the inevitable.

Chapter Seventeen

The house was quiet. Alissia wouldn't be home for three hours and Mrs. James was down for her nap. Clint and the ranch hands had left early to string a fence in the north pasture. Emily was setting the last sleeve in her party dress when a buggy rolled up.

She stepped out on the porch to greet the visitor. "Jessica, what brings you here?" Her friend must have an urgent reason for making a two-hour drive from town. Jessica pulled off her bonnet and used it to fan her face. She drove the buggy up to the water trough to allow the horse to drink, before joining Emily on the porch.

"Business was slow this morning. My boss told me I could take the afternoon off. I can't say I wasn't glad, because I've wanted to talk to you since someone paid me a visit the other day."

Emily's heart skipped a beat. Did Jessica know the truth about her? When Emily could speak, she asked, "Where did you get the horse and buggy?"

Jessica cocked her head to one side. "Oh, I have my ways. Trent, at the livery stable, has taken a liking to me. He let me borrow the rig. But I can't be away too long, or his boss will return and find it missing, Then Trent will be in trouble."

Emily suspected Jessica had also "taken a liking" to Trent. She held the door open for her friend. "Let's visit in the kitchen. We will need to be quiet. Mrs. James is napping. Have a seat at the table and I'll pour us some lemonade. It's fresh and its cold."

Emily filled the glasses and set them on the table before angling her chair toward her guest. Folding her hands together on the table, she asked, "Who was this mysterious visitor?"

Jessica rolled her eyes. "He's not what you'd call mysterious.' It was the mule-faced dentist that Margie left at the church. Thank the Lord, my sister came to her senses in time."

Emily sipped from her glass, swallowing past the lump in her throat. "What was his business with you? Was it a cordial visit?"

"I wouldn't call it 'cordial'. He was asking about you. He's been told your name is not Evelyn, and that you came in on the same train as I did. He wanted to know what else I knew about you."

Jessica sipped from her glass before setting it down. "He hinted that he knew something about you that I didn't."

Emily raked nervous fingers through her hair. "What did you tell him?"

"To mind his own business. But he said you were his business. What did he mean by that?"

Emily cleared her throat. "I-I couldn't say."

Jessica patted Emily's arm. "Is something wrong? You look pale. Anyway, I heard that dentist had ordered three brides. You wouldn't happen to be one of the other two, would you?"

Jessica clapped a hand to her mouth. "I'm sorry, I shouldn't have asked that. It's just that I got to thinking... We came in on the same train, the same day Mule Face was to be married to my sister. I was under the impression that you'd be staying in town with your aunt. Instead, you ended up at this ranch taking care of a cowboy's mother. When I think back, you didn't mention a relative. I just assumed you had an aunt in Abilene."

Emily covered her face and began to sob. "I've wanted to tell someone for so long. I need to tell Clint, but he loathes women who put themselves out as mail-order brides. I would just die if he despised me."

"You're…one of the brides that dentist ordered?"

"Yes." Emily swiped at the tears on her cheeks. "What a mess I'm in."

Jessica patted Emily's arm. "There, there, we'll figure out something. You're in love with Clint, aren't you?"

"No." The denial popped out too quickly. Emily need not hide it from her friend. "Oh, Jessica! I do love him." She sobbed louder. "What am I going to do?"

Jessica clucked her tongue. "Don't cry. We'll think of something. I won't tell ol' Mule Face who you are."

Emily sniffled. "Oh, how I wish I could believe it would be that easy."

"Botheration! What's going on in there?" Mrs. James called from her bedroom.

Emily placed a finger to her lips. "I'm sorry, Jessica. I don't know what came over me. I didn't mean to wake up Clint's mother." She blotted the tears with the hem of her apron and sat at attention as the older woman hobbled into the kitchen.

Emily rose and turned her back to both ladies while she wiped away the residue of tears with her hand. "Mrs. James, we have a visitor. This is my friend, Jessica Dawson. We rode in on the train together. She works as a clerk at the hotel. Would you like a glass of lemonade?"

"Yes, thank you. And you can start callin' me Ma." The older woman settled in a chair across from Jessica and next to Emily's.

Emily sniffed. "Ma it is."

Jessica's eyebrows arched as if she'd drawn her own conclusions from her patient's remark. Emily handed a glass of lemonade to her. Jessica slid her chair back from the table and rose. "I'd better be going so Trent doesn't get in trouble over loaning me the rig."

Ma's eyes narrowed. "You talkin' about that good-lookin' young man who works at the livery stable?"

Jessica nodded. "Yes, ma'am."

"He seems like a right nice fella." Ma winked. "Hmm… seems there's more than one spark of romance in the air."

Emily's cheeks burned and Jessica blushed. "Emily, thank you for the lemonade and the visit. It was good seeing you again." She turned to Ma. "And it was nice meeting you, ma'am."

Ma nodded in response. "Nice meeting you too. I didn't mean to embarrass you none. I just call it as I see it. Jessica, you come back and visit when you can stay for a longer spell."

"Thank you, ma'am. Maybe I will."

Emily followed Jessica out to the buggy. When Jessica had climbed up and taken the reins, she remarked, "Clint's ma speaks her mind, doesn't she?"

Emily smiled, as did Jessica. "Yes, she does." Ma and Jessica would make a formidable pair. She could only imagine the trouble they might get into.

"Are you going to the barn dance next Saturday night?" Emily asked.

"Is this the dance the whole town is buzzing about?" Jessica asked.

"That's it. Alissia says Cooper's barn dance is the biggest event of the year in these parts."

Jessica tapped her chin with her index finger. "Trent dropped a hint about it. I think he will ask me. Are you going?"

"Yes. Clint is taking Alissia. He asked me to ride along to help chaperone."

Jessica winked. "Oh, I'm sure that was the reason."

"It's not what you think." Emily's cheeks flamed again.

"Clint wants to ensure his little sister and Landon don't slip outside and out of his sight."

"Hmm…well, good luck to him. If those two want to be alone, they'll find a way." Her eyes narrowed. "I think I can wangle a date out of that handsome livery stable man."

"Good. I'll look forward to seeing you there." Emily sighed. "Clint will be too preoccupied with his sister and Landon, to notice me."

Jessica's crooked grin spoke volumes. "Oh, he'll make time for you. I saw the twinkle in his eye the first day you two met. When you were seated on the buckboard outside the depot."

Emily's cheeks burned hotter. "I doubt that was it. Clint felt responsible because I sprained my ankle when your sister knocked us off the porch. I should be the one indebted to him. As embarrassing as it was, landing on him did buffer my fall." She giggled. "If I hadn't, I might have broken my ankle, instead of spraining it."

Jessica's jaw dropped. "How did Margie knock you off the porch?"

"She shoved her bouquet into my stomach, and I fell into Clint."

"Then, Margie brought you and Clint McCall together. If nothing else good comes from this mess… How romantic. And that's how you ended up at his ranch? How long will you be here? It looks like his ma has almost recuperated."

"I don't know, exactly. I'll need to find a job in town and move into a boarding house."

"If you get a job at the hotel with me, we could share a room. You'd have to climb two flights of stairs, but I get it at a discount because I work there. And it's a nice room."

Emily mulled it over. "I'll keep it in mind."

"You mentioned Clint keeping a close eye on his little sister?"

"Yes, he's too protective. The young man she's smitten with is a true gentleman."

"Poor Alissia. Clint sounds like my pa. He wants me to take the train home, but I keep writing to explain I don't have money for the ticket. Pa only gave me enough for one of us to return. I let Margie have it because she had to get away from ol' Mule Face. If she'd stayed in town, he would have made her life miserable. The more I talk to him, the more I am sure she made the right decision."

Emily silently agreed. Being near Dr. Clemons had begun to repulse her. Although she hated to admit it, the gleam in his eye frightened her.

Jessica's words brought Emily out of her musings. "I'd better get going. Just make sure you get at least one dance with that handsome cowboy, even if you have to hogtie him."

She shook the reins and waved a gloved hand. "See you at the dance, I hope." With a light slap of the reins, the horse took off at a canter.

ON SUNDAY MORNING when they had reached the church, Clint helped the womenfolk out of the buckboard. Clemons lingered on the porch chatting with Prudence, who plucked imaginary lint from his vest.

He overheard Prudence say, "Wendell, I made your favorite dessert."

Clemons's eyes widened. "Peach cobbler?"

Clint slipped into a pew near the front and stood next to Emily and his family. They opened their hymnals and sang, "Bringing In The Sheaves." When the song ended, Reverend Cole motioned for the congregates to sit. Pews scraped across the wood floor.

Wendell Clemons had leered at Emily from across the aisle

since he'd arrived. She lowered her head every time he looked their way. Clint refused to call him Doctor Clemons. Any man who ordered three brides to ensure he retained his inheritance deserved no respect.

Why the dentist persisted in his pursuit of Emily was a mystery. It was as if he considered her his property. Or that she owed him something. Emily was beautiful, but she was not for Clemons. And if the man knew what was good for him, he'd start looking elsewhere.

Clemons needed to wed before his birthday and Abilene was full of available young women. Some would probably marry him for his inheritance, if not for his title.

The tale of the dentist's disastrous wedding ceremony had spread throughout the county. Alfonso Jones and Joe Grimes still joked about it when Clint took a horse to be shod at the blacksmiths. With only a month left, Clemons would have to work fast.

Why not set his sights on someone like Prudence Wallace, who would enjoy his advances? The redhead obviously adored him. She had turned her attentions on him months ago, but Clemons seemed to brush her off since Emily had come to town.

Clint glanced at Prudence, seated beside Clemons. She glared at Emily from across the aisle. The woman looked to be in her upper twenties, near the dentist's age. She was not hard on the eyes. Not nearly as pretty as Emily, but her looks were palatable if you didn't mind a gazillion freckles and a large nose. Overall, she was still more attractive than the man she pursued.

Would Prudence and the dentist tie the knot? He'd prayed they would. The outcome might depend on how much stock Clemons put in a good peach cobbler.

He coughed to cover a chuckle and slid his arm along the top of the pew, brushing his fingers against Emily's silky locks. He longed to run his fingers through them.

Clint mentally shook himself for the wayward thought, in

church of all places. He hadn't thought of much else besides Emily since their moonlight ride. Bud and Slim had caught him daydreaming several times. They'd ask him a question and he'd answer, "Huh?" making them repeat it.

Focusing on installing new fence wire and harvesting hay had been quite a task. His mind kept straying to the kiss he and Emily had shared the night they took Bowie for a ride. His feelings for her had grown. And from the sweetness of that kiss, Clint believed Emily returned those feelings.

No, Emily Hammons was not for Clemons. He'd better get it through his thick skull. Neither was she interested in the man if appearances were taken into account. The thought of her married to that cocky dentist galled Clint.

He planned to court Emily. The thought struck him like a lightning bolt that their courtship had already begun. Had it begun the night of their moonlight ride, or the night she came to the barn to talk him into loosening his apron strings where Alissia was concerned?

Reverend Coke's voice pulled his attention toward the pulpit. "In Proverbs, Chapter 18 and verse 22, it reads, 'The man who finds a wife, finds a good thing, and obtains favor from the Lord.'"

Clint guessed the reverend had been preaching on marriage, although he hadn't heard much of the sermon. He could guess where Clemons's mind was.

When he glanced across the aisle again, Clemons was grinning at Emily, his buck teeth bared like a wolf's fangs. Even his eyes looked ravenous. To use Alissia's comment, the man could easily eat a pumpkin through a picket fence.

When Clint glared back, Clemons quickly faced forward. Returning his gaze to the front, Clint realized the service was coming to a close and he'd missed the message. He closed his eyes and silently repented for letting his thoughts stray.

He opened his eyes as the reverend announced, "Everyone is

invited to stay for dinner on the grounds. If you are a guest and didn't bring food, don't let that stop you. I've seen that long table, and it is loaded with delicious food. The Lord has blessed us with a bountiful feast."

Today, marked one year since the church had opened and held its first service. It seemed the entire town was present. They would have a meal outside on the grounds, and a singing to boot. The celebration would last all afternoon. Emily had fixed potato salad and fried a chicken. The smells from Ma's iron skillet made him salivate when he came in after feeding the livestock this morning.

The reverend called on Amos Hopkins to say the benediction and bless the food before everyone headed outside. Clint pulled the basket containing their plates and utensils from beneath the buckboard, handing the quilt to Emily.

She smiled at him, a twinkle in her eyes. "I'll find us a spot beneath one of the cottonwood trees."

He returned her smile, hoping he'd put the twinkle there. "You'd better hurry. The good spots are going fast. I think the whole town showed up."

Emily took Ma by the arm and led her to the shade. Clint's heart was touched by the way she treated his mother. He watched her spread their quilt in a shady area before settling Ma on it.

EMILY PLACED a cushion beneath Ma and ensured she was comfortable. "I need to use the outhouse. Will you be all right while I'm gone?"

"Sure. Beatrice is going to bring me a glass of lemonade. You go right ahead. Just watch out for lizards and spiders inside."

Emily opened the door to the outhouse and checked the seat and interior for all kinds of varmints. Satisfied that none had invaded, she made use of the facility. Some thoughtful people had set a small, roughly hewn table against the outside of the outhouse. A basin of clean water and a bar of French-milled soap lay on top of a washcloth, and alongside it, a stack of clean, hand towels.

Concerned about Clint, Emily washed and dried her hands then started back to find him. He had seemed distracted during the service. He'd glanced across the aisle time after time. Was he attracted to the woman in the mustard-colored dress? She had returned his stare. Was she jealous of Emily? Had Clint courted this woman? Did she have feelings for him? Did he have feelings for her?

A man stepped out from behind a tree, interrupting Emily's thoughts and blocking her path. She clapped a hand to her throat and gasped. "Dr. Clemons! You…startled me."

Oliver Clemons wore a smirk and did not look the least bit apologetic. He brushed a speck of something from his fancy vest. "Good afternoon. I've been doing a little investigating, and we need to talk." he rasped.

One look at his menacing eyes and Emily felt the color drain from her face. When her heart began to pound against her ribcage, she raised a clammy hand to her forehead. "Dr. Clemons, I'll explain later. I have to go."

He pasted on a fake smile. "An explanation is not what I want."

What did he want—a wife? No! She almost shouted it. She would not marry him. Not if her life depended on it. Emily started to panic, her breath coming in gasps. She forced herself to calm down. This man could not hurt her. Not with a throng of people as witnesses.

Her gaze darted across the churchyard, searching for Clint. Where was he when she needed him most? "I must attend to Mrs. James," she said. Without waiting for a reply, she took off at a jaunt.

"We will finish this conversation," he yelled behind her, hurrying to catch up. His threats made goosebumps pop up on her arms. She walked at a quick pace, not turning to look behind her. The crunch of leaves and twigs behind her indicated he was gaining ground.

Emily stifled a scream. What would these good folks do if she let it loose? A chill crept up her spine making her hair stand on end, as she cut through the crowd, repeating, "Excuse me," time and again.

She shivered despite the heat, her only thought to find Clint. He would protect her. If she could not find him, she would blend with the crowd so this awful man couldn't bother her.

CLINT CHECKED to ensure the horses had enough browse space before joining the festivities. Quilts were spread in the shade of every tree on the premises. His gaze flitted over the picnic area searching for Emily, his ma, and Alissia. He spied Alissia right away, standing in line in front of the Reilly kid. The two were smiling at each other as if they were the only ones there. At least they were in plain sight.

Clint had turned his back three minutes and his sister had found Landon. He could almost hear Emily telling him to take a deep breath and relax, and to loosen the apron strings on Alissia. He would for now, only for Emily's sake. He hoped her plan worked.

Where was she, anyway? He found his ma sitting alone on the quilt. She waved at him, and he waved back. In the direction of the outhouses, a man was hurrying after a young woman, as if in pursuit. The woman walked at a quick pace as if trying to leave the man behind.

Clint squinted against the sun. He couldn't make out their faces. The woman had on a kelly-green dress like the one Emily was wearing. He started toward them, keeping his eye on them as he walked. Yes, he recognized her, and Clemons was the man stalking her. Emily could be in danger.

Clint sliced through the crowd, keeping his eye on the couple. Before he knew what had happened, he'd slammed into a bowl. Juice splattered across his Sunday shirt. The lady holding the bowl squealed and stumbled backward. He grabbed her to steady her. "I'm so sorry!"

Prudence Wallace's jaw dropped. She clung to the bowl as if it were her lifeline. Clint recognized the remaining contents as pinto beans. The juice and a few beans had splattered onto her bodice as well as his shirt. More beans covered their shoes.

He flicked a bean from Prudence's arm. "I should have been watching where I was going. The sun was in my eyes." He didn't add that he was entirely focused on Emily and Clemons.

He craned his neck to look beyond Miss Wallace. Where had those two gotten off to? He'd lost sight of them. He turned back to Prudence. "Are you all right?"

She ducked her head and smiled meekly. "I'm fine, Mr. McCall. The bean bowl is half empty, but it's no great loss. I saw two other bowls of pinto beans on the table."

Sauce dripped from her chin while beans clung to her dress. Clint would let her pluck the beans from her bodice, but he would help her as much as was gentlemanly possible otherwise. It was the least he could do since he'd caused the accident.

He plucked a bean from her shoulder before pointing to the ones clinging to her bodice. When she had thumped them off, he pulled his handkerchief from his pocket and blotted the juice on her chin. The woman's cheeks turned a rosy pink beneath her multitude of freckles. He hoped she wasn't getting any notions about him.

Clint took a step back to inspect the damage. He owed her a compliment after running over her. "Is this a new dress, Miss Wallace? The color looks nice on you. I hope I didn't ruin it."

"No, you did not ruin it. And, yes, it is new. Thank you for noticing. It's called mustard yellow. I made it, especially for this occasion. Don't worry. The bean juice will wash out."

Clint graced her with a smile. "Well, you did a beautiful job making it, I must say."

Prudence giggled. "Would you like to see the bustle?"

Before he could protest, she did a complete twirl before looking up at him. "What do you think, now?" The woman beamed from the attention. "Bustles are smaller this year. It's the new fashion. Did you know that?"

Yes, he knew about the smaller bustles. Emily and Alissia had discussed it time and again. "I've heard." He'd started to mention how he knew but thought better of it. Anyone listening in might start to gossip. He didn't want to give them a reason. "If you're all right, I'll see about Ma."

"Of course, Mr. McCall. Maybe I'll run into you later." Prudence giggled as she ducked her head and curtsied.

When she raised her chin, Clint touched her shoulder. "Wait. Close your eyes. You have a bean on your forehead, just below your bonnet."

The woman closed her eyes, tilting her head back.

Clint took a step back before plucking the bean from her brow and wiping away the residue with his handkerchief. He leaned in closer to make certain the sticky sauce was completely gone before he straightened. "There." Folding the sticky handkerchief, he tucked it inside his pocket.

Prudence fluttered her lashes at him. "Why, thank you, Mr. McCall. It would have been awful if the latest gossip was, 'Miss Wallace had a bean in her bonnet.'" She giggled again, covering her mouth.

～

WHY WAS Clint standing so close to the redhead who sat next to Dr. Clemons in church? He had leaned down, their faces inches apart. Had he kissed the woman before pulling out his handkerchief and gently blotting her face?

A wave of something akin to jealousy burned in Emily's chest as she reached Clint. The redhead ducked her head and offered her a sheepish smile.

Dr. Clemons caught up and came to a stop beside Emily. "What is going on here, Prudence?" he croaked in his high and mighty tone.

The woman he'd called Prudence, patted the sprig of red hair protruding from beneath her bonnet. "Not a thing, Ollie. Clint, here, wasn't looking where he was going, and neither was I. I had this bowl in my hand when we collided. Some of the contents splattered over my dress and onto his shirt. He was blotting the juice from my face and plucking the beans from my dress. I managed to save half the beans. The juice will come out of this material with a good washing."

Ollie stared down his nose at her. "Did you find us a nice shade to spread our quilt beneath?"

"Yes, I did. I wondered where you'd gotten off to. I also scooped a generous helping of peach cobbler into a bowl, just for you."

Clemons's eyes glowed. "How thoughtful of you, Prudence." He offered her his arm. "Shall we dine?"

Prudence wasn't through yet. "Ollie, Clint complimented my new dress. He said the yellow color flatters my complexion. What do you think?"

Was she trying to make the dentist jealous? It appeared so. Had Clint really complimented the woman on her dress?

Clemons made no comment. His eyebrows rose. "Come along, Prudence. Let's eat before the food gets cold."

Prudence slipped her hand around his arm and turned to Clint. "Good day, Clint." She nodded at Emily. "You, too, Miss."

CLINT FROWNED as the couple walked away. Prudence had called him by his given name. Before, he had been "Mr. McCall". Was she trying to make her Ollie jealous? That was all he needed. He was already mad enough to punch the arrogant dentist. He almost hoped Ollie would instigate something.

Emily wore a smirk. "What's so funny?" he asked, "Do I have dirt on my face?"

She screwed up her face. "Not dirt. A bean particle on your nose."

Before he could wipe it off, she reached up and flung it away. "There. All done."

"I saw Clemons talking to you. Are you all right? What did he say?" Clint asked. "It's probably not a good idea to wander away from the crowd. At least not with a man who's desperate to find a wife. That is, unless you're in the running."

Her eyes flamed. "I am not in the running! And I did not wander off with him. If you must know, I had to visit the outhouse. Dr. Clemons intercepted me when I came out."

"Intercepted? As…in blocking your path?"

Emily chewed her bottom lip. Why had Clemons been stalking her? She had not answered his question. Maybe she was jealous of Prudence. Was that why she appeared upset? Clint choked back a laugh at the absurdity. He should be the one upset. What did Clemons say to Emily? He had no right to ask, but what he didn't know was gnawing at him.

He cleared his throat. "I apologize for jumping to conclusions. I just don't trust Clemons. Did he do or say anything out of the way? I wouldn't want folks gossiping."

Emily propped her hands on her hips. "Gossiping about *me*? You should talk. If you and Prudence didn't give them enough to gossip about, I'll be shocked. You two were standing so close I thought you were going to kiss her." She tossed her head sending her raven tresses flying. "Maybe you did, and I missed it."

Clint's voice boomed. "What? Me kiss Prud—?"

"Sh-h! People are staring. But, yes, that is how it appeared."

"Where did you get that crazy idea? I have no interest in Miss Wallace."

"Well, it's none of my business. You can kiss whomever you like."

Clint shook his head. Did she really think he was interested in Prudence? He looked around to ensure no one was paying attention to them. Then he clutched Emily's wrist. "Come with me…please."

She looked skeptical as he escorted her toward a copse of trees and pulled her behind a large hackberry. Clint pulled her into his arms and kissed her. She stiffened at first, but finally relaxed. When he released her, Emily's eyes remained closed.

"Does that tell you anything?" he breathed in her ear.

Emily's lashes fluttered up at him. "Yes. That you've had plenty of practice kissing."

Clint rolled his eyes and huffed out a breath. "Look, I'll explain about Miss Wallace later, but it's time to eat now. I'm hungry." He peeked out from behind the tree. "Nobody's looking. Let's go." He offered Emily his arm. Her hand trembled as she took it. Whether shaken from their kiss or something else, he could only guess.

They slipped out from behind the tree and walked toward the picnic table. "Ma probably thinks we've forgotten her. Let's fix her a plate. You can help me. You know her favorite dishes."

"I—I don't mind helping." Emily's lips trembled as she spoke.

Yes, Clemons had upset her. Clint and the man would have a talk, and soon.

The line at the table was much shorter. Clint spied his ma

relaxing on their quilt, sipping a glass of lemonade. A thoughtful church member must have attended to her.

A lot of nice people lived in Abilene. Except for the saloons on weekend nights, the town for the most part was civilized and respectable. He was proud to call Abilene his home.

Clint pivoted, his gaze searching the church grounds. Where had Alissia and Landon gotten off to? He hadn't seen them for some time.

Emily tugged on his arm. "If you're looking for your sister, she and Landon have a quilt spread next to your ma's."

Emily had read his mind. Was he that obvious? Clint craned his neck to see where she pointed. "I see them. Mr. Parks and Liam were blocking my view." At least Landon was showing respect by joining them for the meal.

Emily waved at Ma, and she hollered back. "Y'all bring me a big plate of food. I'm starving."

Clint groaned. "The extra attention has spoiled her. She'll expect it from now on."

Emily chuckled. "You only have one mother, Clint. She deserves special treatment."

When they returned with the plates of food, Doc Simmons appeared, his plate heaped to overflowing. "Mind if I join y'all, Vera?"

Ma's face flushed as she gazed up at him. "Why, there you are, you old coot. Where've you been keeping yourself? You weren't in church." She scooted over and patted the place next to her. "Sit yourself down. I ain't had a lively discussion since the last time you came by the house."

"And I've missed your bickering, Vera. Your color is much better." He paused to chew on a drumstick. "I wasn't at morning services because the youngest Garvey boy wasn't feeling too pert. He had stomach cramps last night."

"That don't sound too good," Ma said.

"Nothing much to worry about. He'll get over it. His ma got

him to confess that he'd eaten half a dozen green apples after supper. I instructed her to give him a dose of castor oil to clean him out, and tomorrow give him doses of paregoric as needed."

Ma laughed. "That'll learn him. Experience is ofttimes the best teacher."

Everyone ate while Ma and Doc Simmons bantered back and forth between bites. A gentle breeze stirred the leaves of the tree above them, while a squirrel chattered in its branches. Somewhere a hawk screeched. The sounds of nature and the lull of voices soothed Clint.

Weary from two weeks of extra-long hours of work, he fought sleep. New fences had been installed, and the last cutting of hay was finally in the barn. He finished the last bite of his food and handed the plate to Emily. "Your fried chicken was delicious."

"I thought you liked it. You ate three pieces."

He graced her with a sheepish grin. "I guess I did at that." Weariness overcame him. He lay back against the tree trunk and closed his eyes. A couple minutes of rest couldn't hurt.

Chapter Eighteen

Clint snored softly. His head dropped to his chest as he reclined against the tree. One corner of his mouth drooped. Landon stood and pulled Alissia to her feet. "Mrs. James, may I have permission to escort your daughter around the church grounds? She wants to stretch her legs."

Ma grinned. "Oh, she does, does she?"

Landon's face flushed. Alissia's sheepish expression told Emily they had conspired. Ma flapped a hand. "You young'uns go ahead. Just don't get too far. The singing starts in a bit."

Alissia ushered Landon forward. "We won't, Ma."

The youngsters were taking advantage of Clint's nap. Emily doubted he would have granted them permission. No, he would have accompanied them. She needed to have another talk with Clint.

He had been forced to grow up quickly after his mother married Hank James. As a boy, he had taken on the role of protector for his sister and his mother, against his brutal stepfather. This must have accounted for his overly protective way with Alissia.

Clint's tough facade melted to a softer countenance while he slept. His drooping bottom lip made him look vulnerable. Tenderness flooded Emily. She relived their kiss and a warm sensation surged through her. After the long hours he'd worked to prepare for fall roundup, he had earned this nap. A coppery lock lay across one eye. Emily fought the impulse to brush it back in place.

Ma whispered in Doc Simmons's ear. As he pulled her to her feet, she said, "Doc and I are going to taking a stroll. Unless you'd rather we stayed with you."

"You two, go ahead. Someone has to keep the flies off Clint," she teased, fanning his face.

Ma winked. "And you're doing a mighty good job of it."

Heat rose to Emily's face. She'd hoped Ma had been too focused on Doc to notice. She cleared her throat. "Enjoy your walk."

The doctor took his patient by the hand and smiled down at Emily. "Don't mind Vera. She has a habit of speaking her mind, whether a person wants to hear it or not."

"There ain't no use in mincing words," Ma retorted.

Doc patted her arm. "As, you say, Vera. You could use a little exercise…for your health. Nothing like a good sprint to get a patient's blood to circulating."

Ma scowled at him. "Now, you wait just a pea-pickin' minute, Floyd Simmons. Nobody said nothing about a sprint."

Doc doffed his hat at Emily while ushering his contrary patient away. "We'll be back before the singing starts."

Emily flashed them a smile. "Take your time. I'm enjoying the peace and quiet and the sounds of nature." And watching Clint sleep, she silently added.

She doubted the doctor thought of Ma as his patient. She'd noticed a spark between them the first day Doc had paid a visit. Clint's ma couldn't find a better man.

The doctor was still holding Ma's hand when they disappeared behind the hackberry and cottonwood trees. The same trees Clint had pulled her behind less than an hour earlier.

And what a kiss they had shared. Emily shook her head to refocus her thoughts. She studied the sleeping Clint, her heart aching for the loss she'd experience once this cowboy learned the truth about her.

Dr. Clemons's tone and menacing eyes had frightened her. Had he connected her date of arrival with the expected arrival date of his second mail-order bride? She had been too afraid to ask. But not knowing, frightened her more.

At least Emily hadn't married the dentist. That would have been a disaster. A sigh escaped her lips. She might have if her arrival date had not been delayed. Her day-late arrival had allowed her to see the true character of the man.

God had to be in this. The delay had kept her from making a terrible mistake. She had asked Him to reveal the true character of Dr. Clemons. And he had.

But where should she go from here? The decision was facing her. If Jessica could not get her on as a clerk at the hotel, or if she couldn't find work as a bookkeeper or secretary, maybe she could hire on as a maid at the hotel.

Emily was desperate. She would temporarily settle for anything respectable to pay her board and put food in her stomach. Returning to her brother's home was out of the question. Besides, she would have to work a year to save enough for train fare.

Guilt tugged at her heart. Clemons had dished out a lot for her to come to Abilene. But, offering to reimburse him for the ticket, even if she could, meant confessing she was one of his mail-order brides.

Emily inhaled a ragged breath. Or did Clemons know for certain and was biding his time, waiting for the perfect moment to expose her? This was her greatest fear.

She would not think about that. Instead, she would enjoy the afternoon. She let her gaze drift over Clint, again. She had become attached to his mother and Alissia, but most of all to Clint. The cowboy had worked his way into her heart. Losing him would shred it into a million pieces.

Emily believed Clint reciprocated her feelings. Whether his feelings were strong enough to accept the truth about her, she could only hope. She hadn't let herself dwell on a budding romance between them until recently when she'd admitted her feelings to Jessica.

Her life was complicated by the secret. She had come close to confessing to Clint a couple of times, but the dread of seeing his eyes fill with disgust had stopped her. She couldn't bear his rejection, whatever other emotion he displayed. Blowing out a long breath, she let her gaze linger on Clint's lanky form stretched out before her as he slept, propped against the tree trunk. How he slept against the rough bark, she did not understand. What she did understand was, tomorrow was not promised to anyone. It was in the good Lord's hands.

Soon she must tell Clint everything. Emily looked heavenward and silently prayed, "Father, give me a little more time with the man I love. Then I will tell him the truth. Allow me to savor the time we have left, to share a few more precious moments, so I can tuck these memories inside my heart." She reached across Clint and snapped off one of several goldenrod weeds sprouting up next to the quilt and touched it to the tip of his nose. He frowned, but his eyes remained shut. She tickled his nose again with the weed. He screwed up his face, but his eyes still didn't open. This time she brushed the weed beneath his nose.

~

"Ah-h-Ah-choo!" Clint's eyes flew open. "Something's making my nose itch." He rubbed it and frowned at Emily. Why was she smirking and gripping that weed? She was the guilty culprit who had interrupted his nap. He wrapped his fingers around her wrist and pulled her toward him. "You little minx," he teased. "You will not go unpunished."

She giggled, challenging him with her eyes. As luck would have it, a crowd was gathering around the picnic table. The singing was about to start. He groaned and released his grip on her wrist. "Your punishment will have to wait. Too many witnesses."

Emily arched her eyebrows. "And if there weren't?"

"I'll answer that—no, I'll show you—later," he whispered.

She blushed a rosy pink. Lowering her long, dark lashes, she began to smooth her skirt.

Clint's gaze flitted across the grounds. He found Clemons and Prudence seated on a patchwork quilt beneath a hackberry tree. The woman's animated hands suggested she was talking a blue streak.

But Clemons was not focused on Prudence. He was watching them, or rather Emily. Why couldn't he get it through his thick skull that she would never give him permission to court her?

Which reminded him, where was Alissa? He hadn't seen his sister since he'd fallen asleep. He craned his neck to look around the area. Ah-h, there she was, in line next to Landon at the end of the picnic table. At least the two were in plain sight.

Landon had yet to hear from the medical examination he'd taken in Houston. Clint hoped he would get accepted into the school. The time and distance apart would give Alissia a chance to mull things over. And to mature. His sister needed to consider the responsibilities of adulthood and the repercussions that came from rushing into a lifelong commitment without thinking of the consequences.

Not that Landon was a bad kid, but Clint didn't think he was the one for Alissia. She didn't need any young man until she had furthered her education. If Landon was far away, his sister could keep her mind on her studies.

He returned his focus to Emily, who appeared nervous, picking at her sleeve. Was it from Clemons's gawking at her? "What's wrong?"

She closed her eyes and shook her head. "Nothing. I'm fine."

He could see she wasn't, but it could wait until they were alone. At the moment he needed to locate his mother. "Where's Ma?"

Emily winked. "Doc Simmons took her for a walk. He said she needed the exercise for her health, to keep the blood pumping."

Clint plucked a blade of grass from the ground and stuck it between his teeth. "Likely story. They just wanted to be alone."

A sly grin split Emily's face. "I can't imagine why."

Ma and the doctor emerged from around the corner of the church and meandered toward the picnic table, hands joined. Clint pointed. "There they are, holding hands. It doesn't surprise me."

"Nor me," Emily said. "I've seen the way their eyes light up when they pretend to argue."

"Yeah, Ma thrives on squabbling with Doc. Truth be known, anticipating his visits and sassing him, are probably why she's recuperated so quickly."

On the other hand, his mother's full recovery meant Clint would have to invent another excuse to keep Emily at the ranch. He knew she would not accept charity. She would insist on earning her keep. What he didn't want was for her to move to a boarding house. Abilene could get wild at night. As pretty as she was, she could be assaulted by a rowdy cowhand.

That wasn't the real reason, if he'd admit it. His heart couldn't stand the thought of Emily not being present at breakfast and suppertime, or available to sit on the porch swing with him in the cool of the evening. Maybe they could enjoy more moonlight rides on Bowie. How lonely the house would be without her.

Emily brought joy into their home and had become a wonderful role model for Alissia. She'd been right. As bad as he hated to admit it, her advice about loosening the reins on his little sister had worked. Alissia had begun to treat him with respect again, the way she had before disagreements over Landon had divided them.

Clint refocused his thoughts. It had been a good day. He would not dwell on anything that might ruin it. He would find a way to keep Emily at the ranch. Because he loved her.

Wait. Did he say, "love"? Emily was special, and he was attracted to her. But, love? Yes, he did love her. Reality jolted him. She was eying him again. "Clint, what were you thinking just now?".

He shook his head. "Nothing I want to talk about." At least not yet. He needed to think this through, decide what to do about his growing attraction to her.

He stretched his arms over his head and yawned. "We'd better join the others. The singing is about to start." He tapped the end of her nose. Standing, he reached down for Emily's hand pulling her to her feet. "Remember what I said. I will deal with you later, young lady."

Her sweet smile told him she wasn't the least bit afraid.

AN HOUR LATER, the singing wound down and the congregates scattered to gather their belongings. Clint picked up the picnic basket while Emily and Alissia folded the quilt. Doc took Ma's hand and walked her to the buckboard, trailing the others.

When Doc had helped Ma get seated, he said, "I'll be by soon, Vera. Try to behave, meanwhile."

"You'd best take your own advice, you old coot," she retorted. Doc chuckled before heading toward his horse and buggy parked in the shade.

When everyone was settled in the buckboard, Clint asked, "Ma, are you ready to go?"

"Yes. Let's head for home." Clint shook the reins and clucked his tongue to get the horses moving. Clemons had disappeared before the singing began. Prudence sat alone, looking as if she'd lost her best friend. Too bad. She was a nice lady and would make some man an adoring wife. Evidently, she only had eyes for Clemons.

Unrequited love, Ma would call it. The man couldn't see the gift before his eyes. Instead, he kept reaching for something he could never obtain. Jessica's sister was a pretty woman too, from what he could tell. At least she'd had the sense to run at the last minute.

And now the dentist was eying Emily. Who did he think he was—a Greek Adonis? Far from it. The man's arrogance didn't help. A woman might overlook Clemons's buck teeth and mule face, as Jessica called it, if he showed a little respect for her.

Prudence could likely tame Clemons. She struck Clint as a determined woman who also had a caring nature. If anyone could keep the dentist grounded, she could. Clemons had sent off for three mail-order brides and one had shown up. The other two must have suspected something amiss in his letters. Or had he sent a tintype of himself? That would've done it.

He pulled his attention back to the three ladies in the wagon and determined to focus on something pleasant. Ma and Alissia were chatting about fashions. Well, he was lacking on that topic.

"I thought the Tyler family did a wonderful job. Did you hear the way little Benjamin sang? He can't be more'n ten, but he can bring the roof down," Ma said.

"Benjamin is talented," Alissia agreed, "but the Walker family has amazing harmony."

Emily appeared dazed, her mind miles away. Judging by her countenance, it was not in a happy place. A touch of homesickness? Clint nudged her. "What did you think?"

She blinked. "About what? I'm sorry. What were you saying?"

Just as he'd thought. "Ma and Alissia are debating over the best singers. What do you say?"

"The lady they called Mrs. Rollins, did a nice job on, 'It Is Well With My Soul'. She reached those high notes with very little effort."

Clint licked his lips. Emily was back for the time being. He wished he could keep her with him physically. It was time to start plotting. Ma was up and around now, helping with meals and housework, and even gathering eggs. She would soon take over the running of the house.

He didn't want Emily moving into town. Abilene could get wild, especially on weekend nights. Anything could happen to a pretty young woman living alone. He had not known her long, but she had worked her way into his heart. Was it too soon to have these feelings?

At first, his desire had been to protect her, as he did his sister. At least that's what he'd told himself. Now, he had to face the truth. Her laughter and smile brightened his day. He couldn't imagine one day without her. The thought saddened him.

Clint needed time to work through his feelings. He and the hands were busy moving cattle, preparing for the fall roundup. After the roundup, ranch work would slow down. Then he could figure out what to do about Emily, if she didn't leave the ranch first. Was that where her mind had wandered to a minute ago?

THE FOLLOWING DAY, after a light noonday meal, Emily hummed as she hung the wash on the line. The hot sun and breeze would dry them quickly. She pinned Clint's blue shirt to the clothesline as a buggy rolled up with the redheaded woman from church driving it. Prudence gracefully climbed out wearing an emerald-green dress and carrying a dainty parasol.

Hiking up her print dress with one hand, she marched toward the house. Emily pulled a clothespin from her mouth. "Over here."

Prudence turned and pranced toward Emily, twirling her parasol. This was the woman who had shared her lunch with Wendell Clemons at the church picnic. Emily did not trust anyone connected to the dentist. Had he sent her here? She would not drive a buggy two hours to the ranch unless she had something important to say.

Prudence extended a gloved hand. "Looks like you've got your hands full. I would help, but I would hate to mess up this nice dress."

Emily grasped her hand. "Nice to see you again. I have a few more items to hang. After that, I'll pour up some lemonade. We can chat on the porch swing. I would invite you in, but Mrs. James is napping."

"I understand." The woman's thick brows knit together, but she didn't move. "Your name is Emily, isn't it? I wonder why Ollie calls you Evelyn."

Emily's heart skipped a beat. She hoped the woman wouldn't press her for the answer. "I met you at the church picnic, yesterday. You are Prudence…"

"Wallace," her visitor finished. "I work at the Apothecary Shoppe. I live at the edge of town in the little white house surrounded by a picket fence."

Emily nodded, recalling the neat little house with its beautiful rose bushes in the yard.

Prudence fluttered her lashes and giggled. "I was the lady holding the bowl of beans that splattered all over Mr. McCall. I was mortified."

"Yes, I remember." The lady she'd thought Clint was about to kiss.

When Emily had pinned the last item to the clothesline, they walked to the porch. She gestured toward the porch swing. "Have a seat. I'll be right back."

She went inside and returned with two frothy glasses of lemonade, handing one to Prudence. They discussed the weather, but Emily suspected her visitor had another reason for her long drive.

"Wasn't that a terrifying storm we had two weeks ago?" Prudence asked.

Emily nodded. Her face burned as she relived that stormy night they'd taken Bowie out. She'd clung to Clint for dear life as they raced toward the ranch to outrun the downpour.

She wrung her hands, the suspense killing her. "Prudence, did you come to visit Mrs. James? I'm sorry you picked a bad time."

The woman cleared her throat. "Actually, it is you I came to see."

Emily opened her mouth, but no sound came out. When she had sipped from her glass and collected her thoughts, she said, "You have my permission to speak your mind."

Prudence studied her with a narrowed gaze. "I've seen the way Dr. Clemons looks at you. Are you romantically interested in him as well?"

Emily choked on her lemonade and it spewed from her mouth. When she'd brushed the droplets from her skirt, she squeaked, "Me? Romantically interested in Dr. Clemons?"

Prudence picked lint from her bodice. "I call him, Ollie. Well, are you?"

Emily coughed. "No, I'm not at all interested in…Ollie."

Prudence reached out and patted her arm. "Good. You don't know how relieved I am to hear it. Although, if you had been, it would not have made any difference. I would have fought for him. You see, I've loved Ollie since the first time I laid eyes on him. I went to his office with an awful toothache, and he bent over me and peered into my eyes." She sighed. "Don't you think he's dreamy? His blue eyes were the last thing I remember before everything went black."

Emily searched for a reply that would not offend Prudence. "Dr. Clemons is unique."

The woman clapped her hands. "That is a perfect description of Ollie." Her countenance sobered. "I only wish he would take more notice of me." Fanning her face, she added, "Oh, he likes my cooking, especially my peach cobbler. Otherwise, I may as well not exist."

"Have you told him how you feel?" Emily ventured.

Prudence's eyes widened. "Heavens, no! I could never do that. It isn't proper etiquette."

"Are you from the North?" Emily detected an accent.

"Saint Louis," the redhead explained. "When my parents died last year with smallpox, I came here to live with Aunt Matilda. Unfortunately, she passed away in May. The house felt so lonely that I spent a month with my cousin in Fort Worth. But I missed Ollie and had to return."

She wrung her hands. "While I was in Fort Worth, I saw a newspaper where Ollie had placed an ad for a mail-order bride. I could not understand why, when all he had to do was—" She clapped a hand to her mouth. "Oh! I'm afraid I've said too much."

Did Prudence know she had replied to the dentist's ad? Emily's heart raced and her palms felt cold and clammy.

She patted Prudence's arm. "You should take a chance and let him know how you feel. If you don't, you may regret it. It's worth the risk if you truly care for him. What do you have to lose?"

Prudence's gaze searched hers. "You make a good point." She finished her lemonade, handed the glass to Emily, and stood. "Well, I should get back. Our chat was enlightening. Thank you for the lemonade."

Before Emily could respond, Prudence hiked her skirts and hurried toward the waiting buggy. "Come back any time," Emily called after her. The redhead climbed into the buggy, gave a slight wave, and slapped the reins to get the horse moving.

Emily stood, arms folded across her chest, and watched the trail of dust Prudence left behind. "Well, what do you make of that?"

"What the dickens did Miss Wallace want?" Ma stood at the screen door, holding it open.

"I don't understand," Emily said. "Why would she drive all this way to confess her undying love for Dr. Clemons?"

"Hmph." Ma shook her head. "There weren't no need for that. It's as clear as the nose on your face that Prudence is smitten with the dentist. The sad thing is, the poor girl will be gettin' the short end of the stick."

Chapter Nineteen

The Saturday set for the harvest celebration, fell on October 4th and on a full moon. The temperature had dropped several degrees, a welcome break from the heat. In the late afternoon, Emily bathed in Elm creek with the French-milled soap she'd bought at Payne's General Store. The water was clean and refreshing and the soap smelled wonderful on her skin as she dried off with a towel. Alissia had bathed earlier. Emily donned her clothes and started up the path toward the house. Ma met her with a towel over one arm, and articles of clothing slung over one shoulder.

What in the world? "Ma, what are you doing?" Since Emily had been at the ranch, her patient's bath had consisted of warm water in a washbowl, a washcloth, and a bar of soap, with Emily assisting her.

"I'm takin' a bath in Elm Creek. What does it look like I'm doin'? Now, if you don't mind, I'd like to borrow your sweet-smelling soap. I looked for it and found it missing. Alissia said you were down at the creek, so I figured you had it."

"Mrs. James, are you sure it's a good idea to be dipping in

that cold water?" The last thing the woman needed was to contract pneumonia again.

"I told you to call me Ma." She propped her hands on her hips. "Look here, young lady, I was takin' baths in Elm creek since before you were thought about."

"But, you're not well. What would Doc say about this?"

"I'm well enough," she added with a wink. "Doc is the main reason I'm takin' a real bath. He probably prefers I smell sweet when he picks me up this evening."

"You're going to the dance?" Emily squealed. "When did Doc ask you?"

"At the church picnic." She extended her hand, palm up. "Soap, please."

Emily placed the French-milled bar in her hand. "I'll stay with you and help you dry off and get you into your dry clothes. Let's make it quick, so you don't get a chill."

"Whatever suits your fancy." Ma shoved the towel and articles of clothing at Emily. Hang these on that bush while I get out of these things." She began unbuttoning her dress.

When Ma was bathed and dressed, and they had returned to the house, Emily found Alissia seated at the vanity table, fuming. "Oh! Emily, can you help me pin up my hair? Yours always looks pretty. But every time I stick in a pin, more hair comes loose."

"Give me the hairpins. It's all in the way you position them." Emily stuck a few hairpins in her mouth and went to work, picking up one tendril at a time and pinning each one in place. "Just a couple more pins and I'll be finished." She slipped in the last two and patted Alissia's hair. "There, all done."

Alissia preened at her reflection, touching her hair near the temples, obviously pleased with the results. "This up-do makes me look sophisticated—more mature. Maybe Clint will finally see me as a grown woman."

Emily doubted it. "Landon's approval is what really matters."

Alissia giggled. "Yes. Do you think his eyes will pop out of his head?"

"He may take one look and ask, 'Have we met, young lady?'"

Alissia's eyes held a dreamy look. "Do I really look that different?"

"Yes, you do, but wait until you've donned your new dress. By the way, did you know Doc is taking your ma to the dance?"

"No!" Alissia's jaw dropped. "You're kidding."

"She just told me. He's picking her up here. I just came from helping her bathe in Elm creek. She's excited about going."

"That is really something. Think about it. All three of us ladies have dates for the dance. Ma's going with Doc, I'm meeting Landon, the same as a date, and you're going with Clint."

Emily rolled her eyes. "I don't think you'd call my going with Clint a date."

"Why not? I've seen the way my brother ogles you. And the way you return his looks. You two are in love. And he's crazy if he lets you get away."

Emily shook her head. If only it were that simple. She picked up a strip of white lace left over from the trim on Alissia's dress. "Let's make a bow out of this and put it in your hair. It will match the white lace on your dress."

EMILY BUTTONED up the Napoleon blue dress she'd made for the occasion. Alissia had been ready an hour, and Doc Simmons left with Clint's mother a few minutes earlier. Clint had bathed in Elm Creek and was dressed in the shirt and dress pants his mother had laid out for him.

Emily dabbed Alissia's lilac perfume on her wrists and behind her ears before picking up her wrap. She checked her reflection, made a silly face, and headed toward the living room. Clint's bedroom door stood half opened. He was whistling "Yankee Doodle Dandy" while raking a comb through his hair.

The meal at Cooper's barn was potluck. Every household was asked to contribute a dish or two. She and Alissia had prepared potato salad and fried chicken, earlier. It was wrapped and tucked inside a picnic basket.

As Emily joined Alissia in the living room, Clint's voice rang out from down the hall. "You ladies about ready?"

"For at least an hour. Waiting on you, big brother," Alissia answered.

Clint walked into the living room, a jacket slung over his arm. Emily couldn't help noticing how his emerald green shirt fit his taut body and how the color brought out his sparkling eyes. His gaze raked the two ladies, lingering on Emily. He emitted a low growl. "My, my, you both look beautiful. I am doubly blessed to escort two pretty ladies to the dance."

Alissia looked at Emily, raising her brows, as if to say, "See, I told you Clint would see me as a woman, in this dress."

"Shall we?" He offered an arm to each.

The sun had set below the horizon as they pulled into the Coopers' yard. Swirls of baby blue, apricot, and gold in the western sky added a kaleidoscopic beauty to God's creation as Clint helped Emily and Alissia out of the buggy.

The Coopers' log home looked inviting. From what Emily could tell in the dusky light, it was similar to the one at the L&M ranch. The ladies placed their wraps about their shoulders. Lantern light and violin music emanated from the large barn Emily recognized, "My Sweet Irish Rose."

Clint handed the picnic basket to Alissia. "You ladies, go inside while I park the buggy."

Lanterns hung on the walls inside the large barn to light the interior. Chairs had been placed around three walls, allowing the third wall for tables of food. The remainder of the interior had been cleared out to allow space for socializing and dancing. Everyone appeared to be jovial. Some sat in groups, others stood in huddles of three or four. The violinist seemed to have drifted into another world and become immune to the clatter and chatter, as he played a sweet ballad.

While Alissia set their food on the table, Emily searched the crowd for familiar faces. She spied Doc Simmons and Clint's ma at the opposite side of the barn, laughing as they drank punch and talked with a middle-aged couple she'd seen at church.

Carrie Kramer caught Emily's eye and motioned her over. "Good to see you again, Emily. How is Mrs. James?"

"Very well. She's here with Doc Simmons." Emily pointed to where the pair stood laughing.

Carrie's eyes held a wistful look. "Isn't that wonderful? They make a nice-looking couple." She craned her neck to peer around Emily. "Where's Clint? Didn't he come to the dance?"

"Yes, he brought Alissia and me." Emily's gaze slid to where Clint stood at the entrance, searching the crowd. She hoped he was looking for her. He looked so handsome, she almost swooned. "He's just come in from parking the buggy." She pulled her gaze back to Carrie. "Where is your husband?"

Carrie pointed to two men seated on barrels. "Josh is over there talking to his foreman. He's the tall, dark handsome one. I still can't believe I snagged him." She patted her abdomen and whispered, "And now we're expecting our first baby."

A voice boomed at the front, and the music stopped. A short man of medium build raised his hands to silence the crowd. "May I have your attention, folks? As most of you know, I'm Gerald Cooper, and I'm happy to see all my friends and neigh-bors at our fourth annual barn dance. I want to remind you of the rules. We don't allow liquor at this shindig. Do your drinking some other place. If any of you gets unruly, there are a couple of sturdy cowboys who will be happy to escort you to the door."

Mr. Cooper nodded at two stout, rugged-looking men

languishing against the far wall. Their wary gazes slid over the crowd. "Everyone enjoy yourselves. Looks like there's plenty of food."

He continued. "We'll line up to eat, but before we do, I'll ask Hal Greer to bless the food."

Following Hal's blessing and a round of hearty "Amens," Clint walked over and tipped his hat at Carrie. He then offered his arm to Emily, escorting her to the food line. His breath warmed her ear when he bent to whisper, "As soon as we've finished eating, I'm claiming the first dance."

His smooth baritone sent tingles up Emily's spine, turning her legs to jelly. All she could do was nod in response. How could she dance with Clint if her legs threatened to fold?

The violinist began to play a slow waltz. A few couples were gathering on the dance floor. Clint took Emily's hand and led her to the dance floor. Emily's knees quivered, but she managed to stand as he placed a hand on her back and started to sweep her across the floor.

Clint was a smooth dancer and Emily soon fell into step. Roy had taught her to waltz when she was twelve, but that was six years ago. As Clint whirled her around the dance floor, Emily watched the door, anticipating Jessica's arrival. Instead, she saw Landon and Alissia slipping outside. She hoped they would return before Clint found them missing.

When Dr. Clemons appeared in the doorway with Prudence on his arm, Emily faltered, stumbling over Clint's boot. He tightened his grip to stabilize her.

He grinned sheepishly. "Me and my big feet,"

"No, it was my fault. I'm a little rusty."

She refocused to keep time until the waltz ended. Clint's gaze lingered on the entrance. Oh, no. He must have noticed Alissia and Landon's absence.

He looked down at her, clearing his throat. "Why don't we

take a break? I'll get you a cup of punch and you can rest a bit. There's something I need to check on."

Emily breathed a prayer for Alissia, Landon, and Clint as he handed her a cup of punch and strode toward the door. She longed to intercede but knew Clint would not welcome it. He might call it interference. And Alissia was his sister, not hers.

Taking a deep breath, she watched Doc Simmons and Clint's ma engrossed in one another as they moved across the floor. Ma didn't appear any worse for the activity. In fact, the woman glowed. Emily trusted the doctor. He would make his patient sit down if she looked weary.

"There you are!" Emily flinched as Jessica Dawson plopped down beside her. She leaned closer and whispered, "Clemons is here with that redheaded woman from church."

Emily nodded. "I know. I saw them come in. Where's your date?"

"Trent's seeing to the horse and buggy. I'll introduce you when he comes in. Has that dentist been giving you the evil eye, tonight?"

Emily sucked in a ragged breath. "I don't think he's spotted me yet."

"Let me know if he causes you any trouble. I'll do my best to thwart his plans." She stood and waved at a smiling man with golden-brown hair. "There's Trent now." A tall, muscular man cut through the crowd toward them. Trent's blue eyes twinkled with mischief as Jessica made the introductions. "Nice to meet you, Miss Hammons," he said. "I understand you're taking good care of Clint's ma. Pneumonia isn't anything to sneeze at."

Emily liked Trent's gentle manner. "She had a time of it. Now, look at her. You wouldn't know she'd ever been sick by the looks of her tonight."

The couple turned to where Emily pointed, and Jessica giggled. "Would you look at that? She's dancing with Doc Simmons."

Emily worried her bottom lip. "It's the third waltz, and they've only sat one out."

Jessica clasped Trent's arm. "I'm sure the doctor will make her rest if she gets short of breath. Now, if you'll excuse us, this handsome man has promised me a dance." She winked at Emily as Trent led her to the floor.

"Is this seat taken?"

Emily looked up into Carrie Kramer's blue eyes. "Not anymore."

Carrie sat down in the chair Emily was saving for Clint and let her gaze drift across the gathering. "Last year, when I attended this festival, things didn't start out well."

Emily's curiosity was piqued. "What happened?"

"I'd only been here a few weeks and living at the Kramer ranch to help Josh's aunt with domestic chores. Ben Grady came by and picked me up for the festival, alone. His sister, Nancy, was supposed to come with him. Aunt Em didn't trust the man. I thought she had Ben pegged wrong. That he was a gentleman. She didn't want me to leave with Ben. Her instincts were right."

Carrie sighed. "Ben is a gentleman only when he's sober. Nancy, his sister, was already here with her beau when we arrived. We soon noticed that he and Ben were making frequent trips outside. After their third disappearance, we went out to check on them. ."

"Did you find them?" Emily asked.

"Yes. Nancy and her beau went back inside, leaving me with Ben. The whiskey smell was strong on his breath. When I tried to get Ben to go back inside with me, he grabbed me and tried to kiss me. That's when Josh leaped out from behind a cottonwood tree and yanked him off me. He punched Ben's jaw and threw him in his buggy and sent him home to sober up."

Emily's mouth fell open. "How did it all end?"

"Josh and I rode home on his horse. It was a full moon, like tonight. We stopped at a creek along the way to let his horse drink." Carrie blushed. "It was a romantic evening, stars twinkling overhead. I thought I was in love with Josh before, but that night I knew how much."

Emily chewed her bottom lip. "When we were at the general store, you mentioned unusual circumstances had brought you here. Do you mind telling me about them?"

Carrie laughed. "It's no secret, now. I left Denton in a hurry one night after pushing a nasty drunk off the boardwalk. His head struck a rock. He didn't come to, so I didn't know if he was dead or just unconscious."

"I'm afraid to walk by saloons in the daylight," Emily said. "Why were you there at night?"

"It's a long story. I'll tell you about it sometime, in private. Anyway, because I feared the sheriff and townspeople wouldn't believe my story, I fled town."

"Did you take the train to Abilene too?" Emily asked.

"Yes, but that's not the craziest part. I shared a seat with a woman who was getting off at the stop before mine. Since I was getting off at Abilene, she asked me to tell a tall, dark rancher that her friend had changed her mind about becoming his mail-order bride. I tried, but the rancher wouldn't let me explain. He thought I was the woman he was supposed to pick up at the depot."

Emily's heart clenched. "This is incredible. What did the rancher do?"

"The rancher was Josh Kramer. He tossed me onto his buckboard thinking I was his aunt's domestic help."

"Domestic help? The rancher was Josh?" Emily exclaimed.

"There's a lot more to it, but the next thing I knew, we were heading toward his ranch. I couldn't argue since I didn't have any money left after train fare."

"And I thought I was in a pickle," Emily blurted.

Carrie studied her with compassion-filled eyes. "Are you in some kind of trouble?"

Emily stared down at her hands, wringing them in her lap. Carrie laid her hand on Emily's wrist. "Do you want to tell me about it?"

"It's just that…my brother, Roy, married and moved his wife in. Louise tried to run everything. We were constantly at odds. My being there caused trouble between them. Louise and I argued all the time. I answered a mail-order bride ad to get out of the house."

Carrie's jaw dropped. "Oh, no. Were you one of the dentist's brides?"

Emily nodded. "Sh-h! Clint doesn't know it yet. I don't know how to tell him. Please don't say anything. I'm afraid I've fallen in love with him."

Carrie sighed. "I can see why. Emily, I will pray for you. Mistakes have a way of working themselves out if we give them to the Lord. I thought God was mad at me because both my parents died in a freak buggy accident. But when I saw how He brought Josh and me together, I recognized His hand in it. God made something good out of a messed-up situation."

A male voice boomed above them. "Hey, pretty lady, may I have this dance?"

Carrie smiled up at the tall, dark cowboy. "Of course. Emily, meet my husband, Josh."

Carrie was right. He was handsome. She smiled up at Josh. "Nice to meet you."

"Same here," Josh replied.

Carrie rose, turning back to Emily. "Remember what I said. The Lord will work it out."

Emily wished she could believe the Lord would bring something good from the mess she'd made by not being forthright.

≈

CLINT, Alissia, and Landon had been gone too long. Emily walked to the door and looked outside. To her right, well beyond the barn in a copse of trees, she heard muffled voices. As she approached, the moonlight glinted off three people.

"I know what you said, but I also know what I saw," spoke a familiar baritone voice.

A younger male answered, "Sir, it's the truth. I was just telling Alissia my good news."

Emily hurried toward them before the situation got out of hand. Alissia sat in the wagon, sniffling. As calmly as possible she asked, "Clint, why is your sister crying?"

Alissia raised her chin in defiance. "My big brother jumped to conclusions as usual. He wouldn't let me explain. He caught me giving Landon a hug to congratulate him. Landon just told me he's been accepted into medical school. That was the exact moment Clint showed up."

"What happened afterward?" Emily ventured a look at Clint.

Clint stuffed his hands in his pockets and exhaled a long breath. "Oh, boy, I've messed things up good." Throwing up a hand he said, "When I saw them like that, I thought…"

He stared at the ground and kicked at a rock. When he finally raised his head, he turned to his sister and her beau. "Alissia, Landon, I apologize for not giving you a chance to explain."

"Landon is a true gentleman," Alissia asserted, sniffing back tears. "He treats me with respect. He's never done or said anything that would prove otherwise."

Landon raised his head and looked directly at Clint. "Sir, it's true. I respect your sister. I would never do anything to harm her."

Clint clasped the boy's shoulder. "I believe you. Emily says I'm overly protective. I have my reasons, but I shouldn't allow them to taint my judgment."

He squeezed Emily's arm and whispered, "You go back

inside and wait for me. I want to talk to Landon and Alissia." He flashed her a smile. "You still owe me a dance."

Emily's heart melted at the twinkle in his eyes as she turned to leave. Clint McCall was well worth waiting for. Humming a merry tune, she made her way back to join the festivities. Clint had apologized to his sister and her beau. Admitting he'd been hasty in his judgment was a good start. Carrie could be right. God seemed to be working things out for those three.

Emily was still humming when a dark figure stepped out of the shadows and blocked her path. "We need to come to an agreement, Em-i-ly Ham-mons," he enunciated. "My attempts to talk to you have been thwarted again and again by that rude cowboy."

"Doctor Clemons!" Emily clutched her chest, her heart pounding against her ribcage. She had been found out, and her payday had come.

"Em-i-ly. Is that not correct?" The dentist's eyes burned with a menacing gleam. He folded his arms across his chest. "Old man Ward at the depot, told me a pretty brunette was asking after me on the sixteenth of August. He did not recall her name, but she returned with Clint McCall the next day to pick up her trunk. I took my time and added up the facts." He stared down his nose at her. "Why are you avoiding me?"

"I—I'm sorry." Why was she apologizing to the man who'd broken his agreement with her by repeating his vows to another woman? He should be the one to apologize.

Clemons clamped a hand around her wrist and spoke through clenched teeth. "You owe me for train fare if you refuse to go through with our contract. I shelled out a lot to bring you here."

Emily shook her head. "I—I don't have the money. I'll get a job—pay you back every cent. I promise. Just don't tell—"

A tall figure stepped into the light. His voice boomed. "Clemons take your hands off that lady. Now!"

The dentist dropped her wrist as if it were a hot potato. "Clint!" Emily flung herself into his arms, shaking.

He stiffened before setting her away from him. Gripping her shoulders, he urged, "Please, go inside Emily. Clemons and I have something to settle. Once and for all."

"Clint, I'm sorry," she sobbed as tears streamed down her cheeks. How much had he heard?

"Please go inside," Clint repeated. Controlled anger laced his voice. Emily's heart sank. He despised her and she couldn't blame him. She should have been forthright with him the day they'd met. Instead, she'd acted the coward and withheld the truth.

Emily pulled her wrap around her shoulders and trudged toward the barn. Clint knew her secret. She would surely lose the only man she could ever love.

With her head down, Emily didn't see the woman approaching and ran into her. "Oh!" A fragile hand touched her arm. "Miss Hammons is that you?" the female voice with a northern accent asked.

Prudence Wallace stood before her, eying her suspiciously. Emily forced a smile through the tears. "I'm sorry, Prudence. I wasn't watching where I was going."

"Apology accepted. Have you seen Dr. Clemons? I've looked everywhere and cannot find him. I have something important to tell him."

Emily pointed behind her to a copse of trees. "He's back there, talking with Mr. McCall." Prudence thanked her and hurried away.

Emily trudged toward the barn, her mind in turmoil. What would she do? Where would she go if Clint ordered her to leave?

Chapter Twenty

Clemons straightened his silk derby hat before hooking his thumbs in his vest pockets. "You have no right to interfere, McCall. I paid Miss Hammons's train fare all the way from West Memphis. She owes me. Train tickets do not come cheap."

"Miss Hammons owes you nothing. What kind of man are you, Clemons? The entire town knows you tried to trick three ladies into marrying you. When Miss Hammons found you, you were exchanging vows with your first prospective bride. Because the first woman fled, gives you no right to pursue Miss Hammons.

"She is not interested. As for the third bride, who knows what happened to her? There's a law against bigamy, and what you did could be considered attempted bigamy. You deceived three young women into believing each was the only one for you."

Clemons began wringing his hands. "I—I meant no harm. I received three replies. Each lady sounded like a good fit. I thought if I met all three, that it would be easier to decide."

"Your explanation doesn't hold water," Clint growled. "You

were in the process of marrying the first lady before you even met the second."

"On my behalf, McCall, I was upfront about needing a wife sturdy enough to work alongside me as my assistant in the dental office."

Clint rolled his eyes and drawled, "How romantic. Every man should take courting lessons from you."

Taking Clint's words as a compliment, the dentist replied, "Thank you. And both ladies came of their own volition. Also, I was out an exorbitant fee for their train fares."

"You were, were you?" Clint suspected Clemons's father paid for the brides' train tickets. Nevertheless, he reached into his pocket and peeled a hundred dollars from a roll.

"This should cover half Miss Hammons's train fare. I shouldn't give you anything, but let's just call it your, get-lost money. Take it or leave it. Because it's all you're getting."

"I'll take it."

As Clemons lunged for the bills, Clint jerked his hand up out of his reach. He wagged a finger at Clemons. "Not so fast. This payment comes with one stipulation."

Clemons cleared his throat and rasped, "And what might that be?"

"That you never bother Emily Hammons again."

When he hesitated, Clint said, "I want you to say it aloud."

"Very well." Clemons removed his derby hat, pressed it to his chest, and raised his right hand. Succinctly, as if taking an oath, he announced, "I promise I will never bother Miss Emily Hammons again."

A second time he lunged for the money. Clint jerked the bills out of reach again and grabbed the dentist's vest pocket. He stuffed the money inside.

"I appreciate this, but my problem is still not solved," Clemons whined. "Father says I must marry, or at least be engaged, before the end of the month."

Sarcasm laced Clint's voice. "I'm sure you will think of someone who is willing."

"Ollie? Is that you?" Clint whirled around. Prudence Wallace stood behind him. She swept over to Clemons and grabbed his arm. With a smile, she oozed, "Good to see you, Mr. McCall." Then she turned her attention to the dentist. "Ollie, I wondered where you had gotten off to."

Clint tipped his hat. "Miss Wallace, Dr. Clemons was just confessing how he'd tricked two ladies into coming to Abilene to marry him. Jessica's sister was the first one. We all know how that turned out. The second one was Miss Hammons. Neither lady is interested in keeping the agreement. Now, he's worried his third bride won't show up before his deadline."

Prudence arched her dark, bushy eyebrows. "I overheard your conversation. I had long suspected Miss Hammons was one of the brides. Then I spoke with Mr. Ward at the depot and my suspicions were verified."

She pressed a hand to her heart, searching Clemons's face. "Oh, Ollie. I too have a confession to make. I hope you can forgive me for what I did."

Clemons frowned. "Forgive you? Prudence, what on earth are you blathering about?"

As Clint watched, she exhaled slowly. "Ollie, I am trying to say that I am your third mail-order bride."

Clint's jaw dropped. "What?"

Clemons rolled his eyes. "I like your sense of humor, but this is not the time for pranking."

Prudence hiked her chin and looked him in the eye. "It's true. I am."

Clemons stared down his nose at her. "You can't be, Prudie. Check the facts. Delores Engle was the third bride, and she lives in Fort Worth. I have postmarked letters to prove this."

Prudence's eyelids fluttered. "Of course, you do. Ollie, do you remember this spring when my aunt died?"

"Of course, I remember your Aunt Matilda. She had straight teeth and they were well cared for. She was one of our best-paying patients."

"Do you recall that I left for some time after she passed?"

"You were gone an entire month." Clemons sounded forlorn.

Clint knew he should leave, but his curiosity got the best of him. The conversation had the makings of a good novel, and he'd love to hear how it ended. Neither was he ready to face Emily.

Why had she hidden the truth from him? She'd let him believe she had come to Abilene to seek adventure when he knew it wasn't true. He wanted to hear her explanation, but he needed to calm down before he questioned her.

Prudence explained her part in the tangled web. "I was staying in Fort Worth with my cousin. I answered your ad from there. It was Delores who sent both replies, but it was I who wrote and signed the letters. All Delores did was mail them to you from Fort Worth."

Clemons's mouth gaped. "You don't say! I enjoyed those letters. They were sweet. It was as if Delores knew me personally. Why did you have her mail letters from you, when we lived in the same town? Why didn't you tell me how you felt—especially after Miss Dawson fled the church?"

Clint stepped back into the shadows, trying to make sense of it all. He breathed, "Dear God, please show me what to do."

Emily had not married Clemons. Clint loved her with all his heart but tying himself to a woman who kept secrets could mean heartache. Emily had withheld her real reason for coming to Abilene. Was she also concealing other secrets?

Prudence lowered her head. "Ollie, I was afraid you would think me foolish. You are a prestigious, highly respected man, and also very sweet. Any woman would be insane to turn down your proposal. Yet, I could not bear the thought of your rejection.

I wanted to tell you many times how I felt, but I was afraid you would laugh and not take me seriously."

"Laugh at you? Why would I?"

Sniffling, she raised her head. "Look at me, Ollie. I'm plain —nothing special. But you will always hold a special place in my heart."

Clemons cleared his throat. "Prudence, I never considered that a refined, sophisticated lady such as you would develop an interest in me. I've admired you since the day we met. And I am humbled to learn that you reciprocate those feelings." He pulled off his derby hat and pressed it to his chest. "Plus, your peach cobblers are delectable."

"Oh, Ollie! Thank you." Prudence kissed his cheek. "How could you think I would reject your proposal? If you take me as your wife, you will dine on peach cobbler every day."

Clint groaned. The redhead's peach cobblers might have tilted the balances in her favor, but he would put Emily's cooking up against hers any day. He didn't deny that Clemons and Miss Wallace were well matched. She could dish out flattery and he would lap it up.

Clemons slipped his arm around Prudence. The couple seemed aware of nothing except their blossoming love. Clint had heard enough. The dentist was no longer a threat. He had to find Emily. After the dance he'd promised her, they would find some-place quiet to talk. He knew just the place.

A sweet melody emanated from the violin as he approached the barn. Standing at the entrance, he listened to the merry crowd, his gaze searching for Emily. Where was she?

EMILY SAT IN THE SHADOWS, hoping no one would approach her and notice her puffy eyes. Carrie and Jessica stood arm-in-arm with the men who obviously adored them. The smiles on the couples' faces made Emily long for the same. If only Clint would look at her like that.

She admonished herself for wallowing in self-pity. She had no right to Clint after the way she'd deceived him. She would be lucky if he ever trusted her again.

Emily wiped the tears from her face, raised her head, and stiffened her shoulders. Whatever Clint dished out, she deserved. He'd asked her to wait inside. Would he give her orders to pack her things?

She checked again and found Clint's tall, muscular frame blocking the barn entrance. His rigid stance made her heart hitch. His gaze swept around the room before lighting on her. She held her breath as he cut through the crowd.

RED-RIMMED EYES WERE evidence Emily had been crying. Had Clemons threatened her before he had intervened? Clint should have punched the man for the way he'd talked to her.

He wanted to hear Emily's side of the story. She must have had good reason for not confiding in him. For the life of him, he couldn't figure out what it could be.

Emily looked surprised when he reached for her hand and pulled her to her feet. "I promised a pretty lady a dance, and I aim to keep my promise. Are you ready?"

She offered up a tremulous smile as he led her out to the dance floor, and as he slid his arm around her, she stiffened. A hopeless look flooded her eyes. Was she considering leaving the ranch—and him?

They glided across the floor, staying clear of the other couples until Emily fell in sync with his steps. She was a quick learner. If only she wasn't so tense.

She kept her eyes downcast until he whispered in her ear,

"Loosen up. This is a harvest celebration, not a trek to the gallows." Her grim countenance said she believed the latter.

Emily exhaled and forced a smile. "I suppose you're right."

She seemed to relax a little. "That's better."

When the song ended, he led her away. "Let's take a break. Have you had dessert, yet?"

Emily shook her head. "After chatting with Carrie, I didn't think about it."

"You've been chatting with Carrie Kramer?"

Fear flickered in Emily's eyes. "Yes. Why do you ask?"

"The Kramer Ranch is a short distance south of us. We're practically neighbors."

Emily gave another short answer. "She told me."

"Did Carrie tell you she came here as a mail-order bride?"

Fear flashed in Emily's eyes again, and she looked away. Her gaze darted to the dessert table. "Shall we go for dessert? I saw pecan pie."

Clint rubbed his stomach. "Cherry pie for me." Why had Emily changed the subject? He would not push her, now. But they would talk soon.

CLINT ESCORTED Emily to the dessert table. What emotion had she read in his eyes when he'd first come in? Hurt? Anger? Disappointment? His gentle touch puzzled her. He had to be upset with her, didn't he?

The time had come to tell Clint why she'd answered Clemons's ad. She had delayed it, hoping she could come up with a justifiable excuse. One he would understand. Nothing sounded good enough, not even her desperate need to escape a contentious sister-in-law. Could she make him understand? Before replying to the mail-order bride ad, she should have searched for a job in Memphis. If she had she wouldn't have met Clint. She loved him so much her heart was breaking.

They picked up their desserts. Emily sat down on one side of Clint while Josh Kramer plopped down on his other side. The men discussed cattle and ranching while Emily slowly chewed her pecan pie. Every bite tasted like sawdust.

Clint finished his pie and licked his fork. Leaning toward her, he said, "I'm going outside with Josh. I'll be back in a few minutes."

Emily nodded quickly and the men left. Not knowing the thoughts racing through Clint's mind frightened her. Hands trembling, she fidgeted with the brooch at her throat. He was probably asking Josh's advice on what he should do.

"Hello, again." Carrie smiled and eased down onto the chair Clint had vacated. "Have you seen my husband, by chance?"

Emily exhaled a ragged breath. "He and Clint went outside." She exhaled a ragged breath. "Carrie, Clint knows the truth about me. The dentist told him."

Carrie clapped a hand to her mouth. "Oh, no! He learned it from Clemons?"

Emily nodded, tears pooling in her eyes. "I'm afraid he's outside telling Josh all about me." She wiped her eyes with the back of her hand. "Carrie, what will I do if he orders me to leave?"

Carrie laid a comforting hand over hers. "Don't borrow trouble, Emily. Let's wait and see. Josh may be showing Clint our new buckboard. It has springs under the seat. It doesn't bounce as much when we hit a rough spot." She giggled. "Besides, what could Josh possibly say against you, when he married me after learning I'd come to his ranch under an assumed name?"

Chapter Twenty-One

Clint stood with Josh beneath a hackberry tree where Josh's buckboard was parked. Josh pressed on the seat making it bounce. "Hop up, Clint, and tell me what you think about the springy seat."

Clint climbed up and bounced on the seat "This is nice. A body wouldn't be jarred to the bone when his wagon hit a rut." He hopped down to the ground.

Josh folded his arms across his chest and eyed Clint. "All right, out with it. You didn't bring me out here just to see my new buckboard. What's troubling you?"

Clint leaned back against the buckboard. "I can't pull the wool over your eyes, can I?"

Josh remained silent, kicking at a rock while Clint spilled the story about Emily coming to Abilene as Dr. Clemons's mail-order bride. Did Emily not trust him? Why hadn't she told him about her proposal? She'd made him believe her romantic notions of the wild west had brought her here. It hadn't sounded credible from the start.

Why did Josh persist in kicking that rock? Why didn't he say something? "Well?"

Josh raised his head and looked Clint in the eye. "I have one question for you. It's the only thing that matters."

"What?"

"Do you love Emily?"

Clint hadn't expected Josh to be so blunt. He studied Clint, waiting for his answer. If he said he didn't love Emily, he'd be a liar. "Yes, I'm afraid I do."

Josh gripped both Clint's shoulders. "Then I don't see the problem."

Clint jutted his chin. "Why did Emily keep the truth from me?"

Josh arched his brows. "Clint, how do you feel about mail-order brides?"

"You know the answer to that," Clint growled. "My ma replied to one of those ads and married a drunken lout who got his kicks out of beating her."

He hesitated before adding, "What really bothers me is the men who take advantage of the women who answer their ads. Although, I wish the women would use better judgment."

"Have you voiced your opinion of women who reply to mail-order bride ads, in Emily's presence?"

"I-I don't— Yes, I have. While we were leaving town after Clemons's disastrous wedding."

"Do you remember what you said?"

Clint swallowed hard. "I think I said something like, 'any woman who answers one of those ads has to be either desperate or crazy.'"

"Which category describes Emily?"

Clint shook head. "Emily's not crazy. She must have been desperate like Ma. I'm beginning to see it was my fault she wasn't forthright with me. She was afraid to admit it after I opened my big mouth."

He exhaled a slow breath. "I've been a fool. Thanks, Josh.

Emily needs to know I'm not judging her, that she can trust me to listen to her explanation."

Josh clapped Clint on the shoulder. "That's a good start. I wish you the best. I think Emily's a great catch. She's a proper lady, and she's pretty to boot."

He grinned from ear to ear. "I've never once regretted marrying Carrie. She's beautiful inside and out, keeps life interesting. She's made my life complete." He pulled off his hat and raked through his dark hair. "Carrie's going to make me a papa come spring."

Clint slapped Josh on the back. "Congratulations! You'll make a good one."

"Thanks." Josh's countenance sobered. "Clint, I wonder if you've thought of something. The first thing you need to do is forgive your stepfather. Let go of the bitterness. Ask God to help you with it. You may not realize it, but your anger is hurting those you love."

Clint nodded. "You're right, Josh. I do need to forgive him. And thank you for helping me see this clearly. You go on back inside and dance with Carrie. I need a little time to think."

As Josh traipsed toward the barn, Clint tossed his head back and looked heavenward. "Lord, what I'm asking won't be easy. I need your help to make me willing to let go of the bitterness I've carried for years toward my stepfather. You know what he did to my ma and me. Please take away the horrifying scenes that sometimes sneak into my dreams. Cleanse my heart and heal it. Make me the man You intended me to be—a man Emily can love and respect—and a brother Alissia will be proud to claim." He closed his eyes. "In Jesus' name. Amen."

JOSH SAT DOWN NEXT to Carrie and leaned across her to speak to Emily. "Clint will be in, in a few minutes."

Emily forced a smile. "Thank you." Fear gripped her as she laced her fingers together in her lap. She was afraid to ask him what Clint was doing.

The minutes passed as the violinist played a sweet melody. It seemed as if an hour passed before Emily spied Clint standing at the barn entrance. But it was probably twenty minutes. Her breath caught as his gaze lighted on her and he made a beeline in her direction. His countenance glowed as he caught her eye. She hoped it wasn't a facade.

Clint nodded at Josh and Carrie before turning to Emily. "Are you ready to go?"

"Yes. But I need to get our empty dishes." Emily rose and let him place her shawl around her shoulders. She bent to hug Carrie. "I enjoyed talking to you."

Carrie smiled. "I feel the same way. I hope we will become good friends."

"So do I." Emily meant it. She and Carrie had formed a special bond.

They walked out to where Clint had parked the buggy, but it was nowhere to be seen. Emily whirled to scan the area and frowned. "Our buggy's gone."

"Alissia wanted to go home. I gave Landon permission to escort her."

Clint had allowed Landon to take his sister home without him as a chaperone? "How will we get home? It's a long walk, and it's dark even with a full moon."

Between a cottonwood and hackberry tree, a horse whinnied and shook its mane. Emily peered into the shadows. Moonlight glistened off a golden Palomino's back and mane, giving it an ethereal glow. "Is that Bowie?"

Clint chuckled. "Sure as shootin', it's him."

Emily stepped over to the horse and stroked his forehead. "But how did he get here?"

"Landon's instructions were to saddle Bowie and bring him

back here. No dawdling. I figured that way he wouldn't have any extra time with my little sister."

Emily grinned. "Clint McCall, you are devious."

He shrugged. "Guilty as charged." Taking the empty dishes from her, he tucked them inside the saddlebag. "I hope riding Bowie doesn't damage your new dress. It's beautiful. Like you."

Did he just call her beautiful? Emily's cheeks heated. "My dress will be fine."

He swung up on the horse and pulled Emily up behind him. She clasped her hands together around his waist. Clint asked, "Do you mind if we let Bowie have his head?"

Emily's laugh echoed through the still night air. "I thought you'd never ask."

When they reached the open road, Clint urged Bowie into a full gallop. The horse ran like the wind. Emily's hair streamed out behind her, but she didn't care. She felt as free as a bird. How she wished this ride would go on forever.

Clint soon guided Bowie into a wide-open field, the place he had shown Emily on their moonlight ride the night of the storm. The glowing field and silvery moonlit hills beyond, beckoned them. They reached a group of tall trees where Clint reined Bowie in and dismounted.

Tears pooled in Emily's eyes as he set her to the ground. Her heart began to break. How could she make him understand why she hadn't told him the truth?

Clint spoke first. "Emily, I don't know why you decided to become Clemons's mail-order bride, but I really would like to. I do know why you couldn't tell me. I made it clear how I felt about women who answered those ads."

He huffed out a breath. "You know the horrors my ma went through at the hands of the man whose ad she answered. I'm sorry I let my animosity toward my deceased stepfather make me bitter and distrustful. It's not the ladies who answer those ads, who gall me. They may be gullible, but they aren't to blame for what happens to them after they arrive. I think the unscrupulous men who place those ads to take advantage of ladies, should be held accountable.

"I've let my dealings with my stepfather make me distrustful of Landon, even though he's a good kid. A few minutes ago, I had a good talk with the Lord. I'm letting go of my anger and with His help, will forgive Hank James. Not for him, but for me and for those I care about."

A lump formed in Emily's throat. "I understand bitterness. I've lived the past eight years with anger toward my pa for not sending for us or returning from the silver mines. When your ma told me how your pa was killed by a claim jumper, it dawned on me that the same thing may have happened to mine. I'm ashamed of my anger. I've asked God to forgive me too. Mama always said that Pa would have sent for us, if he could have. Until recently, I didn't believe her."

Clint nodded. "Claim jumping happens. I'm glad you're letting go of your anger too." He lowered his head to look her in the eye. "Back to the ad. You must have had a good reason for answering it."

Emily drew in a breath, her heart thumping against her ribcage. "When I think about it now, no reason seems good enough. It only reminds me there is another person I need to forgive. My sister-in-law. Mama deeded our house and farm to my brother with the stipulation that he look after me. Six months later Roy married. From the first day, Louise moved in, she began hinting for me to move out. After I graduated, she pushed harder. The dissension between her and me was tearing all of us apart, and Roy was caught in the middle."

Emily exhaled. "I had to leave. I couldn't stand by and watch my brother suffer because his wife and I couldn't get along. Roy deserves better. He's been good to me.

"I was born in that house. By all rights, it and the farm should have been half mine. Mama thought if she deeded it to

Roy, he would see to it that I got my share. She didn't know Louise's true nature. Roy didn't marry until six months after Mama died.

"I searched job listings in the paper for months. Then I saw Clemons's ad. It sounded as if he wanted a wife in name only, an assistant at his dental practice. At least, I hoped that was all. I did wonder why he didn't just hire someone to help, instead of advertising for a wife."

Clint's jaw clenched. "Clemons is a selfish lout. He would have taken advantage of you, Emily. You're much too pretty and sweet not to be a temptation to a man."

Emily sighed. "The thought did occur to me. The day I got the reply from Clemons, I was sitting on the back steps, trying to make a decision. I overheard Louise and Roy arguing inside the house. She said if he didn't tell me to get out, she would."

Clint shook his head. "Some are born with a mean streak. And you felt you had no choice?"

Emily nodded. "I walked in and announced that I had accepted a proposal from a mail order bride ad. Until then, I hadn't made up my mind."

Clint planted a chaste kiss on Emily's forehead. "As crazy as it was, I'm glad you did. God must have had a plan in it to bring us together."

Emily gasped. "Do you really mean that?"

"Yes, I do." He chuckled "And don't worry your pretty little head about Clemons. He and Prudence will be very happy together."

"Prudence and the dentist?" Emily clapped a hand to her throat. "You're kidding."

"Nope. It looked that way when I left them, gazing into one another's eyes."

Emily squealed and threw her arms around Clint, then stepped back frowning. "I should repay Dr. Clemons for my train fare."

"No, you shouldn't. I figure his father paid the train fare for both brides. Clemons proposed to three ladies. That was wrong. When I called him an attempted bigamist and warned him he could go to jail for it, he shut up about the money. The matter's been taken care of. I made him an offer, and he took it."

"What did you offer him?" Emily asked.

"One hundred dollars. And he took it without hesitation."

"Emily hiked her eyebrows. "Half price? Is that all I'm worth?"

Clint winked. "I thought that was a good deal. Hmm…maybe I should've offered him fifty."

Emily swatted Clint's arm. "Well! I should be offended."

Clint chuckled and pulled her close, the moonlight reflected in his stormy eyes. "Enough about the dentist. Let's talk about us."

"What about us?"

He pointed to the lush field before them. "What would you say to building a nice cabin over there, centered in front of those hills?"

Dare she hope Clint was including her in his plan? "I'd say it's a wonderful idea. What could be more amazing than a view of these beautiful hills from your backyard? On starry nights you could step out your back door and take in this view. I, for one, would never tire of it."

"Good. I'll start on it soon." Before Emily could get over the shock, Clint removed his hat and fell to his knees, taking her hand in his. "Emily Hammons, I love you. Will you marry me and live here with me?"

"Yes! Yes!" She urged him to get to his feet and embraced him. He swung her around in circles, until she became dizzy.

When he set her down, she clung to him, breathless. "Who will look after your ma?"

"In case you haven't noticed, there's more than one budding

romance in the air. Dr. Simmons has asked me for Ma's hand in marriage. I think she will be in good hands."

Emily laughed. "I agree. Yes, romance is in the air. There's Jessica and Trent, besides Prudence and her Ollie." And Alissia and Landon, she silently added.

As if reading Emily's thoughts, Clint said, "I'll try to be more lenient with Alissia. Anyway, Landon will be gone for a couple of years, only home for the holidays and summer break. By that time, Alissia will be older and hopefully, wiser."

Clint pulled her close. "But, let's not talk about them."

Emily tilted her head back to view his smoldering eyes. "Who shall we talk about?"

"Nobody," he breathed. "Haven't you ever read in Ecclesiastes, 'There's a time to be silent'?" Clint lowered his head, his breath warming her ear before he sprinkled kisses on her cheeks, forehead, and nose. "I'm crazy about you, my half-price bride. What a deal!"

Emily's heart melted. "I love you too." Clint claimed her lips sending shock waves throughout her body and leaving her weak. She thought her heart might burst with love for this redheaded cowboy.

Emily thanked God for leading her to Abilene and to Clint. Even if it took another man's ad to get her to her destination. It must have been in God's perfect plan. And God's plan was better than anything she could ever have imagined.

About the Author

Laurean Brooks lives in rural northwest Tennessee with her flea-marketing/antique-hunting husband, two labs and a cat. She writes inspirational romance with heart, humor, and unpredictable characters. Chivalrous heroes stand by to rescue their ladies from a plethora of disasters along the way. Her sassy heroines are familiar with the taste of their own shoe leather. "Foot-in-mouth" disease prevails throughout her stories.

Ms. Brooks' over-active imagination wrought trouble in fifth grade when she was assigned to write about, "The Adventures of Columbus." Laurean's version should have been titled, "The "Mis"-adventures of Columbus." Evidently her teacher did not approve, because after Laurean read the comical story to the class, she demanded a complete rewrite.

You can learn more about Laurean by visiting her website: LaureansLore.blogspot.com

Also by Laurean Brooks

Taylor County Brides Series - Book One

Not What He Ordered

When Carrie Franklin struggles with a drunk, leaving him unconscious, or perhaps dead, she flees. Forgetting the promise to her deceased mother, she deserts her feckless brother and takes the train to Abilene, Texas.

Carrie shares a seat with Molly, who confides she's a Mail Order Bride en route to meet her fiancé. Molly's friend was set to join her in this adventure. But suspicion made Katy Davis back out of her betrothal. Because Carrie will disembark in Abilene, Molly asks her to explain Katy's absence to the waiting ranch owner, Josh Kramer.

Due to miscommunication, interruptions, and an empty purse, Carrie, seated beside Josh, heads to the ranch, under his assumption she is Katy Davis.

When Josh's aunt pulls Carrie aside to reveal a secret, Carrie finds herself in a quagmire. Aunt Em will also suffer if Carrie reveals her true identity.

Josh is leery of Katy Davis, never suspecting his aunt's deception. Is Katy out to get the ranch? His attraction toward her grows, but he was once burned by a woman and swore, "Never again."

Carrie falls in love with Josh, but her secret threatens to destroy any love he has for her. Did she kill the drunk? Is the law looking for her?

Will God's forgiveness help Carrie and Josh find true love and happiness?

Also from Scrivenings Press

Love's Kindling

by Award-winning Author Elaine Marie Cooper

Book One of the Dawn of America Series

This title includes *War's Respite*, prequel to the

Dawn of America series.

During the American Revolution, Aurinda Whitney lives with her cold and calloused father, an embittered veteran of the previous war. Aurinda's life changed forever when her father returned for her after that war, taking her away from the only place she'd ever experienced affection. Since her father blamed Aurinda for the death of his wife in childbirth, Aurinda is convinced she is unworthy of love.

Zadok Wooding believes he is a failure as he tends the smithy at home while others go to battle against the British. Just when he has an opportunity to become a hero, he is blinded in an accident. Now he fears he will never live up to the Biblical "mighty man of valor" for whom he was named.

When the couple meet, they are both challenged to overcome adversity as well as their inadequacies. Unexpected secrets of their past emerge that can change their lives forever. But can they look past their present circumstances to heal—and find love?

~

The Rancher's Legacy

Homeward Trails

Book One

Matthew Anderson and his father try to help neighbor Bill Maxwell when his ranch is attacked. On the day his daughter Rachel is to return from school back East, outlaws target the Maxwell ranch. After Rachel's world is shattered, she won't even consider the plan her father and Matt's cooked up—to see their two children marry and combine the ranches.

Meanwhile in Maine, sea captain's widow Edith Rose hires a private investigator to locate her three missing grandchildren. The children were abandoned by their father nearly twenty years ago. They've been adopted into very different families, and they're scattered across the country. Can investigator Ryland Atkins find them all while the elderly woman still lives? His first attempt is to find the boy now called Matthew Anderson. Can Ryland survive his trip into the wild Colorado Territory and find Matt before the outlaws finish destroying a legacy?

~

Rose Harbor

Newport of the West - Book Four

All Grace Bauer has wanted to do since she was a child was to fly airplanes. When the Women Airforce Service Pilots (WASP) organizes for female pilots to ferry new bomber aircraft to stateside military bases, Grace applies. She never tires of flying B-17s and other aircraft, and dreams of being one of the first females to pilot a commercial airliner after the war.

A life-threatening illness clips her wings, and she finds herself back home in Wisconsin, thinking that God is punishing her for a past sin. Bored, she joins a ladies bowling league and meets Mac McAlister, a widowed school teacher who helps out at the bowling alley on league nights. He offers to help her restore the old family lakeshore estate, Safe Refuge—now called Rose Harbor and lost during the Crash of 1929—back to the family. She's happy to have a good friend like Mac to help. But despite her efforts to keep their relationship platonic, Grace's feelings for him grow. Before the relationship can move to the next level, she must tell him her secret, and when he hears it, he'll want nothing more to do with her. She should end the relationship, but can't imagine life without him. It is only with God's blessing that she'll be free to love Mac. But after what she's done, she doubts God is willing to forgive her.

Stay up-to-date on your favorite books and authors with our free e-newsletters.

ScriveningsPress.com

www.ingramcontent.com/pod-product-compliance
Lightning Source LLC
Chambersburg PA
CBHW070628100726
47907CB00007B/1904